Porcelain

Porcelain White

Porcelain White

by

Julie Granger

Redwood Series – Book I

a historical romance novel

"All things are possible with God."

Mark 10:27

Printed in the United States of America

Paper ISBN: 978-1-69-900541-5

Chapter One

A Note of Regret

Captain Pichon's buckboard pulled into Calabash, Minnesota, on a sweltering August afternoon in 1876. Dust swirled as strong gusts of wind beat like an unwelcome visitor on the parched buildings of Main Street.

A curtain moved aside, and two sad eyes peered through the opening. Isaiah Grant's luck had run dry.

"He's here," whispered Isaiah to no one in particular.

As the buckboard clamored to a halt, the veteran debt collector stepped down, covered with dust. He looked neither left nor right but walked into the saloon as Isaiah emerged with his hat in his hands.

"Howdy, Captain Pichon," greeted Grant, offering him a timid smile.

"Bring your money and come with me."

Pichon grabbed him by the elbow and pushed him back into the wooden saloon doors without looking at him. Grant stumbled back into the empty saloon. The bartender stopped polishing glasses and slowly touched his revolver under the bar, just in case.

"Pay up," Pichon snarled at the sixty-three-year-old man."

"Well, it's like this, Captain. I need,"

"Pay up before I get mad."

The officer gave him a shove, and Isaiah Grant bumped into the table, unable to explain himself. Pichon whipped a barrel-shaped chair out of his way as he took several steps closer.

"Maybe, now you will remember what you owe me," Pichon growled under his breath as he followed with a fist of steel. Grant fell back and then scurried in total fear to the corner of the saloon.

"I ain't got the money. I needed food for my family," explained Isaiah, rubbing his face.

"You, drunken sot. You drank up the money. Don't lie to me, you, worthless piece of shit."

"Honest, Captain. Just give me a little more time. I promise I'll get you the money."

"I'm tired of waiting for you. I ain't running no charity," shouted Captain Pichon.

Isaiah pulled himself to his feet. "Please, Captain. I need more time to get the money."

Even with Pichon's determination to squeeze every dollar out of this homesteader, he knew deep inside that Grant did not have shit for money.

"Say, you just might have something I want," remarked Pichon with a smile. "You got a daughter, don't you? She ought to be worth fifty dollars."

"No, Captain. Not that,"

"Is she a virgin?"

Isaiah became sick to his stomach as he looked at the Captain.

"Where is she?" barked Pichon.

"She's back at the homestead with her ma. It's a good day's ride from here."

"I know where it is at," snarled Pichon as he winced at the memory of Grant's homestead.

"I'll tell you what, Grant. Put her on the train next week to Redwood.," the Captain.

"That way, she'll arrive like one of those mail-order brides. If she doesn't meet my likin's, I'm sending her back, and the deal is off."

Then, facing the bartender, "Bottle of whiskey and put that on Mr. Grant's tab."

Pichon swaggered out of the saloon with a bottle of whiskey and a smile on his face. He jumped on the buckboard and steered the wagon out of town.

Isaiah Grant slumped into the chair, realizing he now has to come up with a way to pay for the bottle of whiskey and a train ticket to Redwood, Minnesota.

"You owe me for a bottle of whiskey," said the bartender and shoved a broom at him.

* * *

"Please, Papa, No, please don't make me leave. I don't want to get married. I want to stay here with Ma and Ben and you. Please don't make me get married."

Isabel stared at her Pa and blinked back tears at the thought of leaving Ben and her mother and the mountain and their home. She had traveled only a few times to Calabash and never any farther. Fears of never seeing her family or the valley loomed in the back of her mind.

"I don't want to live in town. I don't have any clothes for a town, and they will laugh at me. I can't read and write," pleaded Isabel. "I wouldn't know how to be a wife to a soldier in the army. Please, Pa. Don't' make me."

Ever since Isaiah came home with the news that Isabel was to be a mail-order bride to Captain Pichon, Isabel had screamed and cried in protest. The ideas of running away and living in the cave with her Ma raced through her mind. She even considered running away to live with her ma's friend Grandma Red Bear at the Sioux encampment to the north of their cabin.

"Don't you see this is your chance to start your own life," cajoled Pa.

"I don't want you growing up and becoming afraid of people like your ma and never learning to read and write beyond what your ma can teach you. Besides, I can't afford to keep you. I'm taking Ben with me to the lumber camp next spring to work. 'Bout time that boy starts working like a man and earning his keep."

Ben overheard his dad's biting remarks. At age fifteen, he had always worked hard to provide the family with meat using his self-taught hunting and trapping skills; he chopped wood and took care of his chores every day. His dad's words stung. To have his dad think that he was not pulling his weight around the homestead left a sour taste in his mouth.

The tall, lanky, blond boy slipped out to the barn to escape the tension and fighting in the cabin. He didn't want Isabel to leave, and he did not like the idea of working at the lumber camp next spring. Pa never even asked him what he wanted.

"Why can't things stay the same? Our life is peaceful when papa goes and works for a season and comes back for a few days to bring supplies. I can take care of Isabel and Ma. I am going to make darn sure pa knows that before he takes off again. Why now? Why send Isabel away?" Tears ran down Ben's cheeks as he stood in the silence of the barn, trying to understand his father.

Ellie Grant had spent the day foraging for herbs to dry. Walking had helped her clear her head, and she loved the quiet solitude of the woods. She knew Isabel would have supper started, and every day she thanked her lucky stars for the help and the comfort her children provided to her.

As Ellie approached the yard in front of the house, she overheard Isabel and her father fighting in the cabin. She pushed open the door in disbelief to what she was hearing.

"Why would you have her marry a soldier after what happen to this family?" spat Ellie Grant at her husband.

Isaiah looked at his wife with no answer.

Then, he slammed his hands on the table and said, "Enough. I am the head of this household."

Silence filled the cabin.

“Isabel will be getting on the train to be a mail-order bride to Captain Pichon, and that is final."

He shoved his hat on his head and grabbed his gun. Then, he checks his satchel for a bottle. He walked towards the woods without looking back to see the shock look on their faces from his anger. Isabel collapsed into her mother's arms, and sobs poured from her thin body as her mother tried to comfort her.

Tension remained high at the Grant household for the next week as the preparations for Isabel's departure continued. No one spoke of the details for the trip to Calabash, and sadness prevailed over the homestead.

Ellie dug into her trunk to find old dresses she had worn long ago to alter for Isabel. Mending and sewing occupied her week, as everything needed washing and ironing before packing for the trip.

Ben took on a new project out in the barn. He became unresponsive to everyone's questions. Isabel was the only one who could comfort him.

Pa returned home three days later drunk but bearing skins for processing. He tossed a bundle of smoked fish and one of fresh meat at Ellie as a peace offering, and she acknowledged his contributions with nothing more than a grunt.

Isabel spent the week cleaning and cooking for her family hoping her Pa realized how much she contributed.

The day of departure arrived. The sun backlit the tree line as Pa steered the buckboard to the front of the cabin. Ben tried not to cry as he hugged Isabel goodbye. Her mother gave her some last-minute advice, hugged her and scurried off into the woods like a crazy woman.

On the daylong ride to Calabash, Isabel chose not to talk to her Pa. A flood of emotions filled her mind as she looked at the valley for the last time. She knew she was never going to see her home or Ben or her Ma ever again.

Isabel hated Pa for forcing her into this situation. She remembered the attack on her Ma by the soldiers, and she decided that all soldiers were the same.

"Please Isabel, try to make the most of this opportunity. Lots of young women are mail-ordered brides. They even put ads in the papers and write back and forth. I know this isn't the ideal way to meet a husband."

Isabel's continued silence rubbed Isaiah's nerves raw.

"Please Isabel. Talk to me."

Silence. Isaiah continued for most of the afternoon to talk to Isabel, who remained vigilant in her silence. With every mile, her resolve intensified. By five o'clock, Isaiah and Isabel arrived at the livery on the edge of town. All alone, Isabel set up camp as Isaiah headed to the saloon.

"I should run away right now. I could take one of the horses and the few supplies in the wagon, and I could set out on my own, but where would I go by myself? I have never been on the other side of Calabash. What would I do? "

"I can't go back home. Pa would make me get married to this Captain. I am mad at Pa for doing this to me. I hate him."

With tears falling down her cheeks, sleep eluded her throughout the night. Even when Pa stumbled into the campground, she turned her back and pretended to be asleep.

In the morning, Isabel made coffee and breakfast for her Pa one last time. She pumped a bucket of water from the horse trough at the livery. Isabel moved to the back of the wagon to prepare herself for the day.

Her ma had set her clean porcelain white hair into two tight braids. Isabel watered down the flyways on top of her head with her fingers.

She put on her mother's best dress. The small white flowers on the lavender background seem to match her hair. She smoothed out the front and tied the sash in the back. She remembered the disappointment in her mother's voice when packing.

"Isabel, I am sorry for not doing right by you. I should've been providing a dowry of goods, for when you left home. I don't have so much as any fancy smelling stuff to give you. All I got is some homemade soap and these here bundles of dried herbs that will keep the bugs out of your clothes. I am sorry, Isabel."

"Don't be daydreaming, Isabel. The train is going to be pulling in for water any time now."

As Pa hitched the horses to the buckboard, Isabel broke camp. Silence remained as they both went about their chores. Climbing onto the wagon, Isabel felt funny all dressed up with her Ma's thin brown hat atop of her head.

"Dress looks nice on you, Isabel. Remember when your ma used to wear it," reminisced Pa as he steered the team toward the depot.

Her long brown lashes blinked back the tears that were stinging her eyes with pain. Isabel loved him so much.

Isabel knew that deep down, he loved her, but she didn't understand why he was sending her away.

"Please, Pa. Please. Please don't make me go. I want to stay with you. Please."

He looked at her and heard the frightened panic in her voice. "Now hush up, Isabel. We have been all through this. It will be fine. You're just nervous."

Calabash was a water stop on the rail line. Local freighters lined up ready to receive goods from St. Paul and deliver them to the local businesses in town. Pa pulled up next to the depot and tied the team to the hitching post.

Isabel sat in the wagon, staring at the activity. Pa grabbed her worn satchel and walked around the end gate of the buckboard towards Isabel.

"Isabel, let's not be making a scene now. Git down off that wagon."

Reluctantly, Isabel allowed her Pa to help her down off the wagon, so she would not tear her dress.

"Don't be getting any ideas of running away and coming back here. I won't stand for it."

"I hate you," said Isabel.

Isabel looked into her father's eyes with steel resilience, grabbed her satchel from his hand, and walked toward the depot. Sadness veiled his face as he followed her to buy her ticket.

At the depot, passengers, family members, and onlookers gathered to wait for the train. Her father clutched her elbow and steered her into the lobby of the depot. She stepped away from him quickly and moved over to the farthest wall to stare at a map showing the rail lines and the different types of stops.

"I'll take one ticket for Redwood."

"Is it for you or her?" asked the ticket master.

"It's for my daughter."

"Is she over twelve?"

"No, no sir" lied Isaiah.

"That will be half fare."

Isaiah fished in his pocket and produced the coins to pay the two-dollar fare. Then, he slowly walked over to Isabel, handed the ticket to her and led her out of the lobby.

"Why did you tell that man I was twelve? You know I am seventeen."

"Never mind," he muttered as he rushed her to the end of the platform.

"Let go of my arm," Isabel hissed at her father and said, "I never want to see you again, and I will never forgive you for what you have done to our family and me."

Isabel turned her back to her father; she felt the salty tears run down her cheeks. Slowly, Isaiah backed away, holding his hat in his hand. He shuffled through the crowd towards the buckboard.

Tears clouded Isabel's eyes as she blinked furiously. She found herself the center of attention with onlookers staring at her. The train rolled into sight, and suddenly every ounce of Isabel's courage flowed out of her body.

Chapter Two

New Beginnings

Train arrivals brought unmarried girls to the isolated rural town on the prairie. Mail-order brides were answering ads and starting brand new lives. On this warm August day, Isaiah Grant's daughter was to marry a man she had never met. As the train slowed, smoke blocked Isabel's view of the platform.

Waiting for the train to arrive in Redwood, Minnesota, became a habit for many townspeople. Curious settlers sauntered down to see the fancy new deliveries.

The old-timers declared that the arrival of the train was a big moment for every bachelor in town. Some of the more zealous bachelors climbed up to the tops of feed sheds and watched with field glasses, to see the steam locomotive approaching.

"I see three blondes and a red-head," shouted down a lumberjack lying on a rooftop of a hay shed.

As the train drew near, potential bridegrooms looked inside and studied the prospects. When the locomotive slowed to a halt at the depot, there was a regular stag-line of awkward men, young and old. Every one of them wondered whether his future bride might be stepping down onto the wooden platform.

On that particular late August afternoon, one of the bridegrooms-to-be was Captain Ivan Pichon, a man who went to great trouble to avoid being disappointed. Grant's daughter was due in on the train, but he was not going to meet it.

He positioned himself on a hillside near the train depot, armed with a sturdy pair of binoculars. His sergeant stationed himself several feet behind the Captain to await orders.

At last, the train slid to a halt. Dry dust swirled around the locomotive and rail car doors swung open. The porters dropped down the wooden staircases for passengers to descend.

Isabel looked out the window and watched as town folks greeted the passengers and welcomed them to Redwood.

With the help of the porter, moments later Captain Pichon's bride-to-be stepped down. He recognized her porcelain white hair. Her hair was just like her mother. The Captain, with his binoculars, trained upon her, gave her a thorough going over from a distance. Finding no one to meet her, Isabel Grant walked up and down the platform.

"Damn it! She is nothing more than a skinny school girl. What the hell do I want with an ugly school girl." His disgust turned to anger.

Within moments, he dispatched his sergeant with a note and a leather pouch with plenty of coins to send the girl back home.

Pichon felt he deserved better than her. He needed a wife to impress the Major. The rumors of the fort closing made the Captain nervous. He wanted a promotion with a pay raise and a move to a more comfortable position at his age.

Sergeant John Webster was a burly man, standing six foot three inches and had served Captain Pichon for two years. Readjusting his small, flat-topped, billed cap, the sergeant turned his bay-colored mare toward the train depot. His mind raced to process the generous pouch of coins and the strangeness of the errand.

As he rode, John cursed under his breath. He seemed to end up in awkward situations because of his captain. When he pulled up to the platform, his foot hit the wooden planks with determination to make this short and sweet.

After waiting several minutes outside, Isabel Grant walked into the lobby of the depot to ask the ticket master if there had been a message for her from Captain Pichon. She felt so nervous as she wrung her hands together.

A tall, broad-shouldered soldier rushed through the door with authority.

She caught her breath and thought to herself, "Oh there he is, just like Papa said. Oh My. He is handsome, and he is a soldier. He must be the man who wants to marry me."

Instead of introductions, the sergeant gave her the handwritten note and the leather pouch of coins. Isabel looked up in bewilderment. "I'm sorry. Uh. I can't read."

She handed back the piece of paper and coins with growing embarrassment, John Webster looked at the letter and began to read. "Tell Grant the deal is off, and I want my money, Captain Pichon."

"No. You must be wrong. My name is Isabel Grant, and I'm supposed to meet Captain Pichon; that's what Pa said, and I'm supposed to marry him today."

Her voice faded and tears blurred her vision. As thoughts raced through her mind, she heard a soft, gentle voice speaking to her, and she looked into the soldier's deep green eyes.

Sergeant Webster saw the scared look of abandonment come over her face as she comprehended the situation.

Like a porcelain doll frozen in time, her dark brown eyes filled with emotion. John felt an overwhelming need to protect her.

"I'm sorry Ma'am; I'm just following orders." He handed back the note and the pouch of coins. Locked in her gaze, John felt his heart lurch into his throat. In a wave of panic, fear gripped his chest, and his lungs searched for air. He bolted back outside and left her standing in the empty lobby of the depot.

Isabel turned and looked back at the window and watched the tall soldier walked over to his horse. His tall frame mounted the horse with ease, and he steered it with a commanding presence.

She thought, "Why couldn't he have been the officer who would marry me? He is handsome, and he seems kind. Why did he leave so suddenly? What was wrong with me?"

Isabel noticed the ticket master staring at her. Her thin, cotton, lavender dress with pale flowers looked shabby in the afternoon light. Her hat felt out of place. She clutched a satchel holding her few meager possessions.

Scratching his head, he muttered to himself, "Every woman that has come off that train has been snatched up and carted off to be married before they knew what happened. I've never seen one left standing."

She looked at the sack of coins in her hand. Isabel's eyes stared at the polished wood floors and the potbelly iron stove. The small lobby had two wooden benches with maps and pictures on the wall and windows everywhere.

"You want a ticket, or don't you? Either you buy a ticket for the next train, or you got to leave; you can't stay here," said the ticket master.

"When is the next train?" asked Isabel.

"Where'ya from?"

"I got on the train at Calabash."

"That train runs again in three days."

"Can I buy a ticket, then?", she asked as she clutched the leather pouch tighter into her fist.

"Sure, yah, you betcha. I open every day from 7 a.m. until 5:00 p.m.," said the little man with the striped engineer cap.

"Where will I go until then?" asked Isabel with panic in her voice.

"Maude Renshaw runs the big hotel down on Main Street," he said and then pointed her in the direction of the hotel.

* * *

The walnut clock chimed three o'clock when Isabel pushed open the front door to the hotel. She stood in awe as her eyes absorbed the grand lobby of The Redwood Hotel.

The warmth of the dining room filled her nose with the smell of baked bread and simmering beef stew.

She glanced down the long hallway and then stared at the grand, wooden staircase. The registration desk held a position of prominence next to the stairs, and a velvet sofa and matching chairs adorned the rest of the lobby.

"Well, hello there. Welcome to Redwood. Can I help you?"

From behind the desk, the most beautiful women that Isabel had ever seen stepped forward to greet her.

"I ah, um. I ah, I need a place to stay for three days," stammered Isabel.

The women looked over her half-glasses that hung around her neck with a long-jeweled chain. She discreetly took note of her clothes and said, "Well, right now I need help. We have more settlers coming every day into Redwood, and they have all decided to eat here, which is the best place in town I might add."

Then, she laughed, and her eyes glowed with warmth. "Where are my manners, child? My name is Maude Renshaw, and you are...?"

"Isabel. Isabel Grant,"

"Well, Isabel Grant, how many nights did you say you needed?"

"My train to Calabash leaves in three days," said Isabel.

"If you don't mind me asking, do you have business here in Redwood?"

"No, Ma'am, not anymore," explained Isabel quietly.

Maude raised her eyebrow at the usual answer and then asked, "Honey, how would you like a job along with a place to stay?"

Isabel looked at the beauty that surrounded her, and the thought of going back to Calabash faded in her mind.

“Yes, Mrs. Renshaw, I would like that very much."

She took a long look at Isabel and said, "I tell you what Miss Isabel. How about if the first two days you work for me for free room and board with no wages.

“I will start you out working in the kitchen. If you decided to stay, I offer two dollars a week, paid every Saturday morning."

“I would like that very much,” said Isabel as she smiled at Maude.

Maude handed Isabel the key to the room and then reached out her hand, and they shook on it. Then, she spun around the desk and headed down the long corridor. Isabel held onto her hat and scurried behind her as she climbed the servant's staircase. Her room was located three doors down the hallway from the top of the back staircase.

Inside the room, the meager furnishings included a bed, dresser, and a small table with a pitcher and basin. Maude also brought her a blanket and a uniform, which consisted of a brown dress and a white apron.

"Laundry is done on Saturdays, out back. Take your meals in the kitchen. Now, I have a strict rule that there will be no fraternizing with the customers and no male guests in your room. This hotel isn't a brothel. Change into the uniform, and report to the kitchen. The train brought in new brides today, and they'll be here for supper."

The unfamiliar words left Isabel confused; the last remarks stung her to the quick. Maude noticed her reaction. After she had barked out her repeated litany of rules, Maude realized this one was different.

Maude felt uncomfortable being so blunt with the girl. As the owner of the hotel, she had been through the routine so many times. Maude closed the door, and as she walked down the staircase, she muttered under her breath.

"These girls! Come in, work for a week or two, and the next thing you know they run off and get married."

After Maude closed the door, Isabel stood in the middle of the room and stared. This place was more beautiful than anything she had ever seen.

There was a feather mattress with sheets and bedding, and it was a bed all to herself. Isabel was thrilled to have found a job and a place to stay. She vowed to work hard no matter what the job involved.

She slipped into her new uniform; she had never had a new dress. It was too big for her, but she tied the apron tight and arranged the dress.

Isabel smoothed her long ivory braids and twisted them into a coil at the back of her neck. She secured the braids with pins and looked at her reflection in the glass window.

As she touched her porcelain white hair, she remembered her mother's words.

"Be careful. Listen to him and do as he says," warned her mother.

Then, her mother choked back tears, and Isabel watched as she scurried into the woods.

There had been too many children too close together. Isabel tried to help as much as possible to lighten the load. She knew her mother was not well in the head some days, and it made leaving that much harder.

Her eye caught on the pouch of coins. She knew little about money and that many coins felt foreign in her hands. She clutched the pouch to her chest and looked around the room. Where could she hide it?

Hiding the pouch in her satchel was too obvious, and it was foolish to leave it in the dresser drawer. She spied the mattress on the bed. She lifted the corner and tucked the pouch of coins under the mattress. Isabel closed her door, straightened her apron front, and headed down to the kitchen to start her new job.

Secretly under her breath, she was so thankful that she was not getting married to Captain Pichon, whomever he was.

Isabel reported to the kitchen, and Clara, the head cook put her to work peeling potatoes for the supper crowd. The kitchen was warm and a blur of activity as people bustled around preparing the evening meal.

One woman worked de-boning a plate of steaming chicken, and another woman stood by the stove stirring the gravy and checking the biscuits.

A redheaded waitress was serving up the plates when she bellowed for Isabel to help carry food to the dining room. As Isabel walked behind the waitress carrying hot plates of chicken gravy and biscuits, she saw several officers in uniforms sitting at the long table eating and laughing.

"Captain, I thought you were getting hitched," shouted a young blonde officer.

"No, I got smart. I kept a strong lookout, besides the woman wasn't my type."

"She didn't have what I needed," said Pichon holding his hands in front of his chest, making the other men laugh.

Isabel overheard the remark and looked right at the officer. In all the commotion, another officer leaned back and laughed, which caused Isabel to drop the platter of food right onto Captain Pichon. He began to cuss and swear, and Isabel was turning redder by the moment, as she hurried to clean up the mess.

"You, stupid wench. What the hell do you think you are doing?"

Tears welled up in her eyes as he looked at her. Realizing who she was, he stopped in mid-sentence.

The Captain threw down his napkin and marched out of the dining room. John Webster, sitting at a corner table, had witnessed the whole event.

"Sergeant," barked Captain Pichon.

Webster jumped as he heard his name called from the lobby. He grabbed his hat and headed for the door. Before Sergeant Webster could pull shut the entrance to the Redwood Hotel, the Captain was in his face.

"I thought I told you to give her my note and the money to get back on the train," snarled Pichon under his breath.

"Sir, I did. I gave the sack of coins to her," said Sergeant Webster

"Well, you get back in there and tell that clumsy little schoolgirl to take that money and get back on the next train - you hear me."

"Yes, sir." and he lumbered back into the dining room to look for Maude.

"John, it is her first day; she didn't mean no harm," Maude implored.

"I know. That's not it. I need to talk to Miss Grant. Tell her to meet me in the hallway back by the lobby," said Sergeant Webster.

Moments later, John stood in the darkened hallway listening to the clinking of dishes from the kitchen. In his mind, he was rehearsing what he needed to say to her.

He thought to himself, “I want to tell her she is beautiful, and Pichon is an asshole. I want to tell her to stay right here in Redwood. I want to tell her I will protect her from Pichon.”

Isabel stepped out into the dim hallway and looked up at the tall soldier. Then, she closed her eyes and looked down as she waited for him to yell at her for spilling food on the officer.

"Ma'am, Captain Pichon uh-uh -uh. Ma'am, Captain Pichon,” stammered Sergeant Webster.

If he wasn’t so tongue-tied around women, he could spit it out. She was so small and fragile.

She looked up with those soft, brown eyes, and his heart melted. The humidity in the kitchen had made the ivory hair around her face curl softly into tendrils. His mind turned to mush, and he couldn’t remember a thing. Finally, he took a deep breath.

“Well, Ma’am. Umm. Captain Pichon wanted me to remind you that the money he gave you was for a return ticket home,” he said without taking a breath.

“I can’t go back. I mean I’m not going back,” Isabel stated with conviction, surprising herself.

“Captain thought you were too young. Ah, he was expecting someone older.”

“You mean bigger,” using her hands to indicate. “I saw the Captain in the dining room. I heard what he said.”

Leaning in toward her, he said in a whisper. “Shoot, You’re better off without him. He’s a mean polecat.”

Isabel looked at him, blushed and covered her mouth as she giggled.

He smiled and chuckled. “Wow! Was she pretty when she smiled!” thought John, as he memorized her face.

“Thank you, Mr.,” said Isabel softly.

“Webster, John Webster, Ma’am.”

“Grant, Isabel Grant,” she said teasingly.

John’s eyes twinkled as he laughed. “It was a pleasure to meet you, Ma’am.

“Thank you, Mr. Webster. Tell Captain Pichon I will return his money. I am staying here in Redwood,” said Isabel as she felt her back straighten with confidence.

"That's nice to hear. I mean. I will tell the Captain." He tipped his hat to her and smiled like a schoolboy. John's feet barely touched the floor as he strode out of the hotel into the warm evening air.

Isabel rushed back into the kitchen and plopped down on to the stool next to the butter churn. Joy filled her heart. She had made the decision not to go back to Calabash. She was staying where it was warm and where there were people to talk to every day.

Living with her family in the woods of Minnesota was lonely. Her mother feared strangers and outsiders. Her father was gone for months at a time working at the lumber camps. She and her brother, Ben, had each other to fend off the loneliness of the woods when her mother would spend days in an old cave in the hills.

The noise of the kitchen brought her out of her daydream. The staff was cleaning the kitchen; Isabel helped finish the last of the chores. Then, walking up the back staircase, she remembered there was a fresh, clean bed with her name on it.

Chapter Three

New Discoveries

John Webster strolled down the street, feeling elated. She was beautiful, and she was going to stay right here in Redwood. The image of her soft porcelain white hair curling around her brown eyes just made his heart stop.

He had been nervous to talk to women. He was polite but never able to get past the first few uncomfortable moments of conversation. With Isabel, it was different. John felt the need to protect her, to take her in his arms and never let anyone harm her.

As he walked towards the saloon, he looked in over the swinging doors and saw his Captain involved in yet another card game. Even Captain Pichon was not going to ruin this wonderful feeling.

He crossed the street and found a bench to wait for his Captain. Too many nights, John waited to ride with him back to the fort or break up a fight the Captain had started over cards.

Sitting in the darkness, he thought of Isabel, and memories of when he first arrived in Redwood came to mind. He was ten years old when John and his mother and father traveled from Wisconsin to Minnesota.

An army friend had offered his dad a job as a bank teller. It was a new start for them after the War. They first lived at the hotel, and then they moved into a small room above the café on the edge of town.

The church at the end of the road through Main Street doubled as the schoolhouse during the week. He went to school until his graduation from 8th grade. His mother worked at the café during breakfast and lunch hours.

John was fourteen when both his mother and father passed away that same winter of influenza. They died a month apart. He looked towards the Redwood Hotel.

John remembered when he found himself living back at the hotel. Maude was there for him. She got him through a rough time in his life.

His dad's sister came out to Redwood when she heard that Agnes Webster had succumbed to the flu. She tried nursing her brother Henry, but he died less than three weeks later.

His Aunt Clara made John stay away from the small apartment for fear of the disease spreading to him. He spent most of his days hanging out at the blacksmith shop. The smithy worked with his brother, who handled all of the harness and leatherwork. John learned how to tan leather, fix boots, and make gloves. It took his mind off the new realization that his life was changing.

After his father passed away, his Aunt Clara decided to stay in Redwood and take care of John. She was offered a job by Maude to work in the kitchen at the Redwood Hotel. Life fell into a nice routine, and John continued to work with Gus and Pete in the harness shop.

Now four years later, here he sat waiting for his Captain and counting down the days until he was officially done being a soldier. By the end of the year, he would be a civilian and twenty-two years old.

He wanted to open a shop to make gloves, vests, and coats out of leather. John had accumulated many tools, and he had socked away his pay for the past four years.

Noise erupted from across the street and knocked John out of his daydreaming. A fight had broken out, and John knew his Captain was involved. He jumped up, ran across the street, and tried to pull his Captain out of the fray.

"He cheated me. I want my money back," yelled a sodbuster.

The gamblers scuffled into a fight knocking over the table. A pistol fired in the air, and there stood Shereen.

"Sodbuster pick up your winnings and straighten up this mess. Captain Pichon, you are finished here. I have watched you cheat these sodbusters out of their hard-earned wages too many nights, and I am tired of these fights. Get out. Now and don't bother coming back," said Shereen.

She turned and gracefully walked through the crowded saloon as everyone stepped back to make way for the blond with the pearl-handled pistol.

Sergeant Webster took hold of Pichon's arm and pointed him towards the door. Pichon tore his arm free and stumbled away from Webster.

"Come on, Captain. It's late and time to get back to the fort," said Sergeant Webster.

"Leave me alone. I can take care of myself. I don't need you looking after me," said Captain Pichon.

Pichon made his way to his horse tied at the rail, and Captain Webster helped him into the saddle. They rode in silence back to the fort.

He looked to the night sky and thanked his lucky stars that Pichon had rejected Isabel. He was a piece of shit that didn't deserve her. She was beautiful in his eyes, and John couldn't stop thinking about her.

As he rode, he berated himself for never being able to talk to girls. He would get all tongue tied and say the wrong thing. Then, they would get mad and stomp off in a huff. He never cared enough about any of them to try to explain, and after a while, he just ignored anyone who tried to flirt or talk to him.

Besides, what did he have to offer them? He didn't own his own business, yet, or have a place to live after he received his discharge papers. What kind of woman would want a man who didn't sleep through the night?

Women wanted their husbands to be able to spend the night in bed, holding them and making love to them. What woman would want to wait until one a.m. for her man to come to bed? Most women would be suspicious of a man wanting to stay up late every night. Somehow, he felt that it might be different with Isabel.

Her curly porcelain hair and her soft, gentle face stayed in his mind until finally, he drifted off to sleep with the thoughts of if he worked hard enough, it could work. He deserved to have a wife and a family. John wanted his own business and a house for all of them to live in together. Just maybe.

* * *

Days went by as Isabel worked at the hotel. Every day, she was meeting new people. Having friends was a new concept for her. She had never had friends other than her brother Ben who was two years younger.

At the hotel, she loved the camaraderie of the kitchen help. She listened to the teasing and the local news; even though she did not understand all of the gossips.

"Hey, Marjorie! You could just as well get a job at Shereen's," said Pauline.

"What do you mean?" fired back the waitress with the long red hair pulled neatly back at the nape of her neck.

"I saw you walking past there last night," said Pauline.

"I wanted to see how much money my man was winning. Besides ain't no harm in a girl going for an evening stroll," Marjorie said with a big smile.

Every morning Isabel would scamper down earlier than the other girls would. She loved sitting on the stool in the corner, working the butter churn and listening to the warm laughter.

Hams baked in the oven, and bacon cooked on the griddle along with pancakes, eggs, and potatoes. She has never eaten three square meals a day or been so warm.

"Isabel! Come here! It's time to learn how to make biscuits. If you're going to be here so early, every morning, you might as well learn," bellowed Clara. "Come here. I'll show you."

Isabel jumped to her feet and stood mesmerized by the woman's large hands as she worked the dough. She listened to all the ingredients: butter, flour, salt, baking powder, and all the hints for making biscuits to feed hungry men.

"Timing the pans right is the key; always remember that. Don't be afraid to turn and check the pans."

She looked around and said in a low voice. "I don't always trust them clocks."

From that morning on, Isabel stood by Clara's side and learned how to make biscuits, buns, pancakes, sweet rolls with maple frosting drizzled over the top with streusel topping and chopped walnuts.

Clara told her she was a quick learner, and Isabel was eager to learn everything she could about cooking. Maude knew this, too. In her heart, Maude hoped this one would stay because my, she was a good worker.

"Hey, Isabel – you better be careful. If you eat too many biscuits, you'll start looking like Clara," shouted Maude's son, Thomas.

"Oh, be off with you – you rascal," yelled Clara as she threw a warm biscuit at him.

Showing off his experience, he caught it with his mouth. Then, he smiled and ran out the door.

"Oh, that boy," Clara said, smiling, never missing a beat as she continued to knead the dough. Isabel laughed right out loud. Clara halted in mid-stroke and said, "Finally, you laugh – you should do that more often; it brings the roses to your cheeks." Isabel blushed and smiled at the older woman.

Every day at two o'clock, coffee and pastries sat on a serving cart, and different waitresses took turns staying to work in the dining room. The kitchen staff cleared out until four o'clock, but by four-thirty, the kitchen would be buzzing with preparations for the supper crowd.

Each afternoon, Clara put her feet up and rested while Maude went to her office to do paperwork. Isabel trailed along with the waitresses as they visited the shops and strolled up and down Main Street looking in all the shop windows.

Isabel was in awe. The shops in Redwood had more inventory than she had ever seen, and the shopkeepers displayed beautiful merchandise in all of their windows.

One week had gone by, and Maude was true to her word. Saturday morning, Maude paid wages to the staff, and the waitresses received their extra tip money. Isabel felt the coins in her hand. These wages were the first she had ever earned. The feeling of pride and joy overwhelmed her.

In the back of her mind, Isabel knew she had an errand to run; one she had avoided. She needed to return Captain Pichon's money. Isabel kept his sack of coins hidden under her mattress, checking it every day.

That afternoon she grabbed her oversized coat, tied on her flat brown hat, picked up the coins, and headed out of the hotel.

Fort Smith was located about two miles out of town. The now early September sky was overcast with a delicate chill in the air. As she left the safety of the buildings on Main Street and headed west, the wind stung her cheeks. She drove her hands deep in the pockets and pulled her collar up around her ears.

Finally, Isabel arrived at the massive gates of the fort. She told the guard that she was here to see Captain Pichon. He pointed her towards the wooden building with a porch and a large sign hanging down.

When she arrived at the steps, a wave of apprehension swept through her as she entered through the heavy wooden door. Barely hearing her voice, she asked to see Captain Pichon.

Captain? A young lady here to see you."

A long pause followed as the polite clerk stepped behind the curtain leading to the hallway. Moments later, he reappeared.

"Have a seat Ma'am. He'll be right out," said the clerk.

Fidgeting in the chair, Isabel felt all the eyes in the room looking at her worn-out shoes. She just wanted to give back his money and leave.

"Ain't you the one who works at the hotel – the clumsy one?" said the blonde soldier leaning against the wall.

"That's enough," said Captain Pichon sternly.

"Yes, sir."

Other than the restaurant, this was the first time Isabel had been face-to-face with Captain Pichon. Isabel stared at the man who might have been her husband. His hair was an oily black color with dark bushy eyebrows to match. His paunchy stomach was squeezed in by tight uniform pants held up with suspenders.

Upon seeing her, he immediately had a look of disgust. That look gave Isabel the courage to stand up and address him.

"Captain Pichon, Uh . . . You wanted me to use this money for a return ticket. I decided not to leave, so I will not need your money," she said as she laid the sack of coins on the desk.

He felt sheepish in front of the other officers who were looking at the floor. He looked down at her worn-out shoes and noticed her oversized coat.

"You must be mistaken. Go on. You can keep the money, and don't be coming down here and bothering me anymore."

Captain Pichon moved back through the curtains. His footsteps down the hallway filled the silence of the room.

Isabel was dumbstruck. Was the money hers to keep? She picked up the pouch of coins from the desk and quickly left the office.

She rushed back to the hotel to the privacy of her small room. Flinging her coat on to the floor, Isabel emptied the coins on her bed.

She wasn't sure what kind they were or how much they were worth. Isabel had never had any money to her name. Her mind raced as she looked at the individual coins. She took the money that Maude gave her and set those in a column. Isabel knew it represented two dollars.

Then, she examined the coins from the pouch. Some were the same size, and she began to separate them. Separating the coins into piles reminded her of home when she and her brother and her mother would look for pretty rocks to polish in the stream.

Stacks of flat stones and piles of smooth round rocks laid in the stream as the water gently flowed over them. It was so beautiful and peaceful when they played that game. Funny how good memories seem to surface when you are far from home?

Slamming doors down the hallway alerted Isabel that it was time to return to work. Picking up the coins, she placed them in the leather pouch. Then, grabbing a sock from a drawer in her dresser, she put her wages in the stocking, knotted it and placed it under the mattress.

She was unable to concentrate on her work that evening. There were too many new thoughts racing through her mind. How could she take care of the money? Could she spend it? What would she buy?

She decided to buy only the necessities and put the rest in the bank under her name. Yes, this was what she was going to do; it was what the redheaded waitress did every Saturday morning. Marjorie went to the bank and deposit her earnings. She told Isabel that it was for a rainy day.

Throughout the next week, Isabel window-shopped at Campbell's General Store, trying to decide what those necessities would be. She decided that she would buy a new pair of shoes first and the next week a pair of socks and then at the end of the month a comb and brush set. The majority would go into the bank for safekeeping.

Isabel lay in bed that night with her mind wide-awake. Was she making the right choices? For a few minutes, as she snuggled under the covers in her warm bed, she allowed herself to be happy. Sleep crept upon her as the evening stars twinkled in the still night air.

Chapter Four

Brand New Boots

The next morning, time moved in slow motion. Isabel was afraid that two o'clock would never arrive or that Clara would find work for her to do that afternoon.

As the lobby clock chimed the second bell, Isabel rushed to her room and grabbed her big brown coat. She removed the pouch of coins from her mattress and headed to Campbell's General Store.

A bell tinkled as she pushed open the wooden frame door with beveled glass.

Inside the store were shelves and shelves of beautiful new items: bolts of cloth, canned goods, shoes, clothes, candy, flour, beans, nails, leather goods, and toiletries. Mr. Campbell kept the well-worn wooden floors swept clean, and the air smelled of leather and sweets.

Mr. Campbell knew that every afternoon like clockwork, Isabel would be there to look, just looking at every item. This young girl was inquisitive. He thought that it was strange; it was as if she had never seen store-bought articles before in her life. If he was busy, she never interrupted.

At first, she seemed to be shy, but the past few days, he had noticed a slight air of confidence developing.

"Well, what you expect? Maude and Clara are bound to rub off on a person after a while," he thought as he watched her walk toward the shoes.

"Mr. Campbell, I would like to buy a pair of shoes," Isabel stated.

"Did Maude finally decide to pay you some decent wages?" said Mr. Campbell.

Her face turned crimson as she debated silently on how to explain to him where she got the money and that the Captain had turned her down as a suitable bride.

A lump gathered at her throat, and tears stung her eyes as she stared at the new shoes behind the counter.

Mr. Campbell had seen her demeanor change as he mentioned the money. He cursed himself under his breath. He knew darn well, where she got the money. It was all over town how she had tried to return the traveling money to Captain Pichon.

"By golly," he thought. "I'll help Miss Isabel get a nice pair of shoes for the money."

"Uh – what size did you need, miss?" he said, trying to smooth over the awkwardness in the air.

"I don't know much about sizes, Mr. Campbell. "I have never bought a pair of shoes before."

"Well, let's see." Mr. Campbell handed her different sizes and styles. Isabel sat on the small stool between the glass-topped counters and tried on each pair of shoes. The sunlight streamed through the window, as they tried to find her a suitable pair of boots for work. Mr. Campbell joked and laughed with her, and finally, Isabel picked out black lace-up boots.

"Well, you are in luck today. With every pair of boots sold today, we are giving away a pair of stockings to go with them."

Isabel blushed. She knew Mr. Campbell had seen the condition of her stockings. She looked down and said, "Thank you."

"Let me wrap them up for you."

"Mr. Campbell. Do I have enough for a comb and brush set?"

Mr. Campbell felt the pouch of coins and opened the leather drawstring. He poured half the coins into his hand and smiled. "Oh yes, my dear, you have enough for a comb and brush set. Let's look."

She felt pulled over to the glass cabinet as she stared down at a set that contained an ivory comb with a brush that had a red marbleized back.

This time joyful tears came to her smiling liquid brown eyes. "It's beautiful," she whispered.

It was at that moment that Mr. Campbell realized she was too good for that low-life Captain Pichon. He saw such innocence in her eyes, and he realized she had never owned or seen such beautiful things in her lifetime.

"Will there be anything" else, Ma'am?"

"No, that will be all for today, sir."

Isabel became nervous as she moved closer to the countertop.

"Mr. Campbell, I don't know how to count the coins."

"Here, let me help you. That will be $5.85. Let see what you've got."

She poured out the pouch of coins. On the counter, Mr. Campbell separated several half-eagles each worth five dollars and a few silver dollars.

Then, he took one of the half eagles and one of the silver dollars. He gave her back a dime and a five-cent piece. She slipped the coins back into the leather pouch and clutched it in her hand.

"You still have over twenty dollars left, and that is quite a bit for a young lady to be carrying around. You better put that in a safe place," said Mr. Campbell.

"Thank you, Mr. Campbell. I am going over to the bank. After all, it is my money," said Isabel.

"Yessiree – you're right there, Ma'am."

She headed for the door, turned around, smiled, and said. "Thank you again, Mr. Campbell, for helping count and for the stockings."

Isabel was proud to be carrying packages across the street, packages that belong to her. Her elevated mood diminished as she walked into the First National Bank of Redwood. People were milling around, and they all seem to turn and look directly at Isabel.

She took a deep breath and walked straight ahead to the teller window. A skinny man with a high-pitched voice asked her if he could help her.

"I have some coins I would like to keep in your bank."

The man reiterated, "You would like to open an account with us?"

Townspeople in the lobby of the bank overheard the conversation, Isabel felt everyone staring at her.

"I will need some information – please come with me," said the teller.

He moved over to the intricate, wood-carved gate attached to the marble countertop. Moving with the utmost efficiency, he sat rigid in the wooden chair behind a large oak desk. Silence filled the air as he motioned her to a chair on the other side of the desk. Marvin Phelpson swelled with the importance of the task, and he began to fire questions at her.

"Name?"

"Isabel Grant"

"Age"

Isabel wasn't sure exactly but told him she was 17.

"Current residence?"

"I have a room at Maude's – The Redwood Hotel."

"Where is your permanent resident?

"I got on the train at Calabash."

"Are you married?"

"No"

"Are you employed?"

"Yes, I work at the Redwood Hotel."

"Do you have a permit?"

"No, I don't know what that is."

The skinny young man pushed up his glasses and pointed to a piece of paper hanging on the wall. "Well, there it is. Regulations stated by the Department of Commerce."

Isabel looked at the sheet of paper and then looked back at the young man. She leaned in and whispered to him, "I'm sorry, sir. I can't read."

A high-pitched voice began to read loud enough for everyone in the bank to hear: "All women unaccompanied by a husband, father or mother engaged in housework or industrial employment must receive a permit and travel in a conducted party. Regulations of the Department of Commerce."

"Do you have the forms the young lady needs to fill out to get his permit?"

Marvin Phelpson almost jumped out of his tiny suit when the tall frame of John Webster stepped through the ornate wooden gate.

"Yes, sir, Sergeant. Right here."

Isabel turned to hear the deep, gentle voice of John Webster. She stood up, and her heart melted. Their eyes locked, and the world stood still.

Rushing to a wooden table in the corner, Phelpson was able to locate the necessary forms. He tried giving the papers to Sergeant Webster.

Without looking away, John said, "Give the papers to her, and I'll see that Maude helps her get these filled out."

Isabel looked away and blushed. She took the papers, and John held the gate. As she walked into the lobby, a high-pitched voice squeaked, "Miss, are these your packages?"

"My packages – how could I forget my purchases?" thought Isabel.

"Allow me." John Webster took hold of her packages, and then he opened the lobby door for Isabel to walk out into the brisk September air.

"Thank you, Mr. Webster." She stopped on the wooden sidewalk and looked at the papers in her hands.

"They won't send me back if I don't get that permit – Will they? They can't," said Isabel.

John looked deep into the fear of the soft-brown eyes and thought, "not if I have anything to say about it."

"Don't worry about it. Maude will help you. We won't let them send you back if you don't want to go back," said John.

John offered his arm, and they walked towards the hotel. She told him about her packages, and he told her how he hated how the bank teller treated her.

Isabel laughed at his stories and listened to every word. He smiled as she told him of her new child-like discoveries around a town he had lived in for the last ten years.

That awkward moment arrived as they both realized they were standing in front of the hotel. Isabel knew that it was time to get back to work, yet her heart didn't want him to leave.

"Thank you for your help. I am learning just how difficult it can be for a girl alone in town."

She realized that her words didn't sound like she wanted them to, and she stuttered, "I ah mean with money and banking and."

John let out a healthy roar as his eyes squinted shut.

"I understand what you meant. You had better be careful and get going. Clara will have your hide if you're late. Sure, glad I could oblige, Ma'am. I look forward to seeing you again, Ma'am."

"I would like that, Mr. Webster."

"Please call me John."

"Only if you call me Isabel."

He tipped his navy-blue hat and headed back down the street. Isabel watched him walk away, and she thought she heard him whistling.

Julie Granger

Upstairs in her room, Isabel donned her new stockings and laced up her new black boots. The ivory comb and the red marble hairbrush laid with dignity on the top of her dresser. Placing the sack of coins and the bank papers in the shoebox, she slid it under her bed. Dancing down the hallway, delighted with the feel of her new boots, she headed downstairs for the evening shift.

Chapter Five

Rainy Days

Late that evening, Captain Ivan Pichon paced the small confines of his room with indignation and fire. The more he walked, the more desperate he became.

"How dare Shereen ban me from the saloon! Who in the hell does she think she is? I've been a loyal customer."

He continued to pace and mutter under his breath.

"And how dare she stay here. That skinny scarecrow of a girl. She is nothing, but a constant reminder of another waste of money."

Captain Pichon knew he couldn't handle money. He gambled on cards, left big tips for saloon girls, and paid money to get rid of things that annoyed him. Now in debt and feeling desperate, Pichon itched to play cards, but he needed money, and he needed a plan.

Pichon calculated how he would get back the money he gave to Grant's daughter; it would be enough to get him into a card game, somewhere.

* * *

It had been a long night at Maude's. Some businessmen from the lumber mill were entertaining guests from over by New Ulm, and the people were spending the night at the hotel with no intention of sleeping.

Cigar smoke filled the dining room as the gentlemen enjoyed drinks of whiskey followed by a meal of turkey, stuffing, baked beans and brown bread pudding with pumpkin pie. Festivities continued with brandy and cigars.

The kitchen staff worked late into the evening cleaning. By midnight, every inch of Isabel's feet ached. She never realized that new shoes could hurt so badly. She didn't know if she could walk up the steps. Following the familiar path through the hotel to the back staircase, she climbed the stairs wincing with each step. As she entered her room, she closed the door, and the hair on the back of her neck stood on end. She could feel the presence of someone standing right behind her.

Pichon stepped out of the shadows and covered her mouth with his sweaty hand. He hissed in her ear.

"I want my money... now."

Isabel shook with fright as the familiar tone of his voice became evident. As he eased the pressure against her mouth, Isabel gasped for air and said, "I don't have it."

"Where is it?"

"It's in the bank."

"You listen to me. I want my money back. You get it out of that bank, and you bring it to me tomorrow night."

Isabel nodded her head, obediently.

"If you don't, I'll take you back to your old man, and I'll get it out of him and whatever else he has. I'm sure your old man could turn around and sell you again."

With the realization of his words, she became light-headed and collapsed to the floor. Captain looked around the room and then to the doorway to check down the hallway. Within three steps, he was down the staircase and out into the darkness of the night.

* * *

Isaiah Grant never recovered from selling his only daughter to Captain Pichon to pay off his debt. It was the final straw. He had worked and schemed to provide, but hard living had caught up to his body and mind. He knew he could not work as he used to at the lumber camp. Isaiah had become involved with some bad people who were only interested in making fast buck the easy way, and easy money had a price.

He also blamed himself for his wife's mental state. Isaiah wore the guilt of not being at home when the soldiers attacked Ellie. After the rape and the difficult delivery of another baby, Isabel's mother was never right in the head after that. Ellie was so frightened of people that she would run off to a cave.

She would scamper across the open meadow across the river as if demons were chasing her. The wide-eyed look of fear became etched on her face. After many days in the cave, she would come back and be very sullen and reserved as if she felt bad for her behavior.

Sadness had descended on Isaiah like a heavy blanket of guilt when he returned home from the train station. He lost interest and never left the place. The bottom had dropped out of his life.

* * *

Maude heard the loud footsteps against the pine flooring and decided she needed to talk to those waitresses living across the hall from Isabel.

"There is too much noise this late at night and to be sneaking men up here. What do they think this is a bordello?" She punched her pillow and rolled over, trying to settle back into sleep.

Isabel's eyes opened in pain as the light streamed through the windows. She found herself lying in a crumpled heap, cold and stiff from spending the night on the wooden boards. She rubbed some feeling into her arms and puzzled over the events that led to the floor.

Stumbling to the mirror, she stared at the young woman looking back. "I am not giving that money back" was the first thing her heart told her as she pieced together the strange moments after work.

Isabel checked under her bed. The shoebox with the coins and papers from the bank were still there. She needed to fill them out and return them to the bank.

Isabel looked at the papers and realized she could not read a letter. Isabel had never gone to school or held a pencil. The sheets felt foreign in her hand; it gave her a sickening feeling in her stomach.

She felt her feet propelling towards Maude's room with the papers in her hand. Isabel knocked on her door.

"Good morning, Isabel. Is something the matter? Come in and sit down."

Maude lived in a double room furnished with beautiful burgundy cloth chairs, ornate tables, a full bedroom set with a matching dressing screen. She and her late husband had established the Redwood Hotel and restaurant to the grand status it now held in this booming lumber town.

"I'm sorry, Ma'am to disturb you so early in the morning," Isabel's head was spinning. Her heart was pleading with her to tell Maude about Captain Pichon's visit. She forced herself to calm down and began to explain.

"I have these papers from the bank, and I need a permit, and I can't read or write, and Sergeant Webster said that you might help me."

Maude realized why she looked so frightened. "Why I'd be honored to help you fill out these forms; I'll even take you to the bank this morning to register them."

For the next twenty minutes, Maude explained the papers as she filled in the blanks. Isabel watched in fascination as Maude dipped her pen into the ink well and created these beautiful flourishes on the thick paper of the bank's official forms. When she finished her signatures, Isabel thanked Maude for her kindness.

Moving towards the door, Maude noticed Isabel's shoes and asked, "Is that what you did with the money you got from Captain Pichon?"

Isabel jumped at the sound of his name and then looked down at the floor, embarrassed, "Yes, Ma'am."

"Good for you! Women have to be one step ahead of these men these days. I think you are one of the lucky ones. You got the money instead of the man."

As they walked out into the hallway, two waitresses were walking ahead of them. Maude remembered the noise during the night.

"How dare you two! Bringing men up to your rooms last night."

Isabel realized Maude had heard Captain Pichon leaving. She wanted to tell but held back. The two waitresses continued to protest their innocence all the way to the kitchen.

Maude and Isabel walked into the bank at nine, and then they were ushered back to two chairs across from Mr. Phelpson's desk.

To Maude, Marvin Phelpson's entire suit looked two sizes too small, and she thought he was too tight to spend any money to get a new one. Isabel watched Mr. Phelpson trip all over Maude like a clumsy weasel.

Within the hour, Isabel and Maude were walking back to the hotel. Isabel held her work permit, an address card, a bankbook showing her balance, and an odd amount of coins in the leather drawstring pouch, Maude told her it was her "walking around" money.

The money was hers; she was not giving it back. As she held the paper in her hands, she began to comprehend the feeling of independence. Maude linked arms with Isabel as they strolled back to the hotel in the crisp autumn air.

"I am so glad you decided to stay and work here in Redwood. Payday is this Saturday, and you will be able to add the money to your account. It is so important that a woman have her own money."

"The waitresses told me that it was for a rainy day."

Maude laughed and smiled at this tiny little girl on her arm. "And when it rains, it pours, and somehow it always seems to involve men," said Maude.

As they reached the hotel, Captain Pichon stepped out onto the sidewalk and tipped his hat to the ladies. Maude could feel Isabel grow tense as she hurried by avoiding his eyes. Maude greeted him with business-like politeness as she moved through the double doors of the hotel.

Stopping Isabel in the back hallway, Maude reassured her, "You don't know how lucky you are to be away from him. That man has a mean streak. Thank your lucky stars that you are away from him."

"Yes, Ma'am," said Isabel.

"If only that were true," she thought.

Isabel headed up the back stairs to place these papers of independence into the shoebox under her bed. She had spent almost a full day in her new boots, and her feet were sore and tender.

After removing her shoes and her new stockings, Isabel examined the bubbly red spots on her heels and her toes. She would ask Clara; she would know what to do for her feet. Isabel laced up her old boots and headed to the kitchen to help with the lunch crowd.

Clara bustled around the kitchen, barking orders in everyone's direction. When Isabel walked through the back-kitchen door, Clara pointed to the potatoes.

"The water is already started. The potatoes need peeling," ordered Clara.

As Isabel peeled potatoes, she searched her mind looking for logic and courage on what to do about Captain Pichon and the money.

She knew deep down she did not want to give the money back, but then a stupid, weak voice kept reminding her that it was his money. yet he had told her in front of witnesses she could have it.

Isabel knew that she would continue to see the Captain as long as she lived here. In small ways, Redwood was becoming her home. She didn't want to leave, and she didn't want to go back, back to the isolation of the woods.

For the past three weeks, Isabel could feel herself change. She had spent her entire life void of warmth from soft blankets and busy kitchens and woolen stockings new from the store. She had lived her life isolated from the world. Her world had consisted of trees and bushes and dark, dark, corners of a cabin that smelled of wet dirt.

Now, she was living in a clean room that had a window with curtains and a real bed with sheets that smelled of fresh soap. She had bought her first pair of shoes, and then there was John Webster.

The memory of his laughing, smiling eyes made Isabel forget about the repetitive motions of peeling potatoes. She smiled as she thought of his uproarious laugh and the squinty lines around his eyes. Isabel liked that he was so tall and much better looking than Captain Pichon. She felt safe and protected when she was with him.

She shuddered, trying not to think of the threats the Captain had made the night before.

"I want my money back . . . Tomorrow. I'm coming back for it." The Captain's words seem to play repeatedly in her head.

"Look out! Ah fie, daydreaming!" shouted Clara. "Pay attention to your job."

The potato water had sloshed in all directions.

"I'm sorry. I'll clean it up," Isabel told Clara. Isabel soaked up the spilled potato water and rinsed the wooden floor.

After dumping the gray wash water, Isabel dried her hands and removed her white apron. She took a couple of minutes to admire the cleanliness. She liked the look of polished wood, and the smell of clean swept floors, and she reaffirmed to herself that there would be no more dirt floors in her lifetime.

Chapter Six

Unexpected Surprises

By five o'clock, Captain Pichon had spent over an hour pacing in front of the window looking towards town waiting for her to appear. It was unthinkable that little twit would not show up with my money. "How dare she!" he thought.

His anger burned as he stomped out of the office. He ordered Sergeant Webster to mount up, and they both rode toward the hotel.

Pichon sat alone at the table in the hotel, calculating a plan to confront Isabel tonight. The Captain believed Isabel had the money.

John Webster sat across the room from his commanding officer, calculating his mood. His growing dislike for his commander was starting to rise closer to the surface every day.

John enjoyed the warmth of the dining room, and his Aunt Clara's biscuits. When John had time away from his duties, he spent time working with leather down at a small shop behind the blacksmith's shop at the end of Main Street. It seemed to relax him working on his own.

In two months, his duty was up, and he would be a civilian. He wanted to open a leather shop full time. John made the highest quality boots, gloves, and belts in the area. He only took orders that paid up front in cash. He tucked the money away for the day he could walk away from Captain Pichon. He never regretted his service to the Army, but with the Indian wars moving to the Dakotas, it was time to move on with his life.

As John finish sopping up the last of the gravy with the end of his biscuit, he saw the Captain stride down the hallway to the kitchen. An overwhelming feeling came over him. His need to protect Isabel was pulsating through him. He wiped his mouth and headed down the hallway toward the kitchen.

John heard Pichon talking. It wasn't until he came around the side of Pichon that he noticed Isabel trapped in the corner.

"Isabel, are you all right?" asked Sergeant Webster.

"And why wouldn't she be, Sergeant?" asked Pichon.

Isabel felt weak in the knees as the two men exchanged terse remarks.

John looked directly at Isabel and carefully said, "Are you ready to go?"

Isabel stammered, "No. I have a couple of things left to do in the kitchen."

"Webster, what're you doing? Picking up my leftovers?"

Sergeant Webster looked coldly into his eyes. "Yes, sir, I am."

Isabel listened in disbelief and scampered like a field mouse back into the kitchen. John saw her leave and stood his ground to show he would wait for her. Pichon turned in disgust and walked out of the hotel.

Isabel stalled in the kitchen that night looking for things to clean. Finally, she knew she had to face the hallway and John Webster.

"Leftovers – how dare he! Is that what he thinks of me?" thought Isabel.

Isabel did not have a temper, yet the remarks made her irritated. The more she cleaned, the madder she became.

John sat in the hallway stirring in his mind what he would say to her. What was happening to him? Why wasn't he in his shop? Instead, he was sitting in the back hallway of the hotel kitchen waiting, wondering if she would come out and talk to him.

Her eyes seemed to appear to him at regular intervals throughout the day. His concentration had fogged over, and he found himself daydreaming about those eyes, those soft brown eyes that cried out for protection.

Isabel took a deep breath and walked out into the darkened hallway. John jumped to his feet and blurted out, "Are you all right? Is he bothering you?"

"No. Yes. I'm fine. No, I mean no; the Captain is not bothering me," said Isabel.

Isabel's temper melted away as he asked how she was. His look of concern seared through her.

"You wanted to know if I was ready to go?" asked Isabel.

"I just said that to get you away from the Captain."

"Oh, I see."

"But, if you like, we could go for a walk," offered John.

Isabel smiled and looked deep into his eyes. "I would like that very much. Wait just a moment while I run up and grab my coat."

Although he was 22 years old, John Webster felt like a schoolboy as he paced at the end of the staircase.

When they stepped outside of the hotel, the night air smelled of autumn leaves and wood stoves. The coal-black sky overhead twinkled with stars.

John and Isabel walked and talked with ease as they made their way to his corner shop. The smell of horses and hot coals filled the air.

"Every chance I get, I like coming here to work. Pete and Gus let me have this back-tackle room to store my tools. In exchange, I work on harnesses and repair leather straps for them."

John went about the routine of lighting a lantern and stoking the fire in the corner stove. He cleared off a wooden stool for Isabel.

She looked around at all the wooden-handled tools. Isabel admired the well-organized shop, yet the benches held many projects needing attention.

"I have two months left of duty, and then I hope to work full time for Pete and Gus at first and then eventually build my shop," said John.

Isabel looked at him with pride as he explained his plans.

"Say, let me look at those boots for you. I could polish them up if you like," said John.

She became embarrassed as he noticed her old boots.

"I bought some new boots from Mr. Campbell. I made the mistake of wearing them all day, and now I have sores on my feet from wearing them. I guess I was used to my old boots," explained Isabel.

"Did Mr. Campbell explain to you how to take care of them, so they last a long time?" asked John.

"No, but he did give me a new pair of stockings," said Isabel.

"Blisters are the worse. If I have learned anything about being a soldier, it is how to take care of your feet," said John.

Searching through a wooden box, he found a can of salve.

"Here, rub some of this into your blisters," explained John as he handed her the round tin container. John saw the awkwardness that Isabel felt accepting the salve.

"You can borrow it. Use as much as you need." John grabbed the oil and said, "I tell you what I'm going to do. Why don't you plan to wear your old boots for the next couple of days and give your feet a chance to heal?"

Tomorrow night let me have your new shoes, and I'll use my boot stretcher to loosen them up a little. I'll even put some goose grease on them to waterproof them."

"That would be very nice of you, Sergeant," said Isabel.

"John, Ma'am."

"Isabel, sir."

Then, they both laughed as the fire glowed in the corner. Isabel felt warm and comfortable sitting with John. She asked him questions about how he came to be in the Army.

John found himself telling her about his parents and his Aunt Clara, along with his extreme dislike of his commanding officer.

In the back of his mind, he wanted to ask about the deal that Isabel's father had made with Pichon. He couldn't understand how any man could turn his daughter over to a man like Pichon. It must have felt like selling your soul to the devil.

The silence began to stretch, and John did not want her to leave, not yet.

"I'm sorry, Isabel, but I have to ask. How did you ever get mixed up with a guy like Pichon? What kind of deal did your dad make? If you don't want to tell me, I would understand."

"No, I don't mind. I haven't told anyone. There are nights that I try and figure it out myself," confessed Isabel.

Then, Isabel told John about her home in the woods outside of Calabash and her family.

"Ben is my brother, and he is two years younger than I am. I miss him so much, and I hope someday to bring him here to Redwood, but I know he is needed to run the home place and try to take care of both ma and pa."

John listened with intent, as Isabel explained her home life.

"You see, Pa worked for long spells away from the homestead, and after our home was attacked by soldiers," said Isabel.

"Wait a minute, soldiers attacked your homestead?" asked John. "American soldiers?"

"Yes," replied Isabel. "The men attacked my mother as we hid in the root cellar. I remember the night the soldiers came to the door, and they had been drinking. They wanted food, and my mother didn't have any. When she rushed into the kitchen pretending to look for food, she told us, children, to hide in the root cellar off the back of the kitchen. We could hear fighting and thuds of heavy feet as mother screamed and fought back. We covered our ears, fearing for our lives. I was eight, and Ben was six; Jeb was two, and Noah was one."

"They drank and ate our food. Then, the men left the next morning," said Isabel. "My mother, Ellie, became terrified of everything, including people in general. She would cling to Jimmy, her last baby, like a toy, squeezing him tight and draping him over her arm as she would run towards the cave.

On these days, Ben tried to bring her food and check on her and Jimmy. You see, the cave location was on the other side of the river. Then, we crossed the open meadow near a tree line of pines by the mountain ridge.

Our lives changed after that night, and the cave became our second home. Ever since the attack by the men in blue uniforms, my mother would hide us kids in the cave for days. We played in the area, but Ben and I always managed to sneak back to do chores for the animals. Most of the time, the two youngest boys stayed in the cave with my mother.

When Pa returned home several days later to find the cabin in shambles, and everyone gone; he feared the worse. He saw Ben doing chores, and Ben told Pa what had happened. Ben showed him the cave, and he convinced Ma to bring everyone back home. He stayed for several weeks and helped us put a routine into our lives, but finally, the need for supplies and people drove him to find work.

Ben and I ran the homestead and took care of Ma and the boys. We buried Jeb and Noah and later Jimmy in the cave after they died from winter illness. It was a harsh winter that year, and mother insisted on keeping everyone in the dark, damp areas of the cabin. Malnourished and puny, those babies didn't stand a chance.

We covered their bodies with rocks in the farthest back room of the cave hoping animals wouldn't find their bodies," said Isabel. Before I left, she started showing signs of being afraid of Ben. It was as if she didn't recognize him."

After all these years, Isabel's pain remained. She looked through the pool of tears, which blurred the firelight as she remembered her brothers. Isabel realized how Isaiah Grant had lied to his daughter when he told her he had found a suitable husband, an officer who would take care of her.

She didn't want to leave Ben, but her father became downright violent when she protested. One by one, Isabel remembered the silence that seemed to sever the ties as they rode to Calabash to meet the train.

She looked up into the eyes of John Webster and said, "And that is why I do not want to go back to my life in that cabin."

" I won't let you," said John Webster with conviction in his voice.

He stood up and walked over to her. Ever so gently, he wrapped his arms around her and just held her, hoping his broad shoulders and powerful arms could remove the burden she has carried all these years.

That night he silently vowed to spend the rest of his life removing the pain of her childhood and protecting her from harm. He also realized how deeply he loved this young woman at that very moment.

* * *

It was Saturday morning, which meant washday and payday. Isabel loved Saturdays. Clean clothes and fresh bedding were her two new favorite luxuries. She always stopped at Mr. Campbell's general store on her way to the bank.

This morning, she planned to purchase a bar of scented soap, a pair of stockings and put the rest of her wages in the bank.

She felt beautiful this morning. The burden of finally telling someone her story made her feel lighter than air. She closed her eyes, and she could almost feel John's arms around her. Isabel never wanted to lose that feeling. Isabel grabbed her new boots and headed downstairs to start her day.

The lunch crowd at the hotel included guests and locals alike. Farmers, travelers, and local business people feasted every noon on biscuits and gravy with meat and cooked vegetables. Homemade preserves sat on every table, and the kitchen staff displayed desserts on the buffet.

The dining room doors opened into the kitchen, and Maude smiled with delight when Isabel walked out. Maude had spent most of the morning developing a plan to help her. When Isabel finished setting the last of the coffee cups on the cart, Maude entwined her arm with Isabel and with twinkling eyes said, "Come with me. I have a couple of surprises for you."

They went up to Maude's room, and when Maude opened the door, there was a woman of color working on a dress.

"Isabel, I would like you to meet Sarah. Sarah is married to Joshua, my handyman. He helps me with the hotel and takes care of our carriage house. Sarah helps me with my laundry, and she is an excellent seamstress."

"Oh now, ma'am, don't be telling her stories," Sarah said with an infectious smile. The friendship of the two women filled the room.

Maude walked over to a pile of clothes on the burgundy chair, lifted it, and placed the garments in Isabel's arms.

"Here," she said. "Sarah and I went through some old things of mine, and I want you to have them. Sarah has already scolded me. She told me I need to stop eating biscuits, or else I am going to have to get a whole new wardrobe," Maude laughed.

Isabel was dumbfounded. She had never owned held such a pile of clothes. "Thank you, ma'am. I don't know what to say. Are you sure?"

"Of course, and this week, Sarah will help you alter the dresses to fit."

"I only know how to sew patches," Isabel declared.

"That's a start, Miss Isabel," said Sarah.

"Well, Sarah will help teach you, and she is the best," said Maude as she looked at Sarah with love in her eyes for the young woman.

"Miss Isabel, I would be right glad to help you learn to stitch," said Sara.

"Speaking of teaching," Maude said with a twinkle in her eye. She walked over to the table to retrieve an envelope. She handed the cream-colored envelope to Isabel and said, "I want you to run an errand for me. My late husband's sister lives on the west edge of town in a large two-story house. Thomas needs to take some supplies up to her, and I would be grateful if you could give this letter to her. Wait for a reply. Thomas will need time to upload the wagon and carry her supplies into the pantry."

"I would be glad to run an errand for you, Mrs. Renshaw," said Isabel.

"Oh, I almost forgot. Here. Every girl needs a purse to carry her money and personal things. Just put the envelope in there along with this week's wages and your bank book."

Isabel looked down at the black velvet pouch with small peach-colored flowers.

It had a steel clasp and short silver chain on the top. Inside the purse, dark green silk material lined the velvet pouch.

"It's beautiful. Are you sure?" Isabel looked up with tears of gratitude. " How can I ever repay you?"

"Oh, go on now. You are going to make me cry."

Then, Maude gave her a big hug and told her she was glad these things were going to an appreciative home.

"Besides, if I don't get rid of some of these things, I won't have any room for our spring shopping trip to St. Paul. Isn't that right, Sarah?"

"That's right Ma'am."

Isabel carried her clothes to her room, and then Isabel grabbed her coat and hat. She headed out to the carriage house behind the hotel. She smiled as she climbed up on the buckboard next to Thomas.

"Welcome aboard the Thomas Renshaw Express. Hang on to your hat."

At sixteen, Thomas Renshaw was mischievous with a great sense of humor and adventure. He smiled twenty-four hours a day. The ride was exhilarating as Thomas took Isabel through the homes on the west side of town toward his aunt's house. Isabel's flushed cheeks were beet red by the time he pulled up the reins to slow down in the back alley of Mrs. Henry Beaumont's home.

Thomas's aunt stood in the frame of her back door, clutching a white woolen shawl around her thin shoulders. A cameo brooch accented her throat and complimented the gray dress with intricate pleats and stitching.

"Hello. Come in. Well, come right in. I love having visitors. Thomas, my boy, give me a smooch. There, there, just set those things in the pantry."

"Hello, Mrs. Beaumont. My name is Isabel Grant, and Maude sent you this note."

"Well, come in and sit awhile," said Ruth Beaumont.

Isabel stepped into the magic of her home and became spellbound at the sights.

To the right side were the kitchen and the pantry. Heavenly smells of cinnamon and apples drifted through the house. Her feet seemed to pull her forward as she stared with disbelief at the beauty before her

In the dining room, there was a large wooden table with a lace tablecloth and a large candle centerpiece. In the parlor, there was velvet on the pillows and beautifully carved chairs and sofas throughout the room.

There were books, marble statues, and paintings of flowers everywhere with wire bird cages. Ruth watched as this wisp of a girl with porcelain hair absorbed the beauty of her home. It was refreshing for Ruth to have someone appreciate her home.

"My, this is a delightful offer. Please tell Maude I would love to teach you how to read and write," said Mrs. Beaumont.

"What?" said Isabel as if coming out of a magical spell.

"Didn't Maude tell you?"

"No, Ma'am."

"Do you want to learn to read?" asked Mrs. Beaumont.

"I don't know if I can," confessed Isabel.

"Aunt Ruth?" shouted Thomas.

"Just a minute. I'll be right back," said Mrs. Beaumont.

She bustled into the kitchen toward the sound of Thomas's voice.

"I finished putting the supplies in the pantry," Thomas said. "Is it all right if I go and tinker in the shop?"

"Go right ahead, young man, but sure to help yourself to some of those apple bars."

"Thanks. I already did, and they were delicious."

His smile radiated in the room as his aunt glowed with admiration at her growing nephew. Thomas retreated out the back door towards the carriage house and into the shop, which held tools of every type.

"My late husband has a shop that Thomas finds fascinating. I'm glad someone is getting some use out of all those tools."

"Mrs. Beaumont, I can't begin,"

"Call me Ruth."

"I want to thank you, Ruth," said Isabel.

"Nonsense, " said Ruth Beaumont. "I was a schoolteacher for a few years until I married Henry. Besides I would enjoy the company.

Isabel shared her story of Captain Pichon's money and the bank papers as Ruth served tea and apple bars.

Before Isabel left to go back to the hotel, Ruth dug in the bookshelves and found a primer. She handed Isabel some paper.

Then, Ruth gave her a couple of pencils along with a small pocketknife. She showed her how to sharpen them to a point.

"Take this book. We will start with the alphabet."

Ruth showed her the first few pages of the book and instructed her to copy the letters.

"Thank you. I don't know what to say,"

"Tell me you will be back Thursday and promise to work hard."

"Oh, I will. I promise."

Isabel was radiant throughout supper and chattered to Clara about everything she had seen for the first time in her life.

Clara listened as this child-like girl described these discoveries. Her enthusiasm became contagious throughout the kitchen.

"There were shelves of books to the ceiling with a ladder attached to the side to climb up to the top shelf," said Isabel. As her hand went up in the air describing the ladder, she smacked Sergeant Webster right in the face with the flour packet used to dust the baking powder biscuits.

Good grief. All I wanted to do was to check and make sure Clara had made plenty of biscuits tonight because I'm hungry," John said as he tried brushing the flour off his uniform.

"Well, that's what you get for standing in here eavesdropping in on our conversations," Clara said as she handed him a wet towel to dust off his uniform.

"I am sorry, Sergeant. I didn't see you standing back there," said Isabel.

"It might be safer to wait in the dining room to get my biscuits." He smiled at Isabel with the warmest, widest smile Isabel had ever seen. Then, he leaned in closer to ask her if she had brought her boots with her tonight.

Isabel went over to the corner and grabbed her new shoes, and Clara's eyebrows raised as she watched the exchange between these two. With the boots in hand, he slipped out of the kitchen. Isabel smiled at Clara and gracefully swept up the flour.

Chapter Seven

Growing Pains

On Saturday morning, Isabel and Sarah went through the pile of clothes from Maude. Isabel could not believe her good fortune: it was like a jackpot of beautiful clothes. She sorted nightgowns, chemises, and pantaloons into separate piles.

Sarah hung up the dresses for every day along with two beautiful gowns. Sarah insisted on picking one of the more elegant dresses to alter for Isabel.

"Sarah, where would I wear this?

"Girl, aren't you planning on going to the town celebration next Saturday?"

"Town celebration?"

"The whole town gets together to celebrate the harvest. Why there are apple cider and food stands, a street dance, box socials, and games for the kids."

"Oh, I didn't realize it. I've never been to anything like that."

"Let's try on this emerald green gown; it would match nicely with your white hair."

Isabel slipped the gown over her undergarments, looked down, and started laughing. Sarah smiled and then realized why she was laughing.

"Sarah, I'm not exactly built like Maude."

Isabel showed her the gaping bosom of the dress.

"Well, let's see what we can do about that."

Sarah dug through the undergarments, and she pulled out a whale-boned corset.

"Let's try this with the dress."

Before her eyes, Sara was able to transform her skinny body into the curves of a young woman. Then, she started pinning and tucking the bodice to create a sweetheart neckline to show a modest amount of décolletage.

"I think I will start on this one. I will have it already to go for Saturday. Let's look at these others for fit."

Isabel and Sarah spent the next hour trying and pinning the rest of the dresses. Sarah also agreed to teach her to sew, but she explained the lessons might have to wait until next week with all of the preparations for harvest celebrations.

After the lunch crowd finished, Isabel went upstairs to gather her new purse with her wages and grabbed her coat and hat. At Campbell' Store, Isabel purchased a bar of scented soap, a decorative hair comb and another pair of stockings for winter.

She looked at the cloth and sewing notions as well as the writing supplies. Isabel enjoyed the daydreams of future purchases. After settling with Mr. Campbell, she went to the bank and deposited her remaining money in the bank. She felt so grown up carrying her packages and her bankbook in her new purse.

Maude had tucked the bag full of surprises. There was a beautiful white handkerchief with royal blue stitching, a pot of rouge, a small bottle of perfume, and a leather purse for coins.

Walking back to the hotel, she thought of John and wondered if he was planning to attend the harvest celebration. She looked forward to every night seeing him in the dining room.

It felt so right to be in his arms; everything about him was perfect. For a few fleeting moments, Isabel allowed herself to be truly happy.

* * *

It had been two days since John had seen Isabel. The last time had been when he picked up her boots. Sergeant Webster worked in the shop, polishing and protecting them with goose grease, and then, he inserted the boot stretcher inside to loosen the leather. Tonight, John was going to bring back her boots. If he could straighten out his tongue. John was going to ask her to the harvest celebration on Saturday.

He had heard from some of the soldiers that another train of girls, mainly mail-order brides, was arriving on Friday. He knew every farmer, lumberjack, and single businessman would be at the dance looking for a bride. He did not want Isabel to appear at the dance as if she was available.

All day Sunday, he worked at a fever pace, finishing projects and calculating wages. The holidays were approaching, and he knew orders would start to come into the shop. Also, he needed to prepare his traps for hunting. Rabbit fur was the nicest for gloves, and leather cow hides always took time to cure.

At twenty-two, he had avoided thinking about ever getting married. He did not believe there would ever be anyone who would tolerate his habits. Ever since his parent had died, John had quit sleeping through the night. Working late in the back of the harness shop seemed to fit into the sleepless nights. By eighteen, nighttime guard duty was a perfect fit.

By two or three in the morning, he would lie down and sleep until reveille at six o'clock. This schedule seemed to work for him; he did not believe that anyone else would understand.

During the first year, he lived with Clara; he thought he had deceived her about his nighttime activities until she finally told him not to worry about sneaking around at night. After that, she left cookies or bars on the table for when he returned home.

Daytime duties around the fort included working at the army's livery stable. After breakfast in the mess hall with the soldiers, he would head over to the livery stable and do chores for the horses. He repaired harnesses and saddles, and he kept them in tiptop condition. Stalls needed cleaning, and fresh bedding added daily

John knew he did not want to make the army a lifestyle. He wanted his shop. The fort is the loneliest place to be during the holidays.

There were always so many men without families, and he did not want that. He thanked the Lord every day that he had Clara in his life. They had each other.

Meeting Isabel had changed everything. He knew she was the one he wanted to marry. He just needed to get his affairs in order; he also needed to talk to someone who was married. Pete and Gus were of no help; they were both just old bachelors. The only one he knew who was happily married was Joshua.

He finished up with the last stall and headed to the bunkhouse to clean up before going to the hotel.

* * *

Joshua and his wife, Sarah, lived across the alley from the hotel carriage house. Joshua and John had spent time together when they were younger. After John graduated from the 8th grade, he went with Clara to the hotel in the morning and help Joshua with his chores.

Joshua's pa worked for Maude and her husband. He took care of the carriages and the horses for the hotel. His pa would pick up guests at the railroad depot and drive them to the hotel. Maude hired Joshua fulltime after his father was killed in a carriage accident four years ago. About the same time, John went into the army. Joshua was always a good listener, and John needed advice.

"Hey, Joshua. Long time, no see."

"Same to you."

"How you been?"

"Life' good. Yes, sirree. Had our firstborn few months ago."

" A boy, right? Congratulations."

"We named him Samuel after Sarah's dad."

The silence grew longer as John looked around the carriage house.

The tools were neatly handing on the walls, and the carriages were polished, ready to roll out at a moment's notice.

"You didn't come in here to visit. What's going on?"

John pulled up a stool and sat down in front of Joshua. "I am in love, and I think I want to get married."

"Oooh-wee. No wonder you're all fidgety. Who is she?"

"Isabel Grant. She works for Maude here at the hotel."

"That skinny little girl with the long white hair?"

"That's her. I can't stop thinking about her."

Then, John went on to tell Joshua about Captain Pichon and how the captain rejected Isabel as a mail-order bride. He told him how she came from poverty and that he wanted to make sure she never went back to that life. He tried to describe the overwhelming need to protect her.

"Man, you do have it bad. Have you asked her yet?"

"Hell, I haven't even asked her to the harvest celebration yet," admitted John.

"Well, I know Sarah is working on her dress for Saturday."

"Really?"

"Yeah, it's green."

"Shoot, that's the last thing I want is for her to go with the girls, what with all those farmers in town this weekend," said John

"You're worried about asking her out? How in the world are you going to ask her to marry you?" asked Joshua.

"I don't know."

"Do you have a ring?"

"No."

"Do know where you're going to live?" asked Joshua.

"No, I haven't quite got that all figured out?"

"Does this girl even like you?"

"I think so."

"Have you kissed her, yet?"

"No"

"Well, you're just about as awkward as a newborn calf when it comes to women."

"Thanks for the assessment."

"Anytime," and Joshua let out a big old belly laugh that filled the room and even made John smile sheepishly.

"I have two months left in the army. I thought maybe if she agrees, we could get married during the holidays. I am still looking for a leather shop for my own, and maybe we could live upstairs for the winter. Then, in the spring, I could start to build my own house. "

"Of course, I would need some help," said John winking at Joshua.

"Of course," he replied dryly. "If you already had all of this in mind, what'd need my help for."

"I need a best man, don't I?"

"I guess you do."

"Besides, I had to hear what it sounded like out loud. I haven't said anything to Clara yet."

"Lordy, I love that woman, but the news would-be all-over town, like wildfire."

"Don't I know it? Say one more thing. Would you let me know if you EVER see Pichon hanging out back here by the hotel?"

You hear me. I meant it. If he so much as bothers Isabel, I'll clean his clock," said John.

"And he'll court-marshal your ass right into jail," said Joshua.

"I got two more months to watch my temper around him, but I swear if he so much as touches her, I'll pound him into the ground."

"John and Isabel, sitting in a tree. K-I-S-S-I-N-G."

John and Joshua looked up into the rafters of the carriage house, and there sat Thomas grinning at them.

"How long have you been listening?" said John accusingly.

"Long enough," said Thomas as he swung down the ladder of the loft.

His feet no more than touch the ground, and John had his body raised off the floor. He spoke quietly and directly into his face.

"If you breathe a word to anyone, I will tan your hide within an inch of your life. You won't be able to sit a saddle for a month of Sundays. Do you understand me?"

"Yes sir," said Thomas, and John set his feet on the ground and shoved him toward Joshua.

Joshua wrapped his gigantic arm around his sixteen-year-old neck and said politely, "And I will personally drag your skinny little ass straight to your mama and tell her you have been racing her horses against those sod-busters outside of town. Are we clear?"

Thomas wriggled out of Joshua's hold and straightened his clothes.

"Jeez, you guys don't have to get testy. I ain't gone tell anybody. Besides who wants to hear what you old ladies talk about," he said with a smile.

Thomas never failed to break the tension with that infectious smile. John had always treated him like a little brother, and Thomas loved him for it.

"Come on. Let's go get something to eat, and you can tell me about this horse racing business," said John as he ruffled his hair.

John and Thomas told Joshua goodbye, and they headed into the hotel through the back passageway. Thomas stopped and turned toward John,

"How come you are strong enough to beat up anybody, but you can't ask a girl out to a dumb old dance?"

"That's a good question, Thomas. I guess that is why I needed to talk to Joshua. Someday, you'll understand when a girl looks in your eyes and takes your breath away. You lose all ability to form sentences."

"Well, that doesn't sound like any fun at all. If that's what falling in love is all about, count me out," said Thomas with conviction.

John laughed and smiled at his innocence as he held the back door open to the kitchen.

Chapter Eight

A Misunderstanding

Isabel's heart skipped a beat when she saw John and Thomas sitting in the dining room that evening. He looked handsome. She felt so light as she moved through the tables, taking orders for food and drinks.

"Well, hello, you two," said Isabel.

"Hey, Isabel," said Thomas smirking as he held in his secret.

"Hello, Isabel," said John kicking Thomas under the table.

"I told him that if he didn't mind his manners, he would have to eat in the kitchen."

"How about I bring out two blue plate specials for you both?" asked Isabel with a smile.

"Sound good to me," said John.

"Coming right up," said Isabel as she went back into the kitchen. Within minutes she carried out bowls of vegetable beef stew and a platter of freshly baked bread with different types of cheeses.

Then, she whispered, "Let me know when you are ready for seconds."

Isabel continued through the dining room, filling orders, and refreshing cups of coffee.

Finally, when Thomas and John had worked their way through two helpings of beef stew and a couple of platters of bread, John pushed away from the table and decline dessert. Not Thomas, he ordered chocolate cake. Both Isabel and John smiled at each other as they watched Thomas devour the triple layer slice of chocolate cake and lick up the last smudge of frosting.

"Oh-wee. Tell Clara that cake was the best. Well, I better get going and leave you two alone," said Thomas.

As he was leaving, Thomas turned and said, "Hey, Isabel. You'd better ask John to the dance because he's too chicken to ask you."

Then, he smiled and laughed as he ran out the door.

Under his breath, John mumbled and thought, "Wait until I get my hands on that kid."

Isabel was bright red with embarrassment, and then, she looked at John and giggled at Thomas's antics.

"Is that true?" asked Isabel.

"Sort of," admitted John. "I can explain. Do you want to go for a walk after you get off work? I could come back."

"I should be finished at eight o'clock. I'll see you then," said Isabel.

Isabel nearly skipped into the kitchen. He was going to ask her to the dance.

John appeared nervous. She couldn't believe her ears. It would be like their first date, and Sarah was working on a dress for her.

Being asked out to a dance was almost too good to be true. Isabel rushed through her evening chores that night and even had time to run upstairs to freshen up and grab her coat and hat.

Precisely at eight o'clock, John was back at the hotel to pick her up for their evening stroll. Isabel could tell he was nervous and fidgety. They walked in awkward silence for a block in the opposite direction from his shop.

On the next block was a bench in front of the barbershop, and John slowed down and offered Isabel a place to sit.

"Is everything all right?" asked Isabel.

"About what Thomas said tonight. I can explain it."

"Don't worry about that. Thomas was being Thomas," said Isabel.

"No, you see. Today, I was talking to Joshua in the carriage house," explained John.

"Joshua?" asked Isabel.

"He's married to Sarah, and they live across the alley from the carriage house."

"Oh, I know Sarah. She is helping with some dresses that Maude gave me," Isabel exclaimed.

"Well, Thomas overheard Joshua and I talking about the dance and about how I wanted to ask you to the dance," explained John

"Oh, that is so sweet. Why would you be nervous about asking me?"

"Well, actually, it is because I am kind of selfish."

"What?" asked Isabel.

"You see, on Friday, there are supplies coming in on the train. There is supposed to be some new mail-order brides, also."

"But I don't understand why that would stop you from asking me. Oh. I understand. You would rather wait and see what is on that train rather than be stuck with me. I get it now." and Isabel stood up and took off towards the hotel.

Tears blurred her eyes as she felt so stupid. She should have known it was too good to be true.

"Isabel, wait. That is not it at all. Isabel, come back. I can explain."

Isabel took off on the run and dashed into the hotel. She ran down the darkened hallway and headed straight up to her room. In the safety of her room, she fell upon the bed and cried.

She had not allowed her grief of the past month to surface, and within moments, all the tears of a lifetime poured forth draining her spirit.

* * *

John was flabbergasted and pissed. His male mind couldn't even wrap his brain around what had just happened. He untied his sorrel from the post by the hotel and rode hell-bent back to the fort. He was so upset that he knew he couldn't work on any projects tonight. He pulled up into the livery of the fort and dismounted.

Charlie was sitting up whittling away on a piece of kindling. John put his horse in a stall, rubbed her down with some dry straw. He threw her some oats in the box, checked her water and stared into space with disbelief.

"Hey, Charlie," he said as he drew up a stool to sit on. "Are all women so unpredictable, so complicated?"

Charlie smiled and chuckled.

"I mean I say one wrong thing, and the next thing, I know she's upset and runs off. Now, Isabel won't talk to me. She won't even let me explain," said John

Charlie watched how agitated he had become, and then, he quietly said, "What were you trying to do?"

"All I wanted to do was ask her to the dance."

"Did you?"

"No, I was trying to, but."

Charlie started laughing again.

"What so funny?"

"You"

"I'm serious."

"I know you are. That's what makes it so funny."

"What?"

"You are in love."

"What am I going to do?" John pleaded.

"Women want to be courted."

"I know that. I mean, how am I going to get Isabel to listen to me."

"Don't worry about the explanation. Just ask the girl to the dance, you, big dunce."

"Hey, no need to be calling names now," John said to the old cowboy.

John could hear Charlie chuckling now and then as he walked back into the bunkhouse to bed down for the night. He knew that he wasn't going to be able to sleep tonight. Maybe Joshua was right; perhaps, he did have it bad for Isabel.

* * *

Isabel was late for work the next morning. Her swollen eyes and the dark circles under her eyes stood out in contrast to her pale skin. She could feel Clara staring at her with concern. Isabel went through the motions of her morning chores.

Clara put down her wooden stirring spoon and walked over to Isabel.

"Fie, what is the matter this morning? Do you feel peaked?"

She felt her forehead and looked in her face. Tears welled up in her swollen eyes. Clara pulled her close into her arms.

"There, there. Don't cry. It will be all right."

Isabel felt the sorrow all over again. It was comforting to know that Clara cared for her like a mother.

"Now, tell Clara what is breaking your heart."

"It's nothing. I don't even understand myself," confessed Isabel.

Then, before she knew it, she poured her heart out to Clara in the warmth of the kitchen that morning. She explained how Sarah was altering a dress for Saturday and how Thomas teased John about being chicken to ask her out to the dance.

Then, she told how John said there were mail-order brides coming in on the train. Isabel realized that he was trying to let her down gently and that he was interested in other girls.

Inside, Clara was furious with her nephew for leading her on and then breaking her heart like this; but first, she had to comfort this poor girl who has just had her heart broke over possibly the first boy to show her any attention.

"Well, you plan on wearing that pretty dress on Saturday, and you can help me with the pies. All the businesses in town contribute to the celebration."

"We are bringing pies. Yessirree, you and I will make pies the next two days"

"You can help me serve them at the celebration," said Clara as enthusiastically as she could muster.

"Thank you, Clara. Please don't say anything to John. I was silly to think he liked me. I'll be all right," said Isabel.

"Sure, you will — a pretty thing like you. There will be plenty of eligible bachelors in town on Saturday. I might even take a look myself," said Clara giggling to herself.

Isabel smiled at the thought, wiped her eyes, and started her morning duties. She daydreamed about buying a new hat or a ribbon for her neck, maybe a new shawl. She would ask Sarah's advice this afternoon.

After lunch, Maude met with the dining room staff for a brief meeting. She told her employees that she was offering extra wages for Friday afternoon and Saturday morning for anyone willing to help make pies.

Thomas and Joshua would deliver and set up the serving station at the celebration, but she needed help to make the pies.

Maude continued to explain that she would hand out wages on Saturday at noon, and then the dining room would be closed after lunch on Saturday so that everyone could attend the celebration that evening.

"Also, I am moving this week's laundry day to Monday afternoon instead of Saturday," said Maude.

After the meeting, Isabel headed out the back door of the hotel and crossed the alley by the carriage house to see Sarah. She knocked on the door, and Sarah came to the door holding a beautiful baby boy.

"Hello Sarah, I am sorry to bother you. Oh, he is beautiful."

"Thank you. Come in, Miss Isabel. I am sorry I am not done with your dress yet, but I'm working on it."

"I came to ask you for some advice."

"From me? What in the world?" said Sarah.

"I want to know what I should wear with this dress on Saturday. Should I wear a hat, or do I need a shawl? Should I wear a matching ribbon around my neck? I don't have any jewelry. Do I need any?" asked Isabel.

"Well, let me see. The weather has been warm, this week. Joshua calls it "Indian Summer," but you might need a shawl at night. A hat would be proper for the daytime, but at night, most women won't wear their hats to the dance. I don't think you need any jewelry, but a ribbon would be perfect."

"Maude is offering extra wages for making pies, and I want to pick out something at the store to go with my dress. I was wondering if I could get a swatch of the color to match."

"Why sure thing. I might have to take Maude up on her offer. I could use some extra wages," she said laughingly. "I do make a mean pie if I do say so myself."

Sarah handed the baby over to Isabel, and then, she went into the other room to snip a swatch of material from the hem. Isabel looked into the brown eyes of the bundle. Their baby was beautiful and healthy. He was alert, and he watched Isabel with intent.

It reminded her of her brothers when they were young. They never seemed this healthy or curious of the world around them. They were weaker and more lethargic. Sarah came back and handed Isabel the swatch.

"Here you go," said Sarah as she gathered Samuel into her arms.

"Thank you, Sarah. He's healthy. You are fortunate. Well, I'll see you later."

"Thank you, Miss Isabel. Bye"

Isabel left Sarah's home, walked through the alley up to Main Street, and headed down to Campbell's General Store to look at the hats and the ribbons.

The bell tinkled as Isabel opened the heavy wooden door to the store. She was a regular customer, and Mr. Campbell greeted her with a smile.

"Hello, Miss Isabel. How may I help you today?"

"Hello, Mr. Campbell. I need a ribbon to match this swatch of material."

"Well, let's see what we can do."

Mrs. Campbell and Isabel scanned the ribbon choices in the dry goods section of the store. Isabel spotted a thin, green, velvet ribbon. Mr. Campbell grabbed the roll and pulled out the ribbon for her to compare with the swatch of material.

"I think we have a winner," said Mr. Campbell.

As he pulled the ribbon out to measure it, he realized it was less than a yard. "How much did you need?"

"I'm not sure. It is for my neck. I am going to wear it instead of a necklace."

"Oh then, there is plenty. Let me measure it and calculate the cost. I'll be right back."

Isabel walked over to look at the hats and decided they were too expensive. She looked at the shawls. The lace shawls were beautiful, but not very practical or warm for this time of the year.

"Here is your package. That will be ten cents."

Isabel paid Mr. Campbell and left with the ribbon in her purse. The town seemed busier today, which meant another hectic night at the hotel dining room.

She was thankful she was working for the next few days. It would give her a chance to keep her mind off John. Isabel didn't look forward to seeing him tonight in the dining room. She knew she would have to face him eventually. Maybe Clara was right; there were bound to be plenty of young men in town this weekend. After all, John was kind to her. She is the one that jumped to conclusions, thinking he liked her. She didn't realize the hurt would be this deep and painful.

Chapter Nine

The Unraveling of a Misunderstanding

Illiteracy equated poverty. Every day, Isabel took a step farther away from the cultural isolation and educational poverty she had experienced growing up in the wilderness. Her vows to never return beat louder in her heart.

Mrs. Beaumont had given her lead pencils and ivory sheets of beautiful paper to practice writing the alphabet. The feel of the writing instrument and paper developed familiarity as she practiced writing in the solitude of her room.

It was Wednesday afternoon, and the weather was dreary with rain. John had not shown up in the dining room last night. Isabel now knew he was avoiding her. The hurt cut to the core, and she felt lonely.

Copying the letters on to paper felt repetitive yet calming. Isabel wanted Mrs. Beaumont to be proud of her. She also wanted someday to be able to have beautiful handwriting like Maude. She realized that afternoon how much she had to be thankful for her new life in Redwood

On Thursday, she traveled with Thomas to see Mrs. Beaumont. When they arrived, Mrs. Beaumont was on the bookcase ladder, dusting. She wore a man's shirt with the sleeves rolled up over her dress.

Ruth unbuttoned the shirt and smoothed her hair. "I was just cleaning the bookshelves, and I let the time get away from me."

"Hello, Mrs. Beaumont," said Isabel.

"Please call me, Ruth,"

Thomas carried in the supplies to her pantry.

"Ma, wants to know what time I am supposed to pick you up on Saturday," said Thomas realizing how busy his Saturday was becoming.

"Tell her about eight in the morning that way I can help make the pies."

“Now, go grab some of those sugar cookies and milk before you head out to the shop," instructed his Aunt.

"Thanks, Aunt Ruth,"

"Thanks, nothing until I get my smooch,"

Thomas blushed and walked over to the tiny woman and gave her a smooch on the cheek that made her giggle. He smiled and then walked into the kitchen to help himself before going out to the wood shop.

"Well, let's get started."

Isabel and Ruth sat at the dining room table. Sunlight filtered through the lace curtains and warmed the room. Ruth was surprised to see the progress Isabel was making on her own.

She looked over the rows of practice and saw the development of letters. Ruth then showed Isabel how to combine letters to make words. They moved through the primer pages, and Isabel copied word after word as Ruth instructed her on the sounds of the combinations.

While Isabel copied the words, Ruth fixed tea and sugar cookies for both of them. The discussion turned to the harvest celebration, and Ruth could tell something was bothering her.

"What wrong, Isabel? You seem sad today. Is something bothering you?"

"No, it’s nothing. I'm not very smart when it comes to men."

"Well, none of us are sometimes. What happened?"

"I thought Clara's nephew, John Webster, wanted to ask me to the dance, but it turned out he was just nice to me since I was new in town. You see, there are mail-ordered brides coming in on the train on Friday, and he." The word caught in her throat.

"Well, I can't believe that of John."

"It's true. John told me the other night when we went walking after supper."

"You are still planning on going, aren't you."

"Yes, Clara wants me to help her with the pies, and I got a dress from Maude that Sarah is fixing for me."

"Well, that's the best reason I have heard to go to a dance. It's a chance to wear a new dress. How fun. Do you need anything to go with it?"

"I have a new comb for my hair and a green velvet ribbon to match for my neck."

"Do you have a shawl for the evening?"

"No. I saw some lace ones at Campbell's, but I felt they weren't very practical or warm for at night."

"I think I have got just the thing you can borrow. Come on. Let's go upstairs."

Ruth led Isabel into her spare bedroom. She opened the drawers of a dresser and found an ivory crocheted shawl. She fluffed it out and draped it over Isabel's shoulder.

"Perfect. That will keep the chill off at night.

"Oh, Ruth, it is beautiful. Are you sure? Did you make this?"

"Yes, of course, I am sure. I never did master knitting needles but crocheting seemed to come easier to me. I will teach you if you'd like."

"Thank you so much. You must let me do something for you in return. Please." asked Isabel.

"No, now go on. It just sits up here in a drawer, but I might take you up on that offer."

"Aunt Ruth? Isabel? Where are you?"

"We're up here, Thomas."

Thomas came bounding up the stairs. "Isabel, are you ready to go?"

"We're just finishing up. Doesn't Isabel look nice in this shawl?"

"I guess," said Thomas looking awkward. Both of them laughed at his lukewarm approval.

Ruth gave Isabel more paper and showed her which pages to complete for next Thursday. They all said their good-byes; Isabel and Thomas walked out back to the wagon.

"So, are you going to the dance with John?"

"No."

"How come? Didn't he ask you?"

"No, he didn't. Girls are coming in on the train on Friday," explained Isabel.

"Yeah, a bunch of mail-order brides and some new saloon girls for Shereen's."

"Thomas, how do you know about that?" asked Isabel.

"I have seen it before. There will be sodbusters and single bachelors in town looking for wives. That is why John wanted to ask you to the dance."

"He didn't want you going with the women and having it seem that you were one of those single girls."

Isabel was speechless. A smile of warmth crept over as the misunderstanding began to clear.

"Well, John has a funny way of telling a girl."

"Yeah, he is pretty dumb when it comes to women."

Isabel laughed and clutched the soft woolen ivory shawl to her chest.

* * *

After supper, Clara gathered up a pie and wrapped up some leftovers. She grabbed her black shawl and headed out the back of the hotel toward the fort. It felt good to stretch her legs. The evening had turned out beautiful. As she walked, she prayed for good weather for the weekend.

The town was growing fast. Clara remembered when she first started walking out to the fort when John enlisted. The walk itself was a lonesome two miles with nothing to stop the wind. Tonight, it seemed as if the town was growing closer to the fort. The walk helped her clear her mind.

Clara formulated in her head how she needed to talk sense into her nephew. When she arrived at the fort, she headed to the livery stable. Charlie was sitting outside whittling.

"Is he here?"

"Yep. John has been working these last two days, like the devil himself is chasing him."

"And I got one sad little girl mopping around my kitchen."

"He's got it bad for her."

"Did he talk to you?"

"A little. Enough for me to understand what's going on."

"He didn't show up the last two nights at the hotel, and he doesn't miss too many of my meals. I brought you a pie."

"Pecan?"

"Ain't that your favorite?" smiled Clara.

"Well, I believe it is," answered Charlie with a big grin on his face.

"You coming to the celebration tomorrow night?"

"Oh, I don't know. I might."

"Well, I'll save you a seat. I plan on sitting with Pete and Gus. If you show up, we could play some cards."

"Oh, what do I want to sit with those two old men and listen to them swap lies," grumbled Charlie.

"Suit yourself. Is my nephew inside?"

"Yep. John has cleaned every stall, brushed down every horse, and greased every axel. We have got a pile of supplies coming in tomorrow on the train, and he has made room for them."

"Well, I might as well try to talk some sense into him. Don't know if it will do much good," said Clara. "John? Yoo-hoo, John."

"In here."

"Hello. I brought you some leftovers, in case you might be hungry."

She set her basket down and unloaded leftover meat, cheese, bread, chocolate cake, and a couple of slices of apple pie.

"You didn't have to walk out here to bring me that."

"No, I didn't have to. I wanted to. Besides, I had to bring Charlie some pie."

"That old buzzard doesn't need any pie. If you came out here to yell at me about Isabel, save your breath. I can't feel any worse than I do now," protested John.

"Well, I got a sad little girl in my kitchen. I don't know what happened, but you need to set it right with her."

"If you don't like her and want to see other girls, you need to let her know and not lead her on to the point where she thinks you like her."

"That's just it. I do like Isabel. I think I might even be in love with her, but I got all tongue tied when I tried to tell her, and it came out wrong. Then, she got upset and ran off before I could explain."

"So, now what are you going to do?" asked Clara.

"I don't know."

"Are you still coming to the dance?"

"I don't know."

"Well, you need to swallow your pride and make it right with this girl. She thinks you are waiting for one of those mail-order brides."

"What? No, I tried to explain to her that girls were coming in on the train and that there will be single bachelors in town. I didn't want her going with all of you women, and then one of those sodbusters getting the impression that she was single. Instead, Isabel jumped to conclusions and took off upset."

"Well, you never have been very good at talking to women," said Clara.

"So, everyone keeps on telling me."

"I wanted to let you know that I am going to ask Isabel to the church social on Sunday."

"I expected to see you there. You haven't been coming to church, but you are my family, and I would like to see my family at church this Sunday."

"Will see," said John to his Aunt.

"I better get going before it gets dark. Goodnight," said Clara as she hugged her nephew.

Then, she gathered up her basket and draped her shawl over her shoulders. Clara walked out of the bunkhouse, and Charlie was standing there.

"Goodnight, Charlie."

"Well, if you don't mind, I thought I'd walked you back to town."

"After all, it is starting to get dark, and I can't have a pretty thing like yourself walking all alone."

"Oh, go on, you, old coot," and she smiled at Charlie. "Well, suit yourself." Clara and Charlie walked back into town, and Clara was grateful for his company.

Chapter Ten

Preparing for the Harvest Celebration

Friday was a blur. The farmers began arriving in town early to bring goods to town for trading. Crates of apples, baskets of berries, and pumpkins barely ripe from the vine arrived at the hotel for pies along with eggs, milk, butter, cream, and lard.

The town celebration was being set up with the barbeque pit and a dance floor down by the livery stable. Townspeople strung banners across Main Street.

The Union Pacific train arrived shortly after one o'clock, and wagons were lined up ready for supplies. There were oxen carts and horse-drawn flatbeds. Thomas waited in line for supplies, and Joshua waited for hotel guests.

The highlight, of course, was the different women that stepped down from the passenger cars. It was easy to tell the saloon girls from the mail-order brides.

The saloon girls arrived dressed in bright-colored satin gowns with large plumes on their hats and plenty of décolletage for an appreciative male audience. The saloon-girls had an air of confidence along with the ability to get any male to carry their luggage and drive them to Shereen's.

Many of the mail-order brides had crumpled notes with the name of their suitor who had placed the ad. They seemed to be reserved and shy. Many of them faded into the background until the young men escorted the saloon girls off the railroad platform.

The fresh-dressed suitors were waiting in line to accompany their new brides to the hotel. Awkward introductions took place along with nervous smiles as Joshua loaded luggage into wagons. The girls filled the air with excitement and romance.

Breakfast and lunch ran together that morning. With all the supplies, there was no room for anything in the kitchen or the pantry.

It was after two before the waitresses got a break. Isabel stayed after to help the kitchen staff clean up and prepare for supper. Finally, at three o'clock, Clara chased her out of the kitchen and told her to take her break.

Isabel went upstairs to get her purse and her hat, and she headed out on to the busy street. The town was abuzz with life. She walked down past the general store, and Mr. Campbell was unloading new supplies. He smiled as she walked past his store.

She continued down by the livery stable where they were setting up the barbeque and the dance floor.

The excitement in the air was contagious. Isabel found a bench under a tree by the post office. Before she could even sit down, she heard some talking to her.

"Howdy, ma'am," said this sunburned kid, who was not much older than Thomas, was tipping his hat to her.

"Hello."

"Henry Walker, please to make your acquaintance ma'am."

"Isabel Grant, please to meet you."

"Mind if I sit down?"

"No, go right ahead."

At about the time Henry Walker sat down next to Isabel, John Webster drove past them. He was driving a team of horses with supplies for the Fort through town. He saw Isabel sitting with some sod-buster, and he felt like someone had just punched him in the gut, removing his last breath.

Isabel recognized John immediately. Her thoughts were interrupted with questions.

"Ma'am, do you live here in town? How do you like it? Have you ever lived on a farm? Are you planning on going to the dance? I sure would be obliged if you would consider dancing with me."

"What? Oh, excuse me. I need to get back to work."

"But what about tonight? The dance?"

Before he could get an answer, Isabel was heading back to the hotel. She now realized what Thomas had explained to her. John's worst fear had come true. He was worried about all the extra men in town, and that she would be perceived to be single.

How could she make that big dumb galoot realize that he was the one she liked? He was the sweetest, nicest man she had ever met. She did not need to date other men to know what beautiful qualities he possessed. Why did men have to be so complicated?

Friday at the hotel was the busiest night Isabel had ever experienced in the dining room. The people were non-stop until ten o'clock with drinks and meals. The specials ran out at eight, and the waitresses offered substitutions. Maude was the perfect hostess throughout the evening.

It was after twelve before Isabel climbed the stairs, bone weary tired. Isabel changed and undid her braid. She ran her fingers through her hair to loosen the waves. She jumped into bed too tired to brush her hair. Her thoughts wandered straight to John as they did every night she laid down. Isabel knew she needed to talk to him and explain what he saw today.

She had to make him understand that she was only interested in him. She missed seeing him every night. His dark green eyes, his bright smile, and his genuine laughter filled her memories, but then doubts filled her mind.

"What if he doesn't come to the celebration? What will I do? What if someone asks me to dance? I can't dance. I don't know how. What am I going to do? I need to talk to Sarah," thought Isabel to herself.

Thoughts of Sarah and her beautiful, green dress and dancing with John, being held in his arms drifted through her mind, and soon Isabel fell fast asleep.

* * *

Saturday morning came early. Isabel dressed and headed down to make biscuits. Clara was way ahead of her and set her to the butter churn. Of all days, Isabel needed to be doing something to make the time pass, not sitting here at the butter churn with all kinds of time to think. Before she knew it, there were guests in the dining room by seven, ready for breakfast.

By eight o'clock, the ladies arrived to make pies, and the kitchen was full. Clara was in her heyday as she set about an assembly line of making pie dough from lard and preparing the fruit for the pies. Isabel loved the laughter and the camaraderie of the women in the kitchen.

Isabel kept the orders coming out to the dining room, and Maude had posted a sign that the dining room closed at 1:00 p.m., so the hotel staff could attend the town festivities.

While peeling apples and making pie dough, Mrs. Beaumont and Sarah caught up on latest gossip from Marjorie and Pauline. Isabel listened with intent trying to make heads or tails out of all the local news. Between the two waitresses, no one could get in a word in edgewise.

When the women finished the pies, Maude pitched in with strict instructions to Joshua and Thomas on how slowly they were to drive the wagon and where to set up the table.

By noon, forty pies went out the door. Maude gave the staff their weekly payment along with the extra wages for making pies. As it turned out, Maude received generous tips from the large party of businessmen, and she gave them to the waitresses and the kitchen staff for Friday night's excellent meal and service.

She looked down at coins, four dollars and twenty-five cents, which was over two weeks wages earned in one week. The overwhelming sense of pride filled her with warmth. She had worked so hard this week, and it felt fantastic to be an independent woman earning her own money.

Next, Isabel ran up the stairs to her room to gather her stuff to go to Sarah's. She laid out her new boots, stockings, the corset, her purse, the ribbon for her neck, the comb for her hair, and the borrowed shawl from Mrs. Beaumont.

There was a knock on the door, and Sarah called out to Isabel.

"Open the door, Isabel. My hands are full."

Isabel open to find Sarah holding her gown along with pins, curling irons, and brushes in her other hand. "Good heavens, Sarah. What is all of this?"

"We're going to shake some sense into that Mr. John Webster, that's what we're going to do."

Sarah laid the dress on her bed and grabbed her hand. "Come on, Isabel. I'll explain it to you in the kitchen."

Isabel quickly grabbed her new comb for her hair, and the two went downstairs like partners in crime.

Sarah set up a workstation, and Isabel grabbed the stool from the corner. She stoked the trash burner side of the oven with some kindling and stirred the coals. She removed the lid and set the curling irons close to the fire.

"Oh girl, I have been so excited to do this. I could even sleep last night."

"Do what? Burn my hair?"

"No, silly goose. I am going to fix your hair with style to match your dress."

Sarah pulled out the tie holding her loose braid and began to brush out her hair.

"My, my, you have beautiful hair."

"What are exactly are you planning to do? I have never had my hair fixed by anyone other than my mother. I have always worn it in a braid," explained Isabel.

"Well, today, we are going to curl it and pin the curls up to the crown."

"Where in the world did you learn how to do that?"

"My mother. She was a maid to a wealthy woman in St. Paul, and I'd watch her fix her hair. Sometimes, this woman would have friends come over, so my mother could fix their hair for special occasions. When I got older, I'd hand her the pins and watch her arrange the curls," said Sarah.

"What did you mean when you said we are going to knock some sense into John Webster?"

"I mean that boy needs a little shaking up. Between your hair and that green dress, it ought to do the trick."

"You think so?"

"I know so."

Sarah gathered up her hair in the front and pulled it back, securing it with her new comb. Then, she began to curl the hair in the back, allowing the curls to cool. When Sarah had curled every piece of her long porcelain white hair, she pinned the curls up near the crown just below the comb.

"Oh Isabel, you look grown up and beautiful." Sarah grabbed her hand and pulled her through the kitchen into the closed dining room. There was a mirror next to the hat rack, and for the first time, Isabel saw the transformation.

Sarah stood behind her with her hands on her shoulders; she smiled, beaming with pride at her handiwork.

Isabel was speechless; she almost didn't recognize herself. She turned to each side looking at the curls, and with her hand, she gently touched them.

"It's beautiful. Thank you," Isabel said with a lump in her throat and tears in her eyes.

“Now, don't you start. We still have to get you dressed, and then I'm going to take care of Maude's hair."

The girls gathered their supplies, tidied up the kitchen, and hurried back up the stairs. Isabel hung up her uniform and white apron. She was embarrassed that Sarah saw the poor condition of her undergarments.

As Sarah was lacing up her corset in the back, she told Isabel, "Maybe next week, we can start with those sewing lessons."

"I would like that." Isabel was thankful for her discretion, and it sealed their friendship.

"Sarah, I need to ask you some questions I have never been to a dance, a party, or a celebration. I'm so nervous to see John."

Isabel explained the misunderstanding with John to her and included the part about meeting the young man and talking to him when John drove by with supplies for the Fort.

"What do I do? What should I say to him? What if he doesn't want to talk to me? How do I say no if someone else asks me to dance? I am such a ninny. I don't even know how to act," said Isabel reaching a panic level.

"Take a deep breath, girl. Relax. Everything's going to be fine. When John sees you, he'll forget all about being mad. You smile at him like he is the only man in the world. Once you are in his arms on the dance floor, you will forget all about being nervous."

"You make it sound easy," said Isabel.

"It is. Falling in love happens, and there is nothing you can do about it."

Isabel blushed and then she hugged Sarah and said, "Thank you, Sarah. I don't know what I would do without you."

So, help me, if you start crying on me again," said Sarah. "Let's get you dressed, and then, I will help Maude. Walk downtown with Maude. I am sure she would enjoy the company. Mrs. Beaumont went with Clara to set up the pie stand. Besides, I have to get my men all gussied up for today and change out of this old thing."

Isabel put on her stockings and her boots, and Sara unbuttoned the back of the dress. Carefully, she slipped the dress over Isabel's outstretched hands into the satin-lined sleeves of the green velvet dress.

Sarah had altered the neckline into a sweetheart cut and cinched in the bodice to fit Isabel's smaller frame. The corset gave her curves and made her waist seem tiny. The skirt laid flat in the front and gathered in the back. The dress flowed as she walked with the ruffles in the back.

For the final touch, she tied the matching green ribbon around her neck. Isabel made a full turn slowly for the final inspection.

"Well, how do I look?"

It was Sarah's turn to be speechless. The transformation was almost unbelievable.

The dark green velvet against her fair translucent skin was breathtaking. The green of the garment accented her beautiful porcelain white hair and complexion.

"You better keep Maude and Clara by your side because girl you are going to have to beat them off with a stick. There's going be so many offers to dance that I hope your feet are up to it."

"Oh, go on," said Isabel. Then, she looked down at the dress and said to Sarah, "It is beautiful. Thank you so much."

After Sarah left, Isabel looked in the window to get a glance at her reflection and practiced walking in the dress. She pretended to hold up her skirt and step to the music. She held her arms up and swayed back and forth.

Isabel felt like a lady. She checked her bag for the coin purse. Isabel decided to leave some coins behind in a drawer. She knotted them up in one of her old socks and tucked it under her nightgown. Isabel unscrewed the cap from the bottle of perfume that Maude had given her with the purse. She dabbed ever so carefully on her wrists and her neck.

She looked down toward her décolletage and trailed her finger lightly up to her neck. A feeling of sensuality came over her that felt new yet natural. The thought of John touching her and kissing her neck, kissing her lips left her breathless and flushed.

She put the cap back on the bottle and left it on her dresser. Isabel grabbed her shawl and her purse; she took a deep breath and knew this night might forever change her life. She was ready.

Chapter Eleven

Walking Arm in Arm

Isabel walked over to Maude's room and knocked on her door. "May I come in?" asked Isabel.

"Yes, come on in here. We're are just finishing up." Maude turned around as Isabel walked into the room. She was speechless, and Sarah smiled with pride. Maude teared up unexpectedly.

"Oh, Isabel. Turn around," said Maude.

Isabel slowly spun around, showing Maude her curls in her hair and flow of her dress. "Look what Mrs. Beaumont let me borrow." She held out the ivory crocheted shawl."

"Isabel, I couldn't be prouder of you as if you were my daughter."

It was now Sarah's turn to tear up as she watched the two women embrace each other.

"Thank you, Maude. Sarah told me it would be okay to walk downtown to the celebration with you. Clara and Mrs. Beaumont already went to the pie stand, and the other waitresses had dates."

"Why, I would love to walk downtown with you. I am almost ready. Just give me a few more minutes. Have a seat."

Isabel looked with admiration at Maude's gown. The dress was a gold and burgundy stripe skirt and bodice. The back of the skirt was solid burgundy with gold trim. The fitted bodice showed off a scooped neckline.

She wore a beautiful red-jeweled necklace that lay just above her décolletage, and she had red-jeweled earrings to match. Sarah pinned her dark auburn hair to perfection showing sun highlights and shine.

Maude checked her purse and then walked over to a tall vase and grabbed two parasols handing one to Isabel. Maude checked her make-up and gave herself final approval. Sarah grabbed her hair tools and kissed them both as she headed downstairs to get ready.

The two women walked to the end of the hallway and down the main staircase. Isabel felt like such a young lady walking arm in arm with Maude.

The sheer parasols had ruffles around the edges and were a welcome relief from the warm September sun.

"I am so proud of you, Isabel and all you have accomplished this past month."

"Well, I am so grateful to you. I could not have done it without you. I don't know how I could ever repay you," said Isabel.

"Nonsense. Seeing you all dressed up today is my reward, but I thought for sure John would have asked you to the celebration," said Maude.

"We had a misunderstanding this week before he could ask me," explained Isabel.

"Oh, I see. Is John coming tonight?"

"I hope so. Maude, I like him. I just haven't been able to tell him."

"Maybe, you will find the right words tonight," said Maude.

"But if he shows up, I don't want to leave you all alone," said Isabel.

Maude laughed right out loud. "Honey, I may be getting older, but I have yet to ever be alone at one of these celebrations. Don't worry about me."

"I'm sorry. I meant to say."

"I know. Don't worry about it. I do, however, plan to watch out for you. You are looking stunning this evening, and there are many men in town tonight. Unfortunately, not all of them are reputable.

* * *

On Friday afternoon, when John saw Isabel sitting with that young sodbuster, he felt as if someone had punched him in the gut and removed his last breath. He couldn't get that image out of his mind.

"Damn it. I'm going to lose Isabel. I can't let that happen, but I don't know what to do," thought John. " What if she won't talk to me? I'll end up sticking my foot in my mouth again. Damn it all to hell."

He worked the rest of Friday like a man possessed, hauling and loading supplies to the fort. He didn't go down to the hotel to eat that night. He decided to stay at the fort. He was surly and short with anyone who crossed his path. He couldn't sleep Friday night.

By Saturday afternoon, he was inconsolable, and he had run out of work with nothing but time on his hands. He sat outside the livery, shining his boots again, and he looked up to see Charlie dressed in his best uniform.

"What the hell?"

"What?"

"What are you all dressed up for?"

"I thought I would go into town and listen to Pete and Gus swap lies," said Charlie.

"You smell too pretty for sitting with those two," said John without looking up from his boots.

"There are many people in town, and I want to smell good for all those ladies," said Charlie

"My Aunt Clara doesn't happen to be one of them, does she?"

"She did promise me some pie, and that is hard to refuse for an old bachelor like myself. Aren't you going?" Charlie nodded toward town.

"I don't know. Haven't decided yet," John said as he brushed even harder.

"Suit yourself, but let me tell you, young man, if you want something, then you need to decide if it is worth fighting for or not. If you stay here, there's no telling who might befriend that little lady. Besides, I want to get a look at this girl."

"Why is that?"

"She must be something special because I have never seen you work so hard. Why I have got the cleanest livery and most well-groomed corral of horses I have ever had in my life."

"Oh, go on, you, old buzzard," said John.

"Sure, you don't want to ride in with me. I'm going to take the buckboard in just in case any ladies need a ride home after the dance." Charlie said with a chuckle as he adjusted his hat.

"Go on. I'm staying here."

"Well, I'll tell Clara I tried."

Charlie walked over to the corral, and John sat there, considering his words of advice. Charlie had hit a nerve challenging John to decide on whether Isabel was worth fighting for or not. The concept of another man's hands, even touching her makes his skin crawl. That night Pichon cornered her in the hotel hallway made John sick.

"I need to be there to protect her," thought John.

By the time, Charlie had hitched the team to the buckboard and pulled out of the fort, John was inside the bunkhouse, scrubbing himself clean.

The summer sun had bleached his hair golden brown and left his face and hands dark brown from the sun. He shaved off a three-day beard and used some bay rum sparingly as not to be confused with Charlie.

He put on his best blue uniform and tucked his pants into his black boots. He carefully tied his neckerchief and adjusted his cap. He checked his money pouch and saddlebags.

John headed to the corral and called for Chester. His beautiful sorrel came running up to the fence, looking for a treat. In moments, John saddled and mounted his horse. Riding north toward town, he knew it was after five o'clock as he rode.

He thought to himself, "Isabel is worth fighting for, and I am going to let her know how I feel. Hell, if everything goes right tonight, I may even kiss her."

John flushed with anticipation at the thought of gently taking her face into his hands and kissing her with passion. He tried to picture her in a green dress, and he knew all he needed was a smile from her to let him know everything was fine between them.

* * *

Joshua backed the wagon near the table. The women used the back end like a sideboard for the extra slices. A tarp cloth had been draped over the wagon to protect the pies from the sun and keep them fresh.

Maude and Isabel's walked to the pie stand where Clara and Mrs. Beaumont were serving pie. Isabel greeted the women affectionately. They admired her hair and her dress. Both women fussed with pride at Isabel.

Sitting next to the wagon were several wooden chairs. Pete, Gus, and Charlie all stood up when Maude and Isabel arrived at the stand. Maude proceeded to introduce them to Isabel.

"Isabel, I would like you to meet Pete. He is our blacksmith, and this is his brother, Gus." They took off their hats and shook her hand.

"I am so pleased to meet you, finally. John has told me so much about you both," said Isabel extending her hand.

"Oh, don't believe a word he says," Pete said teasingly.

"No, seriously, he thinks very highly of both of you."

The two older men blushed at her comments, but they both smiled at the praise. Charlie was next to be introduced. Clara jumped in to do the honors.

"Isabel, this is Charlie, and he works at the livery at the fort with John."

"How do you do, Charlie?" asked Isabel.

"Pleased to meet you. I've heard a lot about you from Clara and John both," said Charlie.

"I hope all good."

"Yes, ma'am all good."

Isabel smiled at Charlie, and he fell in love.

All three old bachelors stood looking at this beautiful young lady wishing they were thirty years younger. They stood and watched as she and Maude walked down to the next booths together.

Clara looked back at the three old bachelors and said, "Oh, sit down before you all step on your tongues and fall."

Chapter Twelve

Harvest Celebration

As John approached the town, the noise level of the festivities grew. He smelled the barbeque in the air. Kids were running around with dogs chasing them. Small gatherings of people eating picnic style sat on bright colored blankets.

Booths were selling loaves of bread, delicate pastries, colorful vegetables, sweet jams, and apple cider. Shereen had set up shop by the livery with kegs on makeshift tables and serving beer.

He guided his horse to the back of the blacksmith shop and saw to Chester's needs. John went in through the back door of the shop and walked to the front. No one was around, so he headed to the area where Clara would have her pies set up on a table.

Secretly, he was scanning the crowd looking for Isabel with her porcelain white hair, and thanks to Joshua, he knew she would be wearing a green dress.

Walking toward the table, he saw Clara and Sarah serving pie and Pete, Gus and Charlie sitting on wooden chairs. He noticed Joshua sitting on a bench holding his baby in his arms. John sat down and greeted his friend.

"Hey"

"Hey yourself. I heard you weren't coming," said Joshua.

"Well, I changed my mind. Have you seen Isabel?"

“Yes, I have, and I must say my wife has outdone herself this time."

"What do mean by that?" John said, accusingly.

"I mean, wait until you see Isabel. You may not recognize her," explained Joshua.

"Where is she?"

"She walked downtown with Maude, and I believe they are over by the barbeque visiting with some local town businessmen.”

“I believe she is talking to the banker and his son who just arrived back from out East."

"Damn it to hell. I knew it," said John.

"You need to get over there and ask Miss Isabel to supper. Miss Maude will be fine by herself. She will have those rich suitors fawning over her all night long," said Joshua knowing he had finally made John realized he needed to act quickly.

"Maybe you're right."

"Course I am."

John stood up and decided he needed to see Isabel. He needed to straighten everything out and let her know how he felt.

He spotted Isabel and Maude talking to the banker and his son. He stopped in his tracks. John made a double take with his head. Was it her? She was beautiful, beyond beautiful. She had her hair up in curls, and the emerald green dress made her look regal. She was laughing and smiling as the banker's son and the story he was telling.

Suddenly, John lost his nerve. He felt inadequate, but he couldn't take his eyes off of her.

"Excuse me. Look out." Two guys carrying another keg of beer to Shereen's table brought John out of his daydream.

He followed them to the table and laid down money for a draft of beer. He moved closer to the barbeque area and finished his beer, setting the mug on the table. He took a deep breath and stepped forward.

"Hello, Isabel, Maude."

"Why hello, John," said Maude with so much charm that John felt immediately thankful for her manners.

Hearing a reassuring voice seemed to relax him, but he only had eyes for Isabel. Then, Isabel looked at John and smiled from ear to ear.

"You look beautiful, Isabel."

"Thank you."

“I was wondering if I could have a word with you, Isabel?" asked John.

"I'm sorry, soldier boy. Run along. Isabel is busy this evening," said Randall Wainwright.

John bristled and stepped toward Randall, who was a half-foot shorter than himself. John could feel his arms tighten in his uniform shirt.

"No, it's okay Randall. I want to talk to John, so if you'll excuse me," said Isabel with the manners of a well-bred lady.

“I do hope to see more of you this evening. I was hoping we would be able to dance later."

"Thank you, Randall, but unfortunately, I don't dance," said Isabel.

"Oh, but my dear, that is half the fun." and he reached for Isabel's hand to kiss.

"If you will excuse us," John said firmly holding out his arm for Isabel.

Isabel took his arm and looked right into John's eyes. All of his doubt faded.

He was hopelessly head-over-heels in love with Isabel. He just had to figure out a way to tell her tonight.

Isabel's heart was skipping beats, and she could not feel her feet on the ground. She doesn't know what happened, but the smile worked just like Sarah said it would. She could not believe he came to the dance; he was here.

"You look beautiful this evening. Your dress is becoming."

"Sarah altered one of Maude's old dresses for me, and she did my hair," explained Isabel.

"It looks nice."

"You think so. Until today, my mother was the only one who had ever done my hair, and it was always into braids."

Silence came between them as they walked. Neither one knew where to begin. Both John and Isabel talked at once.

"About the other night.”

“The other day.”

“You, first.”

“No, you were saying."

Then, laughter erupted from them both as they realized how silly the misunderstanding had been. All that mattered was the present moment. John and Isabel were here and together. They drifted over to the pie stand where everyone was watching this beautiful young couple-walking arm in arm.

Clara was the first to speak. "Well, it is about time you got here. I'm almost out of pie."

"I bet you saved some for me, didn't you?" and John as he hugged Clara.

"Oh, go on. You know I did," said Clara as she bustled under the tarp.

"Isabel, I would like you to meet some friends of mine," said John politely.

"Maude introduced us," said Gus.

"What?"

"I meet these gentlemen earlier," said Isabel with a twinkle in her eye.

"I don't know if I would go that far," said John teasingly as he looked with affection at these three men who have raised him for the past ten years. He smiled with admiration on how cleaned up these three old buzzards were.

Usually, Pete and Gus always wore heavy aprons working around the livery. Tonight, Pete's full head of white hair and his bushy white mustache were well groomed. He wore a black coat and pants with a new white dress shirt and a black ribbon tie.

Gus had a large belly to cover, and even he had squeezed into some dress clothes. His brown hair was streaked with gray and slicked back. His jacket hung on the chair, and he rolled the sleeves of his dress shirt tight.

"Miss Isabel, have you had any of that barbeque, yet," asked Pete.

"Not I haven't, but it smells wonderful," said Isabel.

"Well, Gus, don't you think John should go over get a plate a barbeque for Miss Isabel before it is all gone," said Pete.

"Why I think that would be the gentlemanly thing to do," responded Gus.

"Okay, Okay. I can take a hint. Miss Grant, would you like some barbeque?" asked John.

"Yes, Sergeant Webster, that would be nice," said Isabel affectionately.

John left to get two plates of barbeque, and as he walked, he plotted mischievously on how he was going to get those two old coots back. He couldn't help but smile. Everything was going to be all right.

As John was walking away, Thomas showed up. He jumped up on the wagon wheel and said, "Hey Clara, got any pie left?"

"Do you think I would forget about you?"

She handed him a pie tin with a couple of pieces and then she went to look for a fork. She found one and gave it to him. He handed back the empty tin.

"That was great, Clara," Thomas sputtered with crumbs all over the front of his shirt.

"Thomas Renshaw"

"Now, you're in trouble, boy," said Gus. "Here comes your Ma."

"Thomas Charles Renshaw, where have you been?" said Maude looking over his appearance.

Thomas shoved his hands in his pockets to keep the rattling of coins in his pocket quiet

. He looked over to Joshua and then back to his Ma. She noticed immediately and knew she would have to check with Joshua. She knew he has been up to something, and she has not been able to quite put her finger on it.

"Thomas, you smell like an old horse blanket. Now, you march right up to the hotel and get yourself cleaned up. Then, put on that new dress shirt I laid out for you."

"But ma."

Maude took him by the arm and walked him toward the hotel.

"Listen, Thomas. You are getting to be a young man. I am a businesswoman in this town, and I expect my family to look respectful."

"Now, get cleaned up and come back here, so we can dance together."

"Ah, Ma," said Thomas reluctantly.

"What do you mean? I look forward to it every year," said Maude.

"I know you do," he said with a smile sheepishly. "I'll be right back."

"Thank you, Thomas. It means a lot to me."

Maude watched her pride and joy walk to the hotel. She worried whether she was doing a good job raising him without a man's influence. Maude had her choice of suitors, but none of them caught her fancy.

Thomas was the most important thing in her life, and she needed to let him know that more often.

"Maybe tonight, we are all searching for the words to let those people in our lives know how important they are to us," thought Maude as she walked back to the people who had become like family to her.

Mr. Wainwright and his son Randall had joined the small gathering by the pie stand when Maude returned. Maude noticed Randall had wasted no time moving up next to Isabel.

"Miss Isabel, would you allow me to teach you a few dance moves," said Randall as he reached for her hand.

"Why thank you, Mr. Randall, but Charlie here has already offered to teach me to dance," said Isabel as she turned toward Charlie with a look of "please rescue me."

"Why sure, Charlie, go on and show Isabel some of your dance moves," said Gus with all mock seriousness.

"Why, I would be glad to Miss Isabel," said Charlie glaring at Gus.

The rest of them tried hard to hide their smirks behind their hands because not one of them had ever seen Charlie on the dance floor. Charlie and Isabel walked arm in arm toward the dance floor as John was walking back with two plates of barbeque.

John thought, "What in the hell is going on?"

Then, he saw Randall Wainwright standing there watching Isabel walk away with Charlie.

"Thank you, Charlie, for dancing with me."

"Well, ma'am I don't dance very well,"

"That's okay. I don't either.

"Then, I guess will be just fine together," said Charlie feeling twenty years younger.

Isabel observed the other couples on the dance floor, and she tried to mimic their hand and arm movements. Charlie held her as if she was going to break any moment.

Slowly but surely, they started to move to the fiddle music swaying back and forth. Charlie gently held her hand and supported her other arm. He placed his other hand in the middle of her back and swayed to the gentle strains of the music.

Before you know, Charlie and Isabel were gently two-stepping around the dance floor. To Isabel, this was magical. There were lanterns hung on the posts, and the sun was slowly starting to set in the west.

"Cra-ack!"

Their enjoyable dance was interrupted by a slap to the face.

"How dare you say that to me," screamed a brunette saloon girl who was dancing with Captain Pichon. "I am not a prostitute. I am a singer and a friend of Shereen. How dare you talk to me like that?"

The woman stomped off the dance floor, creating a scene and leaving Pichon in the middle of a cleared-out area.

"You're nothing but a whore," yelled Pichon in a drunken slur, and he staggered off the dance floor. He walked over into the shadows where the men were drinking moonshine out of fruit jars.

"Right sorry, you had to hear that ma'am," said Charlie.

It made him sick to his stomach, thinking that Isabel might have had to marry that worthless piece of shit. Charlie was usually an even-tempered old cuss, but there were days that Pichon just rubbed him the wrong way.

"It's all right. Do you care if we head back?" asked Isabel. "But thank you for dancing with me. You are a wonderful dancer."

"Well, I had a good partner," said Charlie, making Isabel smile.

"Why does Pichon have to ruin every moment of happiness I have? Why can't he disappear?" thought Isabel.

"Stop it, Isabel, don't let that louse ruin this beautiful day. You are safe and among friends."

"I know you didn't want to dance with me, but I appreciate it," said Isabel. "I didn't want to dance with Mr. Wainwright's son. I am afraid it would have made John mad. Besides, I think Mr. Wainwright is girlish-like for a guy."

"I have always thought so, ma'am," said Charlie in a deadpan manner that made Isabel giggle.

Charlie and Isabel no more that got back to the group when Clara said,

"Okay, Romeo, now that you are all warmed up, it's my turn to dance."

"Dang, you Gus, do you see what you started?" said Charlie glaring at Gus.

Then, he held out his arm to Clara and headed right back to the dance floor.

"Mrs. Beaumont, would you care to dance?" asked Pete, leaving John and Gus to look at each other in disbelief.

"I would love to," said Mrs. Beaumont.

"Oh, don't look so surprised, John. We all were young once. Come on, Mrs. Beaumont, let's show Charlie how it's done," said Pete.

"I am going to get a beer," said Gus, and he walked up toward Shereen's table.

Finally, John and Isabel were able to sit down and eat barbeque. Sarah was cleaning up the pie stand, and Joshua joined them and introduced himself to Isabel. The four of them talked and laughed; mostly everyone teased John.

Samuel started to get fussy, and Sarah knew it was time to go home and put him to bed. Joshua and Sarah took turns comforting their infant son but to no avail.

John helped Joshua hook up the horses to the wagon. The horses seemed restless and were jumpy.

"Too much noise and commotion today. Even the horses are ready to go home," laughed Joshua.

"Tell Clara, Joshua will unpack the wagon into the pantry, and once I get Samuel to bed, I will come over and finish cleaning up. There is not much to put away. Forty pies, gone just like that," Sarah told Isabel.

John and Isabel said their goodbyes to this young couple with each of them feeling a twang of jealousy. Joshua and Sarah were going home together with their new son to their own home.

"Isabel, would like to dance?" said John, wanting nothing more than to hold her in his arms.

"I thought you would never ask," Isabel said, looking into his eyes. She hooked her arm into his, and he covered her hand with his. Together, they walked toward the dance floor.

John took Isabel into his arms and held her close. He whispered into her ear, "I have been waiting for days to be able to do this, to be able to hold you in my arms." She smelled heavenly, and he felt intoxicated by her beauty

Isabel felt right to be these strong arms. She could feel his muscular chest as his arms encircled her tiny waist. The lights of the lanterns showed the blonde streaks in his hair and the depths of his green eyes.

They slowly danced to the music, and time stood still. Gradually, John and Isabel danced to a stand-still, and John's hands moved up gently to Isabel's face. He moved closer to her lips as he tilted her face upward. Isabel's breath caught in her throat, and she was shaking in anticipation.

"FIRE, FIRE on the prairie," shouts cried out along the street. The alarm bells were ringing. A bugler called all the troops.

John looked up and then looked back at Isabel. He grabbed her around the waist and kissed her gently at first, and then he devoured her lips.

Isabel returned his passion with innocence. She was shaking with desire as her hands felt his beautiful head of hair.

"I have to go."

"No, stay."

"I can't. Please wait for me. I'll be back," and John kissed her long and hard, leaving her breathless.

Porcelain White

Chapter Thirteen

Prairie Fire

Isabel stood frozen amid chaos. John kissed her right there in front of everyone. Her hand reached to her lips, and she closed her eyes. She still felt his lips on hers. His kiss was gentle and warm yet given with passionate urgency. John's kiss awoken feelings of desire in her; then in a fleeting moment, she had them torn away with the urgent call of "FIRE."

Sergeant Webster was in charge and held his commanding presence for everyone to see.

His blonde hair curled in the back below his army-billed cap. His muscular arms were at his hips, and moments before they had held her so gently as they danced.

From across the dance floor, Isabel watched John listen to some soldiers as they assessed the situation. The men pointed and shouted over the excitement of the crowd. The shouts of "FIRE" had brought instant panic out in everyone, yet John seemed calm and in control. With the ringing of alarm bells, people immediately searched for loved ones. Then, hand in hand, husbands, wives, and families ran to their wagons and horses. They left town hoping and praying their homes were safe.

She heard questions throughout the streets from farm families and townspeople alike: Where was the fire? What should we do? The smoke curled in the southwest as the sky glowed.

The soldiers told Sergeant Webster that Captain Pichon was nowhere in sight. As a sergeant, he took command and shouted orders to the other soldiers.

Soldiers ran to their mounts and rode for the fort for tools and supplies. Sergeant Webster formed brigades and gave orders to each soldier in charge of a squad.

John saw Isabel walking toward the pie stand as he ran for his horse. She was breathtaking. His stomach churned at the thought of leaving her, especially after that amazing kiss. He had planned to kiss her gently, but his passion had taken over impulsively. To his surprise, she had kissed him back with desire.

Cursing the fire under his breath, he reached the back of the blacksmith shop. His sorrel had been stamping to get loose and chewing his reins in a panic. John realized his horse had sensed the fire, and that explained why Joshua's horses were so jumpy when they tried to hitch them up to the wagon.

Down by the livery, the moonshiners had lit out with the panic of their hidden liquor still being found. They drove off into the chaos and fear of soldiers rushing to arms; Captain Pichon laid in a drunken stupor next to a tree.

Staff Sergeant Charlie Anderson hurriedly escorted Clara back to the pie stand, and he quickly gave her peck on the cheek.

"Oh, go on now. You don't have time for that."

"I'll see you later and don't be worrying about me," said Charlie.

"Oh, I can worry if I want to."

He jumped on to his buckboard and allowed the first wave to ride out of town. Being staff sergeant, he plotted strategy knowing he would be riding scout on the backburn.

Charlie knew that he needed his binoculars and extra rags for the horses' eyes. He thought he had better grab extra bandanas to protect from the smoke. It was going to be a long night.

Pete guided Mrs. Beaumont and Isabel back to where Clara was standing watching Charlie leave. The women gathered as a feeling of helplessness overcame them. They watched as panic swirled around them in every direction. Maude arrived, and all the women quickly asked her questions to see what she knew.

The mayor fired gunshots three times in the air, and for a moment, the panic quieted to a din. Standing on the back of a wagon, Mayor Thornton shouted through a cone-shaped megaphone to the townspeople to bring hand tools, tarps, and blankets.

"The fire is on the southwest end of town and approaching. It is about two miles away. Men, I want you to hook up one-bottom plows and drags to horses and oxen alike. Hook up anything that will dig up dirt to create a firebreak. The army will start a back burn to meet the fire. Load the wagons with water barrels and buckets. All hands are needed. I am asking every man, women, and child who can work. We need to pull together to save our town."

After the mayor's plea for help, people seemed to rally to the call. The women walked back to the hotel, holding on to each other for support. Maude spotted Thomas talking to Joshua and Pete. She knew he was safe.

"Sarah. What on earth?" exclaimed Clara. "I plumb forgot all about these dishes. Oh, you"

Sarah was in the kitchen finishing the last of the pie plates. Sara explained how fussy Samuel has been. She suspected he might be cutting his first tooth, so she had brought Samuel in a basket with her to the hotel. Maude, Clara, and Ruth filled Sarah in on all the details in the mayor's speech.

Isabel headed straight upstairs to change clothes. She changed into her oldest dress and tied a handkerchief around her hair and hid her purse in a drawer. She put on her old boots and ran back downstairs with determination.

Clara noticed Isabel looking through the basket of old aprons. "Isabel, where are you going?"

"I'm going to help. The mayor said he needs everyone: every man, woman, and child able to work. They need help beating back this fire from destroying our town. This is my town, and I plan on helping," said Isabel with conviction.

Marjorie and Pauline walked in during her speech to Clara. They raised their eyebrows, knowing she was standing up to Clara.

"I am going to see if I can help Pete and Gus. Don't worry about me, Clara. I'm strong," said Isabel. "The mayor expects everyone to help. Let me do my part for what this town has given me."

"Okay, but you be careful, girl," said Clara.

"Mrs. Beaumont, would you keep an eye on Samuel? asked Sarah. "He is sleeping for now, and I will be back to feed him.

"No problem," said Ruth Beaumont. "He will be safe here."

"Isabel's right. I am strong, and I can help, too. We'll stay close by with Pete and Gus," said Sarah.

Sarah grabbed a handkerchief from the basket for her hair. Clara found them both an old pair of Thomas' leather gloves. The two girls rushed out the front door of the hotel to help where they could.

Pete and Gus changed out of their dress clothes and threw on their heavy leather aprons over jeans and cotton shirts. They dug through their shop for extra tools and threw them into a wagon. The men loaded water barrels and buckets into two buckboards.

Thomas filled the water buckets from the horse trough with Pete, and Gus loaded the water barrels in the wagon. When Isabel and Sara arrived, the men stopped working.

"Where do you think you two girls are going?" asked Gus.

"To help and don't tell us no. We can work hard. We can fill buckets, and we can dig dirt if we have to," said Isabel.

Joshua walked through the open doors of the blacksmith shop carrying tools from the carriage house. Sarah ran to him and answered his question before he even had a chance to ask.

"Mrs. Beaumont is watching Samuel. He is safe. I am fine. I can help." Said Sarah.

She grabbed some of the tools from his hand and put them in the wagon.

Prairie fires were dangerous to work with because they often jumped firebreaks. The mayor organized plows to dig dirt furrows around the town, three to four rows wide. Townspeople followed chopping and turning over anything that remotely looked like it could burn.

The soldiers were up ahead, beating down the prairie fire and back burning off patches. The wind gusted, and the fire flared. Cries for help went out when breaks in the line occurred. Wagons of water rolled up with horses jerking and spilling water as they went. Wet rags and shirts covered the horses' heads to keep smoke out of their eyes and noses. Oxen continued to plow and voice their discontent as the farmers walked behind, hanging on to the one and two bottom plows.

Isabel and Sarah worked at the horse trough, loading water buckets. When they looked up, they saw Maude, Clara, Marjorie, and Pauline walking towards them with handkerchiefs on their heads.

"What are you smiling at, you two? We are young and strong, and we can help."

"This is our town, too," said Clara to Isabel and Sarah. The women started laughing.

"Besides, we couldn't let you have all the fun," said Maude.

The women held lanterns and carried water buckets. Isabel and Sarah kept hold and calm the horses, as water barrels were re-filled. Pete, Gus, Joshua, and Thomas drove wagons with water barrels out to the soldiers.

Townspeople of all ages worked the fire brigades of buckets to fill carts from every water pump in town. The work went on for hours until finally, the prairie fire met up with the backburn, and the backburn met with the furrows. The water brigade emptied the last of their water barrels. Smoked- covered townspeople joined with farmers and soldiers at the empty benches, tables, and chairs that were remnants of a celebration, which seemed a lifetime ago.

Town folk served coffee and pulled barbecued beef sandwiches as daylight was upon them. The mayor stood on a wagon and thanked everyone for their hard work and dedication to the town of Redwood.

"I want to reassure the townspeople that the army is going to stand guard, in case the wind comes up or switches directions. They will be on guard throughout the day," said the Mayor.

"The reverend will still be holding church services today at eleven 'clock with the church social to follow. Ladies and gentlemen, I hope to see all of you there, for we have much to be thankful for today. Our town has been saved from the fire; thanks to all of you."

Bone tired, the women walked back to the hotel.

"I need to go back to feed Samuel," whispered Sarah to Isabel.

"I will be fine," Isabel assured Sarah. "I am going to stay with Pete and Gus."

Clara walked back towards Isabel.

"Isabel, please come back to the hotel to clean up and go to church with me. It would mean a lot to me."

"I need to wait for John. He told me he would meet me back here, and I need to see him and make sure that he is all right. Then, I will come back to the hotel."

Isabel had not attended church yet, even though Clara invited her every Sunday. Clara explained to her the services, but Isabel felt uncomfortable attending a meeting to pray and worship.

The worship concept was foreign to her, and her limited education held her back from understanding prayer. Isabel knew it was important to Clara, and she decided that was all that mattered. Isabel and Clara hugged, and Isabel told her she would think about it.

Right now, her main concern was to check on John. The thought of him hurt by the fire or overtaken by smoke inhalation raced through her mind. She needed to see him, to know that he was safe.

Pete and Gus admired how Isabel had worked and pitched in like a farm girl. John would be proud of her, for she was a good worker. She was smart and caught on quick.

After Clara left, these two old bachelors realized a little too late that she was unrelenting. She tried to convince one of them to drive her out to the fire zone to see John. After much persuasion, Gus agreed to take Isabel out toward the area of the soldiers to check on him, and then, she promised them she would come right back and go to church with Clara. Isabel and Gus took off in the wagon and head to see the damage first hand.

The amount of land burned was unreal. The fire brigades saved the Taylor home outside of town, but farther down the line, three homesteads smoldered in the distance.

The first set of soldiers gave Gus directions and pointed to Sergeant Webster, who was on horseback. Gus drove the wagon to where the soldiers looked. He saw the urgency in Isabel's face, and he slowed the buckboard to a halt to let her jump down to the ground. She took off running, and John dismounted.

They gathered in an embrace. Isabel leaped into his arms, and he lifted her into the air. She clung to him thankfully, knowing he was safe and unharmed. He laughed at her handkerchief, and she told him he looked like a bandit with his bandana tied around his mouth. Their smiles were infectious as they stared at each other. It made no difference that neither had slept nor cleaned up before seeing each other.

The sun was coming up in the east; they were safe, and they were in love. John and Isabel walked arm in arm over to the wagon, and John shook Gus' hand.

"Thanks for coming out here," said John as he smiled at Isabel. "Turned out I had to take over command. Pichon was nowhere in the area."

"They found him dead drunk this morning behind some trees where the moonshiners had parked their wagon. His horse gave him away," said Gus.

They all laughed at Pichon's expense, but John said, "I need to stay as second in command."

"Charlie worked the back burn and rode scout on the fire sending in orders all night. He did a great job, but I am worried about Charlie. He is getting too old for this kind of work."

"He'll be all right. He is a tough old bird," said Gus, defending his brother.

"Clara wants you to come to church as her family because we all have a lot to be thankful for," said Isabel.

"I'm not going to be able to make it. We have to re-organize this morning, and then send out a scouting party to investigate how this fire got started. If it was Indians trying to burn settlers out, then we may have a situation on our hands and will need to call in another unit."

Then John told Gus and Isabel, "I am suspicious that something is going on at the fort. A bunch of supplies were brought in and stored, but nothing unpacked for the fort. Rumors flew around amongst the men all night. There is everything from Indian risings to a possibility of the fort closing and relocating. I am not too fond of rumors. I got get back."

John walked back around the wagon to help Isabel up on to the backboard. He whispered in her ear, "I can't wait to see you again."

Isabel felt his warm breath on her face, and she hated the idea of leaving him out there. He looked tired.

On the ride back to town, John's suspicions left both of them with a feeling of uncertainty. Gus thought about what the townspeople would have done without the army last night.

Isabel's thoughts only asked one question; if the fort closed, would John have to leave even if he only has two months left to serve?

As the wagon pulled away, John thought about his Aunt Clara, and he knew how vital church and family were to her. He rode to check with some junior officers as he made his rounds to each checkpoint.

He ordered small brigades to cut in half by seven o'clock; Sergeant Webster gave men orders to go back to eat and sleep. He assigned the men to guard duty on rotations throughout the day.

Pichon's horse, tied to the tree since yesterday afternoon, was distraught by morning. The horse continued pawing at the ground by his master and lick his face to rouse him. The sun was up and shining brightly.

Pichon looked around in disbelief at last night's festivities. The downtown area was a mess, and then he smelled smoke. He stood up, wobbly and shaking, holding on to the tree. His head throbbed like a sledgehammer.

His guts were churning, and he still felt drunk. His skin felt clammy, and he was stiff and sore from sleeping all night up against a tree. He walked down toward the livery, and men were cleaning up the town's celebration.

"What the hell happened here last night? "Where's all that smoke coming from?" asked Pichon with a dry slur.

"Where have you been, Pichon? Town almost burned down last night. Prairie fire. Army's out there now on guard duty, in case the wind comes up," said one of the workers.

"Whose is charge out there?" grumbled Pichon.

"Webster, I think."

"Oh, is that so?" Pichon walked over to his horse, was barely able to mount his horse, and with sheer determination rode hell-bent for Webster.

Charlie was selecting a scouting party when John rode up to him.

"Before you start arguing with me, I am sending these guys back to the fort so that they can get some supplies together. We should be able to grab fresh horses and possibly ride out this afternoon," said Charlie.

"Where the hell do you think you're going? asked John.

"I've been scouting long before you were walking, I know what to look for on the prairie. We need to be sure about who or what started this fire. Besides, it may be my last scout trip," admitted Charlie.

"I'll take these guys and ride out this morning. We'll stay overnight and report back tomorrow."

"Are you sure about this?" asked John.

"Yep," said Charlie looking into the distance. "Don't look now, but we got company."

Chapter Fourteen

Count Your Blessings

John called the small brigade of soldiers to attention as Captain Pichon rode up to the soldiers. His disheveled appearance surprised even John for he had seen him in many drunken stupors before today.

"Report, Sergeant Webster," barked Captain Pichon.

"Sir, the fire is contained, and the brigades have been cut in half to allow men to eat and rest. I gave instructions to rotate guard duty," reported Sergeant Webster.

"Staff Sergeant Anderson?" asked Captain Pichon.

"Sir, a squad has been selected to ride out to investigate the cause of the fire. We will be riding out this afternoon; we hope to return tomorrow evening with a full report," said Staff Sergeant Anderson.

"Permission to be dismissed, sir, said Sergeant Webster. He waited for a returned salute.

Pichon gave the salute before realizing this left him in charge. Webster, Anderson and the scout team rode back to the fort for food and rest.

"Get something to eat and get some rest. Be ready to ride out at three o'clock," ordered Anderson.

When they reached the livery, John told Charlie, "I am going to church with Clara. I know how much it means to her to have a family at church."

"Mind if I come along?" asked Charlie. "I want to tell her I will be gone a couple of days."

"Don't mind a bit. I think Clara will love it," said John. "Church starts at eleven. I'm going to get some rest. Wake me at ten."

* * *

The joy in Clara's heart was over the moon that morning. Isabel agreed to go to church with her. Clara fixed food all morning and packed a picnic lunch for a full family. It was a beautiful day for church services.

She walked back to her small apartment that she had one time shared with John. Fie, how she hated those steps to the second floor, especially as another winter was approaching.

Clara cleaned up at the water basin and undid her hair. She brushed her long brown hair. Grey streaks blended in across the crown. She braided and twisted the braid in the back of her nape, securing it with hairpins.

Clara changed into one of her best church dresses. It was navy blue with small red flowers. She found her matching navy-blue hat with a red rose attached. She put on her small ruby earrings that belonged to her mother. She sprayed some perfume and smiled at the finished product. She loved community services and the chance to visit with townsfolk.

Isabel pulled out hairpins from her hair and cascades of curls fell across her back. She slipped out of her old dress and boots. The water in the basin was cold, but it felt refreshing as Isabel cleaned her hands and arms. She scrubbed the dirt from her nails and used her new soap to lather her arms, neck, and chest.

Isabel sorted through the dresses of Maude's that Sara had altered. She found a beautiful royal blue cotton dress with small icy blue cornflowers. She slipped it on along with her new boots. Then, Isabel pulled up the crown of her hair and reinserted the comb to hold back the hair. She decided to let her hair remain loose down her back.

She needed to check with Clara to see if it was proper. She dabbed on some perfume and found her purse. Isabel reminded herself that attending church was important to Clara.

When Isabel walked downstairs, she saw Clara in the kitchen, checking the last-minute details in the baskets.

"Clara, you look beautiful," exclaimed Isabel.

The women in her forties blushed. "Oh, go on now with you."

"No, Clara, that dress and hat look nice on you."

"Well, you don't look too bad, either," said Clara.

"Clara, is it okay for me to wear my hair loose like this? I don't want to embarrass you."

"It is beautiful. You are a young girl who is not married. It is fine."

"Then, I guess we are ready to go," said Isabel. "Let me get that basket."

They each took a picnic basket and walked out the front door of the hotel and headed west to the church at the end of the street.

Townspeople arrived and gathered in the schoolyard. The school became a church on Sundays, and many people talked of the day they would build a new church.

People claimed picnic spots in the shade of the large oak trees, and tables were set up with food to share. Clara and Isabel found a place next to an old maple tree, and they spread out a blanket and set their baskets on top.

The minister stood on a small wagon and rang a hand bell, calling all parishioners to worship.

Clara took Isabel's arm and walked proudly to the gathering. Everyone greeted one another in the act of pure fellowship. The minister sang the opening hymn, "Blest Be the Tie That Binds." People joined in to sing praises to the Lord. Isabel looked around and realized how many people she recognized in this community.

Pete and Gus were standing next to Mrs. Beaumont. Maude and Thomas stood next to them. She recognized Mr. Wainwright and his son Randall who waved his fingers at her. She started giggling, realizing how silly it looked. Mr. Campbell and the mayor sang with deep booming voices.

Just as the opening hymn finished, Isabel felt a presence standing behind her, and John was there, cleaned and scrubbed, smelling heavenly. Her heart skipped a beat, and inside, she felt giddy. He came; he knew how much this meant to his Aunt Clara.

Clara turned to see Charlie standing next to her, and she smiled like a schoolgirl. Then, she saw John, and her joy overflowed. "My family," she wistfully thought.

The minister read the morning announcements and led the congregation in prayers of thanksgiving for the blessings the Lord had given them on this day.He also added special prayers to the three families who lost their homesteads in the fire. The minister asked everyone to donate clothes, tools, blankets, bedding, and money to help the families. The minister passed the collection plate for these families.

After the sermon, the parishioners sang more hymns, and the minister offered the final blessing. Families dispersed for the community-wide picnic.

Isabel showed Charlie and John the location of their blanket and picnic baskets. Clara visited and helped at the community food table. Isabel pulled out food and dishes, overwhelmed by the amount of food Clara packed.

Charlie and John had no problem digging into fried chicken, deviled eggs, homemade buns, jelly, and canned pickles. Also, Clara packed an apple pie plus carrot cake for dessert. There were two-quart jars of apple juice.

John and Charlie ate until they thought they were going to pop. Clara joined them for her meal, and she was in hog heaven fussing over those two men.

"Enough Clara. I can't eat another bite," said John in protest.

Charlie located a spot up against a tree, and he propped his hat over his face to block the sun. He was ready for a nap.

"That looks like a good idea," said John, following suit.

Isabel and Clara knew the men worked hard last night. They packed the leftovers and dishes into the picnic baskets.

"Come with me, Isabel. I want to show you the schoolhouse," said Clara.

Isabel and Clara walked arm and arm towards the schoolhouse. Isabel saw families enjoying their picnics.

The young parents rested while small children played next to them. Some of the teenage boys were playing a game with a stick and ball showing off for some young girls sitting in the shade. Young couples held hands and walked down toward the river's edge.

A bittersweet wave of emotion overtook Isabel. The scene made her realize what it looked like to grow up in a typical family, to grow up in a community.

She felt the bitter resentment of bile bubbled up in her throat. Isabel felt cheated out of childhood, and she felt resentful for her mother, teaching her not to associate with others and to stay isolated and lonely. These thoughts swirled in her head as they approached the steps of the schoolhouse.

Inside, the building was immaculate. The desks and woodwork shined in the sunlight. There were desks of all sizes with slates and books. On the chalkboard in the front was a welcome message to parents and community members written in beautiful cursive script.

Isabel realized the opportunity these kids had to go to school. In the back of her mind, she knew her parents received little education from their parents. Still, it felt unfair that her parents denied Ben and Isabel a chance to be educated.

The thought of Ben stabbed through her. She missed him so much. She needed to get him away from that desolate cabin and introduce him to this community.

She realized how lucky she was to have met Maude and Mrs. Beaumont, and Isabel knew she was on her way to learning to read and write.

Isabel sat in one of the desks and opened a book that had numbers in it. She looked at another with stories and a drawing of a steamship on a large river.

Tears sprang to her eyes, and she was overwhelmed with emotions. Nearby, Clara visited with some women by the coatroom.

Isabel interrupted, "Clara, I need to get some fresh air."

Clara saw the tears in her eyes, yet she nodded and told her, "I' will meet you back at the picnic area."

Isabel stepped out of the schoolhouse. Not wanting anyone to see her cry, she took off towards the river's edge. Maybe, it was a lack of sleep from working through the night or the fact that she missed Ben, but the faster she walked, the faster the tears came.

It felt good to stretch her legs. Her arms ached from last night, but her legs felt strong. Isabel walked along the river until she found a secluded spot next to some running water.

She sat on a big flat rock and pulled her knees to her chest. Isabel allowed the tears to run, and yet the bitter taste of a lost childhood remained. It felt safe to be alone with her thoughts. She forgot how much time she spent in nature and how calming it felt.

She tried to review everything that had happened in the last few days. Her mind returned to John's kiss. He kissed her with passion. It awoke feelings in her; she never knew she had. Just thinking about the kiss made her legs weak, and her stomach churned with butterflies. John was handsome. Images of his strong chiseled face, his muscular arms, and broad chest floated through her mind She felt his gentle hands upon her face. She closed her eyes and remembered that first kiss.

"Penny for your thoughts," said John.

Isabel blushed bright red. "Oh, it's nothing."

"Clara said you left the schoolhouse, upset. She came back to the picnic spot, looking for you. I know Charlie wanted to talk to her. He is going to be leaving for a couple of days. He needs to scout out the source of the fire," said John. "Care if I join you?"

"No, of course not. I would like that very much," said Isabel.

John sat down with his back to the rock, and Isabel sat next to him. He put his arm around her and pulled her in close.

"What upset you in the schoolhouse?"

"Oh, it's just silly."

"You can tell me."

"I'm just tired, and I'm missing Ben. I realize what Ben and I missed out on years of days like this, growing up in the woods. I see all of these happy families and that beautiful schoolhouse with books and slates. I see those young guys showing off for those young girls and think Ben is that age, and he should be playing with kids his age instead of working like an old man on that homestead," said Isabel.

"Isabel. I wish I could remove the hurt from your life. I am sure Ben is fine. He is looking after your mom and dad. Work never hurt young boys. It makes them better men," said John reassuringly.

"I want to bring Ben here to live with me. I am going to save up," said Isabel.

"What if he wants to stay and homestead?" asked John.

"Well, I will bring him here for a visit, and he can decide. I will respect his decision."

"Sound reasonable. Now, let's talk about you and me."

"I don't want to fight anymore. I was miserable when I didn't see you for a few days."

"I didn't want to leave you alone last night," said John.

"I didn't want you to leave," said Isabel.

"By the way, Miss Grant, where were we last night? Oh yeah, I remember," said John taking her face in his hands. He reached down to kiss her gently on her lips.

Isabel breath caught in her throat. His lips were warm and salty from fried chicken. His hands felt gentle, and her mind swooned into a pool. She reached her hands to the back of his head and brushed the soft, golden-brown curls.

John pulled back and looked into her eyes, brushing her hair to the side.

"Do you realize how beautiful you look with your hair down and in curls? I love the softness. Come here," said John, and then, he sat her on his lap and began to kiss her again.

Each kiss became passionate as Isabel kissed him back with desire causing her body to tingle. Her hand caressed his chest, and she felt his muscles; his heart was pounding. His muscular arms wrapped around her, pulling her close. He felt her chest against him, and he was on fire, ready to burst.

Time stood still as they kissed in the seclusion near the riverbank. When they finally came up for air, they both laughed with joy. John never wanted to leave; moreover, Isabel felt she could stay in his arms forever.

"I didn't realize church and fried chicken had this kind of effect on you, Mr. Webster," said Isabel teasingly.

"I believe it is all you, Miss Grant. You drive me wild," said John, and he began to kiss her repeatedly all over her face making her giggle.

"Uh -hmmm," said Charlie hoping these young lovers would hear.

John and Isabel heard Charlie, and Isabel stood up to brush her dress and straightening her hair.

"Sorry, to interrupt, but we need to get back to the fort," said Charlie.

"Yes, sir," said John. "Two months and I won't have to leave," he whispered to Isabel.

John and Isabel walked hand in hand back to Clara, who had everything packed up and ready to carry back. Charlie walked over to get the horses.

John told Isabel, "I will come by Tuesday night, and we will go for a walk after you get off work. I can't wait."

Charlie and John galloped through Main Street toward the fort. Isabel and Clara started toward the hotel when they heard Isabel's name called.

"Isabel," said Mrs. Beaumont. "I am so glad I caught up to you before you left. Would you care if you came over on Tuesday instead of Thursday this week? I want to go to the church meeting on Thursday."

"Oh, that will be fine, Mrs. Beaumont," said Isabel.

"We are going to organize the donations to give to the families next Sunday," said Mrs. Beaumont.

"Mrs. Beaumont, I hate to interrupt you ladies, but I was wondering if you would like to go for a buggy ride this afternoon," said Pete Anderson in a most eloquent manner.

"Why, I would love to Mr. Anderson. It is a beautiful day," said Ruth Beaumont, and she took his arm. They smiled and whispered as they headed to a beautiful black carriage hitched with a blue roan stallion.

"They do make an adorable couple," said Isabel to Clara.

"Yeah, they do. There is so much love in the air, you'd think it was spring," said Clara laughing to herself.

When they reached the hotel, they put away the food and the dishes. Clara thanked Isabel for going to church with her, and Isabel told her she enjoyed it.

Then, Isabel went upstairs to discover a new pleasure: a Sunday afternoon nap.

* * *

Monday brought washday for the staff at the hotel. Main Street was quiet as farmers left town with supplies. A few hotel guests remained, and the day went by with everyone feeling the effects of a busy weekend.

Isabel worked diligently on her lessons for Mrs. Beaumont after the visit to the schoolhouse, and she knew she was receiving a good education just in a different route. She wanted Mrs. Beaumont to be proud of her.

On Tuesday, the weather turned cold, and the wind brisk as the calendar flipped over to the first of October. Isabel covered up her legs with a woolen blanket as Thomas drove the buckboard over to Mrs. Beaumont's house. They walked in carrying supplies.

"Aunt Ruth? Aunt Ruth?" called Thomas.

"Up here, Thomas. Come upstairs and bring Isabel," shouted Ruth.

They both walked up the wooden staircase and found Ruth in the spare bedroom with clothes strewn all over the bed and chairs.

"Here Thomas, I want you to take this crate of clothes and this carpet bag with clothes to the church.

“This box, I want Isabel to go through," instructed Ruth.

There were three woolen dresses and matching stockings. One dress was navy blue, another was grey with a white collar and cuffs, and the last one was a dark chocolate brown. There was also a winter nightgown, a black and red woolen scarf, black leather gloves, and a red woolen hat. In the bottom of the box was a winter coat of black wool.

"Try it on and see if it fits," encouraged Ruth excitedly. "I sorted for two days through these old clothes. I want to donate to those families that lost everything in the fire.”

“I also pulled out some things for you to try on today."

"Oh, Mrs. Beaumont, you did not have to do that," said Isabel.

"Of course, I didn't. I wanted, too," said Ruth, beaming a wide smile.

The coat was a perfect fit, and it was beautiful. Isabel felt the warmth of the wool. She gave Ruth a big hug, thanking her repeatedly, and Ruth felt the rush of generosity from giving to a worthy recipient.

Thomas carried all the clothes out to the buckboard. Ruth gave him strict instructions once again, and he assured her that he would take care of it.

Isabel kept back the coat, gloves, and the scarf to wear home. Thomas left and told Isabel that he would be back before dark to give her a ride to the hotel.

After Thomas left, Isabel and Ruth sat down at the dining room table to work on lessons. Their friendship developed as Ruth worked with Isabel. Ruth loved having the girl visit her.

Ruth's heart swelled with pride as her eagerness to learn was contagious. She found herself looking forward to the afternoons with Isabel.

Enthralled with the lessons, Isabel was like a sponge absorbing every word. She listened to every hint and every suggestion on learning to read and write. Words popped off the page. In less than a month, Isabel was able to read and write simple sentences.

When the lessons finished that afternoon, Ruth brought out tea and cookies. Refreshments signaled the end of the lessons for the day along with assignments given for the next week.

"I was wondering Isabel if you would like to write a letter to any family or friends during the upcoming holidays?" asked Ruth.

The word "family" felt empty inside as Isabel blocked out the flood of emotions that words seemed to bring to her Friends? All of her friends were here in Redwood. She felt at a loss for words as she pondered her answer.

"I'm sorry ma'am, but even if I did send a letter, there isn't anyone in my family that could read it," explained Isabel.

Within moments, Isabel was telling Ruth everything about her childhood, her mother's fear of other people, living in a dark cabin, her father leaving them to work for months, her brother, Ben, who was Thomas's age, her feeling of independence and her determination not to go back and Captain Pichon. Isabel was overwhelmed with feelings of relief at finally telling another woman the whole story.

Ruth listened with the concern of a mother. Ruth held her hands and reassured Isabel that everything was fine. Ruth told her that she had grown beyond the point of going back to that lifestyle again. Education was her ticket to independence. She reminded Isabel that she had a job; Isabel had friends, and she now had a female confidant.

She also had a problem. Darkness covered the two-story house on the edge of town, and Thomas was not back with the wagon. Isabel needed to get to the hotel. She jumped up and knew she had to leave. She put on her new coat, gloves, and scarf.

Then, Isabel gathered up her precious school supplies and the satchel with her new clothes. Opening the door, Isabel came back and hugged Mrs. Beaumont, thanking her for listening and for the clothes. She stepped out into to crisp air of the October evening.

The stars were out in full force. Since living in Redwood, Isabel rarely went outside of the hotel after dark alone. If she did venture out, she had John with her. She hated the dark. Years of listening to her mother's ranting and warnings of the darkness felt ingrained into Isabel's psyche.

Isabel tied her scarf around her head to cover her ears, and she was so thankful for the leather gloves. Many times, she rode through the streets with Thomas but often too fast to notice many details. The houses were large with two and three stories with many sheds and outbuildings surrounding the property.

Block by block in the darkness, Isabel walked in the direction of Main Street. Soon, she realized she made the mistake of coming along a small saloon several doors from the hotel. A tinny honky-tonk piano played as smoke filtered out of the top of the door of the saloon. She quickened her pace as she walked by, trying not to look in the windows.

"Look where you're going?" slurred Captain Pichon as he stumbled out of the alley. He was drunk.

Captain Pichon grabbed hold of Isabel and pulled her close. His rough hands squeezed her arms as he looked intently at her face.

"I know you. You're that girl, aren't you?" said Pichon with some clarity.

Isabel's empty stomach churned as the smell of stale whiskey and strong tobacco assaulted her face with every word he uttered.

"You and I could be married right now, and I could be headed home to my wife for a little loving. How about it? You're bought and paid,"

BAM!

Out of nowhere came the iron fist of John Webster. One punch and Captain Pichon slumped to the ground.

Chapter Fifteen

One Punch

Isabel flew into John's arms with a sob. The incident left Isabel so shaken that she could not speak. Her body shook with fear at the thought of what took place. The cold air seemed to penetrate right through her gloves, leaving her hands raw.

"Are you all right? Did he hurt you?" asked John. He noticed her thin black gloves. He pulled her close allowing her to warm her hands inside his coat next to his body.

"Oh, John, I was so scared," whispered Isabel.

"Are you sure you're not hurt?" asked john. "Isabel, my brave girl," and John kissed her head in desperation.

The thought of Pichon touching her tormented his mind. He kissed her forehead and cheeks, her hands, and her eyes. He kissed her mouth and whispered, "Thank God, you're safe."

"Thank you for saving me," Isabel whispered as he kissed him back.

"Let's get you back to the hotel. We'll go around the back way through the alley," said John. Inside his body, John was shaking with anger.

Knowing that son of a bitch touched Isabel made him sick to his stomach.

He was furious, yet he had to get his Captain back to the fort, or did he?

John led Isabel through the alley to the back of the hotel. They opened the back door of the kitchen, and Isabel ran into Clara's arms.

"Oh, Clara," said Isabel.

"What's the matter?" asked Clara, searching her face for answers.

"Pichon attacked her in the alley next to Sam's Saloon," said John.

"Oh you, poor thing. There. There. It will be all right," said Clara as she comforted Isabel.

"Clara, do you have a cold rag for my hand? I don't need this swelling showing up on my hand," asked John.

Clara looked at both of them trying to piece together what just happened.

"Did you hit Pichon?" she asked John and then turned to Isabel and asked, "What were you doing at Sam's Saloon?"

"I walked home from Mrs. Beaumont because Thomas never showed up, and I didn't want to be late for work," explained Isabel.

"I didn't recognize you in that coat until I saw your white hair, and I knew it was you," said John, tying the cold rag to his hand. "Wait until I get a hold of Thomas."

"Mrs. Beaumont gave me this coat and scarf. Oh no! He tore off two buttons," said Isabel checking her coat for other tears.

"I'll look for them when I go back," said John. Then under his breath, "I hope that piece of shit didn't see who hit him. I don't know if I am going to be able to contain my anger,"

"Now, you listen to me. You have just hit your commanding officer. If he saw you, he is going to remember when he wakes up, and you could be in a pile of trouble," said Clara.

"I know," said John as he paced the kitchen holding cold compresses in a towel to his swollen hand.

"John, thank you. I don't want to think of what might have happened if you hadn't shown up when you did," said Isabel.

"Come here," said John as he wrapped his muscular arms around her tiny frame. "I am always going to protect you. I had that feeling the first time I saw you. All I could think of was how much I wanted to protect you and take care of you," said John.

"You did?" asked Isabel in the comfort of his arms.

"Are you all right? " asked John.

"Yes, I'll be fine," said Isabel.

"I got to get back," said John, and he held on as if he never wanted to let go. He took a deep breath and strode down the hallway towards the front door.

Isabel watched him walk out the door. Using the back of her hand to wipe her eyes, she walked back in the kitchen in a daze. Seeing Clara setting up plates made Isabel realized that there was food to serve. She hung her coat on the hook next to her apron.

Walking over to the basin to splash cold water on her face made her feel better. Then, Isabel grabbed a clean towel and dried her face. She smoothed down her hair and tied on a clean apron. Her eyes looked at Clara, and she said, "Pichon is never going to leave me alone, is he?" asked Isabel.

* * *

Captain Pichon laid in a crumpled pile face down in the alley. His nose bled down his face in the dirt. The saloon customers were oblivious to what had taken place just steps from the front door.

When John arrived, the first thing he did was check to see if he was breathing. Then, he looked in the dark for the buttons to Isabel's coat. Darkness enveloped the alley, so he gave up the search. John gathered up his commanding officer by throwing one arm around his shoulder. They started towards Pichon's horse.

"You son of a bitch, Webster," said Pichon, wiping the blood away from his nose.

"Yes, sir," said John politely through his teeth.

"What the hell do you think you're doing?" yelled Pichon. He struggled to walk and fell forward on his face.

Once again, Webster picked up his commanding officer and put him on his horse. John held on to the reins of his horse.

John mounted his sorrel and led Pichon's horse through town and back to the fort. The captain faded in and out of his drunken stupor as they rode back to the post.

When they arrived, Sergeant Webster motioned for help. Two recruits on guard duty opened the doors and helped him put Captain Pichon into his room. They removed his boots and wiped the blood from his face. His nose looked broken along with two very black eyes.

Then, Pichon groaned and rolled to his side. John grabbed the spittoon, and Pichon vomited into the brass container. The recruits scattered to get more water and rags. One of the recruits laid a cold compress on his forehead and agreed to stay with his new commanding officer.

John ordered the other recruit to stand watch as he went back to the barracks to change uniforms. He wanted to remove the stench of Pichon. John wanted to explain to Charlie what had happened, and then, he needed to plan his next move.

Yesterday, Charlie arrived back to the fort late in the evening. The scouting party camped two nights out on the prairie. One of the soldiers discovered a tree struck by lightning. It appeared to be the source of the prairie fire. Also, they saw no Indian tracks or disturbances of a war party on the trip.

Charlie was plumb tuckered out after this trip. Working through the night, getting no sleep, riding for three days and sleeping on the ground for two nights took its toll on him.

Propped up in his bunk bed, Charlie was scratching some figures on paper when John walked in to talk to him.

"Hey, got a minute?" asked John.

"Sure. What's up?" asked Charlie, setting his paper aside as he swung his feet to the ground.

"Pichon attacked Isabel, and I hit him. Knocked him out, in fact," said John.

"Humph," said Charlie shaking his head. He knew exactly how much trouble John was in now. "How's Isabel? Did he hurt her?" asked Charlie as his hackles rose in the back of his neck.

"She's fine but scared. I took her back to the hotel. She is with Clara," explained John. Then, he whispered to Charlie, "I was afraid I struck him so hard that I killed him."

"Did he see you hit him?" asked Charlie.

"I don't think so," admitted John.

"Where is he now?"

"I brought him back on his horse, and he is in his room. He has two black eyes to go with his broken nose."

"That son of a bitch is lucky. I didn't break every bone in his body," said John with a vengeance in his voice.

"Quiet. Keep your voice down," admonished Charlie. "If no one saw you throw the punch including Pichon, you will be all right."

Then, John showed him his hand, which was as big as a squash.

"I'll get some water," said Charlie. Grabbing a bucket, his friend walked toward the small hand pump. He filled the bucket half full and set down in front of John. "Stick your hand in there. You need to take that swelling down."

John flinched as he immersed his hand into the cold well water. He held it in there until in turned numb. Then, rubbing his hand to retrieve circulation, the Sergeant flexed his fingers to make sure everything worked.

"You better lay low and stay out of his way for a couple of days."

“Wear gloves and don't let anyone see that hand of yours until the swelling goes down," explained Charlie.

* * *

Isabel and Clara finished the last of the dishes that night. Isabel hauled the wash water out the back door to the cistern.

Out of the corner of her eye, she saw the buckboard that Thomas had driven that day. The lanterns were still on in the carriage house. Isabel walked down the path towards the lantern light.

Inside sat Joshua holding a piece of meat to Thomas's eye. Isabel walked in, ready to yell at Thomas until she saw his face. She ran over to Thomas, fearing the worst.

"Thomas, what happened to you?" asked Isabel as her anger disappeared.

"I got in a fight. I'm sorry Isabel that I didn't pick you up," said Thomas.

"It's okay, Thomas. Who did this to you? Does your mother know?" asked Isabel quickly.

"Don't tell ma, please Isabel," pleaded Thomas.

"She is going to find out when she sees you," said Isabel.

Then, Joshua spoke, "She is right, you know. You need to tell her everything."

"Everything? What's going on, Thomas?" asked Isabel.

“After I left, Aunt Ruth's house, I went to the church to drop off the clothes for the donation. Well, Henry Walker was there by the schoolyard. When he saw me, he started dogging me around and wouldn't let me leave," explained Thomas.

"Why not?"

"On Saturday afternoon of the harvest celebration, I was racing some of the sodbusters. Everyone was betting money on the horses. In one of the races, I beat Henry Walker by four or five horse lengths and took his money. He wanted a rematch. I told him no, that I had work to do. He called me a coward, and he wouldn't take no for an answer," said Thomas.

"So, you Had to fight him," asked Isabel. She felt like she was scolding Ben.

"Yeah, I Had to fight him," Thomas said, defending himself. "I was holding my own until he knocked me out. Then, I don't remember too much after that.”

“I woke up the back of the wagon, and it was dark. I'm sorry Isabel," said Thomas hanging his head.

Isabel and Joshua exchanged looks, and she knew Thomas felt terrible. She put her arm around him and then looked closely at his face.

"Well, it doesn't look that horrible. I think you'll heal, and then, you will be just as handsome as ever," said Isabel, as she tried to cheer him up. "Your ma needs to know."

"I know," said Thomas reluctantly.

Isabel walked back down the path and picked up the dishpan. She walked into the kitchen and startled Clara, who was lost in thought as she swept the kitchen.

'Fie, you frightened me. I was worried. Where were you?" asked Clara.

"Thomas's buckboard was sitting in the alley. I went to see what happened to Thomas and find out why he didn't pick me up today," explained Isabel.

"What happened to Thomas? Is he all right?" asked Clara with urgency.

"He got in a fight, and he is beaten, mostly in the face," said Isabel.

Before Isabel could say another word, Clara was out the back door running to the carriage house. Isabel found Maude at the front desk checking in a late-night guest to the hotel.

Maude saw the urgency in Isabel's face and excused herself after handing the man the key with directions to his room. "What is the matter, Isabel?" asked Maude.

Briefly, Isabel told her about how Thomas had not picked her up from Mrs. Beaumont's house and that she walked home.

She left out about the attack by Captain Pichon. Then, she told her that Thomas was beaten up and left at the schoolyard.

"He is at the carriage house, and Joshua and Clara are seeing to him," explained Isabel.

Maude picked up her skirts and flew down the back hallway towards the back door.

Chapter Sixteen

The Fallout

Bruised, but no broken ribs, was the verdict. Thomas allowed Clara to examine his black eye and bruised knuckles, and Clara ordered two days of bed rest. Thomas allowed Maude and Clara to fuss over him that night and the next morning.

By the next day, he rested for an hour after breakfast and decided enough. Thomas needed to be outside and not confined to bed. He dressed and walked to the carriage house to see Joshua.

"Thanks for taking care of my eye last night, Joshua," said Thomas.

"No problem, little man, but didn't I tell you, I'd tan your hide if I found out you were racing those top-notch horses? In a cow pasture, no less. You fool! A horse could step in a hole and break a leg. Then, you would have to shoot it. Did you think about that?" asked Joshua.

"No, I didn't. I didn't think," said Thomas with frustration and anger at his friend. Thomas kicked at the dirt and then said, "Joshua, I need to learn to fight. Could you teach me? I want to be good at it, so this never happens to me again."

Before his eyes, Joshua saw Thomas grow, and he realized he was looking at a young man who was almost seventeen.

"All right. When do you want to start?" asked Joshua.

"Now," said Thomas.

* * *

The next morning found Pichon hung over. When he looked in the mirror, Pichon saw a worn-out soldier with two black eyes and a crooked red nose. The Captain felt sick to his stomach. He had been drinking that rotgut moonshine from a flask at Sam's Saloon. Sam caught him not buying drinks and threw his ass out into the street. Pichon stepped back in the alley to finish the flask before going back to the fort, and that was when he ran into Miss Isabel Grant. Damn it! That girl was a thorn in his side.

On the other hand, she was prettier than he had given her credit for when she first arrived. Hell, Isabel was a warm body, and that is all he wanted at this point. Then, bam out of nowhere, a hammer punch knocked his lights out until Webster picked him up off the ground. Webster? Hmmm.

Pichon splashed cold water on his face, combed his hair, and changed his uniform. He ordered a black coffee and told the private to tell Webster to report to his office immediately. He wanted to get to the bottom of what the hell happened to him last night.

Charlie had been working on the descriptions of the morning, detailing the fire timeline and their scouting trip. He worked on duplicate forms, just in case, someone decided to destroy or rewrite the reports. Under Captain Pichon's command, reports often disappeared. Charlie wanted the descriptions to show dereliction of duty by Pichon for the night of the fire, and the details needed to be in writing and given to the proper authorities.

That morning in the livery shop, John finished working on some harnesses that Joshua had given him to fix. The young private interrupted his thoughts and told him to report to Captain Pichon's office immediately. He set his harnesses down but left on his leather gloves. Sergeant Webster grabbed his hat and followed the young man to Pichon's office.

"Webster," said Pichon in acknowledgment.

"Captain Pichon, Sir," answered Sergeant Webster with a salute. He stood at order, received a salute, and then placed his hands behind his back as he stood at ease.

"Do you mind explaining to me what the hell happened last night?" asked Captain Pichon.

"Ah sir, I found you laying in the alley next to Sam's Saloon, and I picked you up and took you back to the fort," said John.

"What about the girl?" asked the Captain.

"I escorted her back to the hotel," said Webster, realizing the question of truth was coming.

"And who hit me, Sergeant?" asked Pichon. By now, Pichon had moved to the point of standing toe-to-toe with Webster.

No answer.

"I said "Who hit me, Sergeant'?" demanded Captain Pichon.

No answer.

"Answer me," screamed Sergeant Pichon.

Sergeant Webster refused to answer, knowing it would incriminate him.

"Let me see your hands," requested Pichon, as Webster ignored his questions.

Sergeant Webster pulled off his gloves to show his swollen hand.

"I hit you, you son-of-a-bitch. I hit you because you were attacking my girl. You were drunk, and you assaulted her in the alley." Then, he stepped closer to tighten the gap. He muttered with ferocity into his face, "Don't you ever touch her again, or I'll break every bone in your body, you swine."

"Is that a threat, Sergeant?" asked Pichon.

"It's a promise, sir," said Webster with conviction.

"Private, Lock him up. Webster, I hereby charge you with insubordination for striking a superior officer. Thrown him in the stockade," ordered Pichon.

"You piece of shit," said Webster. "So, help me, you stay away from Isabel, or I will hunt you down."

"Well, Private, this man is making dangerous accusations. Put him in shackles," said Pichon mockingly serious. Pichon grabbed some shackles from a box and handed them to the private.

He snapped on the right arm bracelet himself, being sure to bump his swollen hand a couple of times.

"I will telegraph Major Jamison to preside over the proceedings," said Pichon. "Now, gets this piece of shit out of my office. It is beginning to smell."

John walked out of Pichon's office in shackles, and the young guard led him to the stockade.

Soldiers stopped what they were doing and shook their heads at the site. The men liked John, and they knew how many times he bailed Pichon's ass out of situations. All along, Sergeant Webster remained loyal to Pichon.

The door to the stockade opened, and John ducked to go through the doorway. The small dark cell had one window with three iron bars. The young guard placed him in his cell, which contained a cot and a three-legged stool with a chamber pot next to it. John heard the wooden door shut.

John looked through the small window with three iron bars in the opening, and Sergeant Webster was alone with his thoughts. A couple of tears ran down his face in pure frustration at his situation. John thought, "Why won't that son of a bitch leave us alone.?"

"Why is he so determined to ruin our chance at happiness? That pathetic piece of shit. What is going to happen? Could I be court-marshaled? Whipped? Both? Would he be dishonorably discharged? Jailed for months? All of the above? What about Isabel? Will she wait?

After seeing John locked up, Charlie knew the army procedures. He grabbed the finished reports and the fixed harnesses for Joshua. Charlie stuffed the statements in his saddlebags. He threw the tackles into the other saddlebag.

Staff Sergeant Anderson mounted and rode out of the fort to town. Charlie told the guards that he was taking back harnesses.

No one questioned him as he calmly rode out the front gate.

In his mind, Charlie needed to send a telegram to Major Jamison. Sergeant Anderson had a great deal of respect for him and knew him to be a fair man. Pichon has been derelict in his duty, and Major Jamison needed to know the full story.

When he arrived at the carriage house, Joshua and Thomas were sparring in the open doorway. After Charlie saw Thomas's black eye, Charlie saw why Thomas needed lessons from Joshua. Charlie handed the harnesses to Joshua.

"Why didn't John bring them by tonight? That boy always needs an excuse to come in and see Isabel," said Joshua with a smile.

"Pichon locked up John in the stockade," said Charlie. "John is charged with hitting his superior officer."

Joshua and Thomas looked at each other and back at Charlie in utter confusion.

"What? What are talking about?" questioned Thomas, in disbelief.

"When did this happen?" asked Joshua.

"Last night, when Isabel was walking home from Mrs. Beaumont's house, Pichon attacked her in the alley, and John hit him," said Charlie.

Thomas felt even worse than before. He sat down with his head in his hands. His stomach churned, and tears stung his eyes.

"I'm going to telegraph Major Jamison. If John is court-martialed, it will be a military trial for military personnel only," explained Charlie to Joshua. "Will you tell the womenfolk? Make sure Maude gets this report to Major Jamison when he arrives at the hotel. I need to get back."

Charlie walked into the telegraph office and sent a telegram to Fort Snelling in care of Major Jamison. The telegram stated: COME TO FT. SMITH. STOP. SEE CHARLIE FOR FULL REPORT. STOP.

After paying his two bits, he left the telegraph office, and Charlie saw Captain Pichon tying his horse to the railing. Pichon exchanged curt greetings with Staff Sergeant Anderson. Pichon looked at him very suspiciously.

Charlie noticed Pichon's hat pulled way low to hide the black eyes. It was the first Charlie had seen his face. Wow. One punch had done all that damage. His nose was crooked, his eyes were coal black underneath, and his skin looked gray.

John saw Charlie ride back into the fort. He thought in his mind; what the hell is that old buzzard up to now? John paced back and forth in the cell. The concept of not having anything to do with his hands was driving him crazy. He needed to be outside or doing something. John watched Charlie dismount and then carry some papers into headquarters.

Moments inched by, and then finally, John heard that familiar voice talking to the guard stationed outside his cell.

"The guard is going to get you something to eat. I told him I would stay here," said Charlie quickly. "We don't have much time."

"What the hell are you up to?" asked John.

"I took a copy of the fire report to Joshua to give to Maude, said Charlie.

“She will make sure Major Jamison gets the report. I saw Pichon at the telegraph office. He looked suspiciously at me. Man, you did a number on his face. Remind not to get in front of your fist," said Charlie.

"What were you doing at headquarters? asked John.

"I gave him a copy of the report, and he wanted to know what I was doing at the telegraph office. I told him it was personal," said Charlie with annoyance in his voice.

"What do you think is going to happen to me?" asked John cutting right to the quick.

"I don't know. I do know that in 1872, the Army made it so the punishment could be no more than 50 lashes," said Charlie.

"Thanks, that is comforting to know," responded John. "I am afraid I'll be court-martialed and dishonorably discharged with no pay or pension."

"That is the least of your worries, but Major Jamison is a fair man. He will hear all of the evidence before he passes judgment," said Charlie with conviction. "Also, I wanted you to know that I'm not going to re-up. I'm going to retire from the service. I want to talk to the Major first."

"Then, what are you going to do?" asked John.

"Don't worry. I'll see you through this, and hell, I might even stay around and help you open that leather shop," said Charlie with a smile.

John smiled and then said, "That's the best news I've heard."

The next morning, Pichon declared everyone confined to quarters with no passes to town. He wanted reports and paperwork caught up and filed, and the fort cleaned for inspection. Work details commenced immediately.

After issuing orders at roll call, Pichon eyed Charlie with growing suspicion. He knew he was up to something.

Also, these past two days, Pichon suffered through withdrawals of drying out his body. The shakes developed from the start along with irritability. Pichon knew he was a drunk, and the moonshine made him sick to his stomach. Throwing up blood this past two days made him realize he needed to heal his stomach and lay off the corn liquor.

Telegrams arrived the next day with one delivered to Charlie and one for Pichon. Pichon told the news at roll call. He announced that Major Jamison will be traveling to Fort Smith by train in two days for the tribunal and inspection.

Charlie's telegram said, "Will talk privately upon arrival."

Scrubbing and polishing kicked into full gear. Even Pichon worked to sweat out the alcohol from his system. To prepare for the Major's visit, he planned to dine at the hotel the first evening and made reservations for the Major to stay at the hotel. Pichon arranged for the inspection to be the first thing the following morning with the trial procedures conducted and punishment implemented immediately afterward.

With the thought of carrying out the punishment, Pichon reveled in the idea of issuing lashes to Webster. Finally, that smart ass was going to get his. He was too perfect in soldiering, and he always made Pichon look bad without saying a word. With John jailed in the stockade, Isabel was an easy target for the next step in his plan. He needed to send her back for the last time.

Chapter Seventeen

Consequences

The October sun showered the backyard of the hotel in the sunshine. After Charlie left, Joshua worked with one eye toward the back door. He waited for Clara or Isabel to step out back with the wash water. When he saw Isabel, he crossed through the rays of sunshine to bring the expected news.

"Miss Isabel, I need to talk to you and Miss Clara and Miss Maude if she is available," said Joshua.

Isabel ran in to tell Clara that Joshua had news. Then, she peeked into the dining room to look for Maude. Isabel walked through the dining room to the front desk. Maude was working on the books when Isabel told her Joshua needed to talk to her.

"Miss Clara, Miss Maude, Miss Isabel, Charlie stopped this morning. They arrested John, and he is in the stockade," said Joshua as the women gasped.

"When is the trial?" asked Maude.

"Charlie telegraphed Major Jamison. Charlie wanted Maude to have these here papers and to make sure they get to the Major, safely," explained Joshua as he handed the papers to her.

"When is the trial?" asked Clara.

"Day after the Major arrives, and it will be a military trial, closed to the public," said Joshua.

"Can we see him?" asked Isabel.

"I don't know, Isabel. Maybe, Clara could because she is kin, but I don't think they would allow you after what happened with Pichon," said Joshua.

Deep inside, both Maude and Clara thought the captain had it coming. Maude had seen him drunk and heard the rumors of his growing gambling debts. He had a mean streak, and she did not trust him. Maude left and went up to her room; she knew she had some letters to write.

Isabel found herself unable to concentrate the rest of the afternoon. John occupied her thoughts. Twice he had rescued her, once in the back hallway and now in front of Sam's Saloon. She felt safe around him, yet he was in jail because of her, leaving her devastated.

That afternoon in her room, the thought of practicing circles felt useless. She stood and stared at the ivory paper spread across the bedspread. Her courage took shape as she decided to write a letter to John. For the next hour, she spoke to him on paper, writing her feelings and thoughts, hoping to raise his spirits. She folded the paper and gently dabbled a little perfume on the corner of the letter next to her signature.

Grabbing her black wool coat and red woolen scarf, she headed downstairs. Isabel made the long, windy trek to the outskirts of the post. The large wooden gates remained closed to any traffic in or out.

"Sir, could I see Sergeant John Webster?"

"I'm sorry ma'am. Sergeant Webster ain't permitted to have visitors."

"Could you see that he gets this letter?"

"Are you kin?"

"No, just a friend from the hotel," said Isabel.

Then, for the first time in a flirtatious manner, she smiled ever so sweetly at the guard.

The tall, gangly private was smitten with her porcelain doll face as she smiled. He winked at her and quietly agreed to give John the letter.

When she was out of sight of the fort, laughter slid from her lips. She had watched the waitresses at the hotel flirt with the customers regularly. The power of a smile had worked.

During her walk back from the fort, she found herself praying for John and asking the Lord to watch over him and allow them to be together. A warm feeling came over her as she walked. She smiled, knowing that everything was going to be all right.

When she arrived in town, she walked into Mr. Campbell's general store and looked longingly at the beautiful types of paper, envelopes, quill pens, black bottles of India ink, unsharpened lead pencils. She contemplated her next purchase.

* * *

John Webster stared in shock when the guard pushed the letter through the bars of the door. He didn't have any family or friends that were letter-writers. Letters were priceless gifts that caused everyone a moment's hesitation.

His mind searched, paused, and then devoured every individual, handwritten word. On this envelope, the penmanship was flawless, the sign of an educated woman. Then, in the corner of the letter, John saw the return address of Isabel Grant.

He took a deep whiff of the fragrance and closed his eyes. After opening the letter, he savored the simple sentences that thanked him. Dark swirls of the King's English spelled out a genuine affection. He smelled the richness of the paper and visualized the hand of the letter writer until it became painful.

As the sun set in the west, John missed seeing Isabel's eyes and holding her in his arms. Jail time gave a fellow too much time to think. It forced a twenty-two-year-old man to sort things out, devise a plan, and calculate every last detail. He savored the letter next to his heart that night and knew he was head over heels in love with her.

On Friday morning, Pichon barked orders to soldiers to shape up the outpost. Captain Pichon's commanding officer was to arrive in Redwood on the 2:40 train from St. Paul. Major Jamison was to preside over the court martial of Sergeant John Webster.

John was awake early knowing that he had to face judgment for hitting a superior officer. The Army was not going to let it go. He watched the large table and several chairs carried out to the center of the flagpole. Then, they brought in a buckboard with special hardware place strategically on the sides. Pichon was serious.

As the fort whirled with activity, John Webster was glad he missed out on the opportunity to help Pichon look good for his superior officer. John needed to prepare for the lashing mentally. Pichon gave him fortitude; he will not be giving him the satisfaction of so much as a whimper.

The train pulled into Redwood on a bright, brisk October afternoon. Fort Smith officers were at the station in their full-dress uniforms awaiting his arrival. Mounted and stuffed, Major Pichon had donned his dress blues and felt miserable.

Major Edward Jamison stepped down from the platform, and Charlie recognized him right away except his hair was whiter. The barrel-chested man with white hair flying out of the back of his hat shook hands with every officer and army personnel at the train station.

From the train station, Major Edward Jamison rode in the open buckboard with Charlie to the Redwood Hotel to freshen up and change for his evening meal; his sergeant took his luggage to the guest quarters.

"Maude, darling," drawled Major Jamison, as he walked through the double doors into the lobby of the Redwood Hotel.

Maude stood behind the front desk of the hotel wearing a burgundy pinstripe gown with lips to match and one arm on her hip.

"Major Jamison. How are you, darling?" cooed Maude.

From that moment on, the evening turned into a tornado of activity throughout the hotel.

The officers from Fort Smith joined in with the officers in Major Jamison's entourage. The waitresses were back and forth with extra breadbaskets and more wine.

The kitchen served juicy red steaks with baked potatoes and homemade butter. As the officers finished their meal, Clara dished out generous pieces of chocolate cake with cream. Waitresses served coffee and brandy. Cigars followed along with sipping whiskey.

The conversation was lively as Maude and Major Jamison laughed and told stories, and Pichon had the shakes. The wine helped calm him down during dinner.

The Captain sipped on brandy the rest of the evening. He needed to be sharp for tomorrow morning.

The best part of the night was that he was able to study Isabel. He watched her every time she entered the dining room. She did not look as skinny as he remembered her from the first day, he saw her. Pichon daydreamed of how he was going to get her alone.

Finally, Major Jamison ordered his officers to ride back to the fort for the night. The festivities wound down as the waitresses cleared the dining room and set it up for breakfast the next morning.

Maude knew this would be a perfect chance to talk to Edward, and she wanted Isabel to tell her side, also. After Major Jamison went upstairs, Maude and Isabel walked up to the back staircase, walked down the long hallway, and knocked on Major Jamison's door.

"May we come in?" asked Maude.

"Why, of course, my dear?" said Major Jamison sincerely.

Isabel realized what a true gentleman he was. He treated Maude with the utmost respect.

"Charlie Anderson wants you to read this report. He gave me a copy to hold on to in case something happened to the copy he filed with Captain Pichon," explained Maude.

"Thank you, but I don't understand," said Major Jamison bewildered. "I was to meet Charlie and speak to him privately.

A gentle knock at the door and Major Jamison opened it to find Charlie standing in the hallway. Charlie came into the room. The events unraveled as everyone told their story and confirmed facts on each other's conclusions.

Major Jamison shook his head in disbelief. He assured Maude and Isabel that matters were under control. Charlie stayed to talk late into the wee morning hours as he and the major strategized the morning court-martial.

Chapter Eighteen

Military Tribunal

The sun filled the courtyard of Fort Smith. Major Jamison set the inspection for oh-eight-hundred hours. Major Jamison, Major Randall, and Captain Pichon stood out on the platform of the headquarters office surveying the premises. The bugler blew the call for an inspection, and soldiers reported to their designated spots.

Major Jamison looked over the troops; he felt deep admiration for their efforts at the spit and polish decorum on the open prairie. After inspecting the soldiers, the Major and a court reporter sat at the large wooden table. Officers signaled the guards to bring the prisoner forward.

John walked out of his cell in the same clothes and boots from four days ago. He squinted at the bright sunlight trying to adjust his eyes. He looked disheveled in his appearance. The guards brought him up front and center.

"At ease, soldiers. I have a few announcements before conducting this disciplinary trial," said Major Jamison. "First of all, I would like to announce to all personnel who have served with loyalty here at Fort Smith. As of November 1, 1876, the US Army will officially close Fort Smith and transfer all supplies to a new fort in North Dakota.

Fort Adams will be on the supply front for the current Indian Wars that are raging in the Dakotas. In light of this news, all personnel will be required to meet with their commanding officer to discuss future deployments. At this time, I would like to address Major Pichon,"

"Yes sir," said Captain Pichon, saluting.

"Captain Pichon, we will no longer be needing your services. Major Randall will oversee the transition, as he will be the new commanding officer at Fort Adams. So, thank you for your service," said Major Jamison.

"I don't understand. My enlistment aint' up yet," said Pichon defensively.

"Thank you, Captain, now, if you would stand over there with the other officers. We have more business to conduct," explained Major Jamison.

Pichon stepped to the right side of the table, confused beyond belief.

"Step forward Sergeant Webster and Captain Pichon," ordered the new commanding officer.

Major Randall stepped forward, unfolded a sheet of paper and read, "Sergeant John Webster, charged with striking a superior officer. How do you plead?"

"Guilty, sir," John said in a gravelly voice.

Major Randall cleared his throat as he stood before his new unit. He read:

"Gathered testimony reads as follows: Sergeant John Webster witnessed the attack on a young woman by a drunken Captain Pichon recently thrown out of Sam's Saloon for drinking moonshine and not buying any drinks. Sergeant Webster saw the young woman struggling, hit the Captain once in the face and knocked him out cold. Webster then proceeded to escort the young lady back to the hotel. After seeing to her safety, Webster went back and secured the Captain to this horse and brought him back to his quarters and put him to bed."

"Sergeant Webster, how much of this is true?" asked Major Jamison directly to John.

"All of it. Every word, sir," said Sergeant Webster.

"Would you be willing to sign your name to the testimony?" asked Major Jamison.

"Yes, sir," said John, and he signed the piece of paper.

"Captain Pichon, how much of this is true?" asked Major Jamison.

"Major, the girl and I were merely talking that evening. It is the second time Sergeant Webster has interfered while I was trying to talk to the young lady."

"Major Jamison, I saw no reason for him to use force against his commanding officer," said Pichon with an air of superiority.

"Yes, you are correct. Striking a superior officer is a serious offense. Now, answer my question, how much of this is true?" asked Major Jamison impatiently.

"Most of it, sir," said Pichon. "I did not attack her; we were talking."

Anger crept up the back of Major Jamison's neck as he gritted his teeth to maintain his composure. Major Jamison grabbed the gavel and banged it several times on the wooden table.

"Captain Pichon, I have spoken to the young woman and other witnesses. In my judgment, I believe that punch in the face you received from Sergeant Webster was justified," said the Major.

Then, he took a deep breath and slowly released it.

"Would you be willing to sign your name to the testimony?" asked Major Jamison.

"Yes, sir," said Captain Pichon reluctantly.

"Sergeant Webster, striking a superior officer, is a serious offense. I sentenced you to twenty lashes and confinement to quarters until the closing of Fort Smith," said Major Jamison.

The guards led John to the buckboard parked to the left of the flagpole. It was the wagon with specialized irons. One of the privates removed the hand shackles along with his shirt. The other guard tied his hands tight to the hardware. The guards stepped back and found a position at each end of the wagon.

Major Jamison handed the whip to Major Randall who nervously took it in his gloved hand and walked out into the center of the yard. Slowly, he took his position, testing the snap of the whip. He adjusted the grip and took two more practice snaps at the air.

One.

John felt the whip burn his skin. He told himself to stay calm.

Two.

Inside, Captain Pichon's mind exploded with fury. He was the commander; he should be the one to issue the punishment at this fort.

Three.

Major Randall knew the men were watching to see what type of disciplinarian he would be. He needed to prove to these men that he was a leader despite his age.

Four.

It felt like cold water running down his back. John knew it was blood. The lashes were coming harder and closer together.

Five.

"I should be whipping the hell out of that son of a bitch," thought Pichon as he stood with rage, boiling inside.

Six.

Major Jamison knew his new commander was trying to prove himself. He, himself, never had the stomach for long severe punishments.

Seven.

Charlie winced at every slice of the whip through the air. He wanted it to be over soon.

Eight.

John saw Pichon staring at him, waiting for him to break. He was not going to give him the satisfaction. He held his ground and gritted his teeth.

Nine.

He closed his eyes and pictured Isabel's eyes. Her soft brown eyes would glisten in the lamplight. He could spend all night looking into her eyes and kissing her lips.

Ten.

Charlie's words rang home; "Is she worth fighting for?" It became clear to him. "Hell, yes, she is worth fighting for."

Eleven.

Charlie was mentally going through what he would need to take care of John's back. Infection and fever were two things that Charlie detested. He had watched too many people die during the war.

Twelve.

John opened his eyes with determination as he stared at Pichon. He was feeling the wrath of the whip but did not utter a sound.

Thirteen.

Major Randall's arm tensed up with each stroke. As he approached fifteen lashes, he felt his strength wavering. He adjusted his position and stepped back. There had been enough blood.

Fourteen.

The sun beat down on his back, and John could feel flies crawling on his face. Sweat ran off his cheeks, and his muscles strained against his restraints with each lash.

Fifteen.

"Scream, you, stupid boy. Let everyone know you are not perfect. You feel pain just like the rest of us," thought Captain Pichon, glaring at him.

Sixteen.

Soldiers noticed the change in stance and handhold of their new commander. The men realized the severity seemed to lesson with each stroke.

Seventeen.

John felt a tear fill his eye as he bit down to endure another lash. Frustration and anger felt close to the surface. He closed his eyes and searched for familiar faces. Clara, Isabel, Charlie, Isabel, Pete, Isabel, Gus, Isabel, Joshua, Isabel.

Eighteen.

Major Randall knew he had two left in delving out this punishment. Major Jamison was wise in having him tested in front of the men. He gained whole new respect for his new commanding officer.

Nineteen.

John felt light headed. He fought to stay alert. To bear through. To endure.

Twenty.

On the twentieth lash of the whip, everyone let out a silent deep breath that they had been holding. Shoulders and stomachs relaxed. The guards quickly untied and propped up Sergeant Webster against the wagon. Then, he swung his arm around each of the guards, and they led him to the bunkhouse in the livery.

"We have one more order of business," said Major Jamison. "Captain Pichon, would you step forward."

Pichon stepped front and center to Major Jamison. Major Randall laid the whip down, removed his gloves, and took a spot next to Major Jamison.

"Captain Pichon, in lieu of some recent events involving this fort and the personnel who serve the United State Army, it has come to my attention you were derelict of your duties on September 28, 1876, when a fire broke out that almost engulfed this town. Is this true?" asked Major Jamison.

Pichon looked right at Staff Sergeant Charlie Anderson, and under his breath, he said, "You son of a bitch."

"Captain, is this true?"

"I believe my report is on file concerning the activity of the fort and the personnel on hand that evening," replied Pichon.

"For your information, I have read several reports of that evening. You, sir, were derelict in your duties as commander of this post. You are fortunate to have such fine soldiers who can step in during a crisis and lead. These men deserve better leadership at the top," stated Major Jamison.

Then, the major reached down to his chair and pulled out a large hunting knife.

"Captain Pichon, you have been drunk and disorderly in public, in uniform; you have been seen gambling, cheating at cards, thrown out of saloons, attacking young women in public, fighting; your appearance at time has been unkempt and unbefitting the office of Captain, and when your men needed you the most, you were derelict of your duty."

Major Jamison grabbed the unsheathed knife and stepped forward to face Captain Pichon.

"Captain Pichon, you are hereby dishonorably discharged from the United States Army," said Major Jamison. He ceremoniously cut off each uniform button, pulled off each stripe, and removed the Captain's bars.

"You are no longer part of this man's army. There will be no pension, no pay, and no horse. Gather your personal belongings, and the guards will escort you to the gate."

Chapter Nineteen

New Assignments

John drifted in and out of consciousness. The familiar smells of the livery, and the dusty warmth of the bunkhouse invaded his nose. His back was numb. If he laid perfectly still, it did not hurt. When he moved, the dried blood cracked apart, and the pain surged through his system.

Major Jamison dismissed the unit, and soldiers lined up to meet with the commanding officer to go over the new assignments and the potential promotions that Pichon was behind on giving to the men. These promotions moved a soldier's pay grade up and gave them more privileges, better lodging, and additional benefits. Staff Sergeant Anderson had been in the army long enough to know paperwork could wait. Charlie went into the bunkhouse to check on John.

He spread a sheet on John's bunk and then ordered a couple of soldiers to move John carefully to lay face down. The soldiers removed his boots and his socks. Charlie laid another sheet across his belt line and cleaned the wounds with cold water. Charlie made a brine solution and took bandages and soak them it the salt solution.

Then, he rinsed them out in a bucket of cold water and laid them on the wounds. The brine solution sterilized the open wounds. After covering the cuts, he took another sheet and wrapped the bandages to keep them in place. He forced John to drink water mixed with laudanum to ease the pain, and then, he let him sleep.

If infection or fever took over, John could be in for the fight of his life. Charlie positioned himself to be there with him night and day until the crisis past. Within minutes, John was asleep, and Charlie sat back to let out a big sigh of relief.

"How is he?" asked Major Jamison as he walked into the livery.

"Oh, he is going to be all right, I guess," said Charlie, feeling bitter about the whole experience.

"Have you met with Major Randall, yet?" asked the Major.

"No sir," said Charlie respectively.

"You need to, so he can make arrangements," explained Major Jamison.

"Edward, step over here a minute," said Charlie. They both moved out of the livery towards the fence and away from any ears. "I want to retire from the army. I want to move on and do something else with my life. I am tired of sleeping on the ground or in a bunkhouse."

"When is your enlistment up?" asked Major Jamison.

"January 1st," said Charlie.

"Oh, I see the dilemma," sighed Jamison.

"Yeah, two months of Indian Wars and relocating to Fort Adams," said Charlie.

"We could use a good man like you to help us organize the livery," answered Jamison with encouragement.

"What will happen to the livery, this barn, and these fences?" asked Charlie, looking over the expanse of what he had built.

"In the past, the forts fall to ruins, or the settlers tear down the buildings and reuse the lumber," said Major Jamison as a matter of fact.

"Can a person ever buy or homestead the property?" asked Charlie.

"I don't know, but I could look into for you," said Major Jamison.

"I'd appreciate it," said Charlie. "I want to build a house on the far end of this corral."

"You still need to go meet with Major Randall, Charlie. He is a good guy. I think you'll like him if you get to know him. Give him a chance," said Major Jamison.

"All right," said Charlie. "Baxter, keep an eye on him for me while I am gone."

"Yes, sir," said Private Baxter.

Charlie and Major Jamison walked over to the headquarters building and walked inside to meet with Major Randall.

* * *

Pichon headed out of the gates of the Fort and walked towards town. His uniform sleeves torn, and the buttons cut off, leaving his protruding stomach showing. He needed a drink. How could he show his face at either saloon? It was morning; where they even open? He needed to find some liquor.

Pichon walked towards town and noticed both saloons closed until 1:00 p.m. He walked through Main Street until he reached the end near the river. Pichon plopped down at the bench back from the road. He reached into his pocket and pulled out his leather pouch. The pouch measured half full of coins, and it represented all the money he had left in the world.

Pichon found a cool spot down by the river out the way of anyone seeing him. He reached in with his hands to cup a cold drink and then found a comfortable place down near the shoreline to do some thinking. He leaned against the tree and adjusted his cap.

Asleep under the tree, Pichon did not hear the horses approaching. It was not until he felt a kick at his boots that he pulled the cap from his face to look up and see who was bothering him.

"What are you doing here?" asked Henry Walker.

'Who wants to know?" grumbled Pichon.

"I do," said Henry. "This is our look-out spot. I mean our fishing spot."

Henry exchanged looks with Alvin.

"Who are looking for?" asked Pichon as he sat up. "Say, ain't you Ernie Walker's boy?"

"Yeah. Who are you?" asked Henry.

"I need to see your old man. Let me have your horse," Pichon said to the younger Walker brother. "You can ride double with him.

“I’ll follow you out to your pa's place, and you can tell me about your spying out here," said Pichon.

"We ain't spying; we are just watching them when they drive by," said Henry defensively.

"Who?" asked Pichon.

"Thomas Renshaw and Isabel Grant," admitted Henry.

"Henry's got a crush on her," laughed Alvin.

"You shut up. Renshaw owes me money, and I plan on stealing that horse of his," said Henry.

"Well, boys, we may be able to help each other out. Now, let's ride out and see your Pa.," said Pichon thinking only of drinking until he passed out cold.

* * *

John hallucinated through the first night; by morning, the fever broke, and he was able to drink and sit up. He straddled a chair as Charlie changed the bandages. John sipped on some broth.

After changing the dressings, he took half of a teaspoon of laudanum in his coffee. John slept for the rest of the day.

By evening, Charlie made him get up and walk around to get his circulation going.

"I owe you, big time, you, old buzzard, "said John leaning on Charlie.

"Shut up and stay upright. I don't need you falling in this dirt."

"How did your meeting go with Randall?" asked John.

"How did you know?" asked Charlie.

"Major Jamison told me last night when he checked on how I was doing. He told me you were getting your next assignment," explained John, who winced with pain.

Charlie found a couple of stools, and they sat down outside the livery.

"Yeah, I'll be leaving in a few days with the first supply wagons. My enlistment finishes on January 1st, and then I'm coming back," said Charlie. “Major Jamison wants me to set up, organize the livery, and train a recruit to take over my position.”

“You’re the best man to do the job,” said John.

“And they bumped me up a pay grade to Sergeant Major. It seems Pichon was negligent in his paperwork. The army promoted me and upped my pay grade a couple of times. I even have back paychecks coming from the army," said Charlie with a smile on his face.

"Congrats. I'm proud of you, you, old son of a gun. What do you say once more around the corral fence? This fresh air feels good, and I have slept too long on my stomach. I need to stretch my legs," said John standing ready to walk around the corral fence.

Silence fell into step as they walked around the corral fence, knowing their days together were narrowing.

Finally, Charlie spoke. "John, there is something I have meant to ask you. I want you to look at something out here."

When they reached the end of the corral fence, Charlie looked and pointed to the land between here and town.

"I want to homestead and build my own house out there, and I want the old livery and this corral to be part of my property. Major Jamison is going to look into it for me and see if I can buy it from the government."

"That is a great idea," said John with pride at his futuristic thinking.

"When I get back, I am not going to have a place to stay unless I stay here in the bunkhouse or bunk in with Pete and Gus," said Charlie.

"I have thought of that also. Where am I going to live? I am getting out at the end of the month. I know Clara will be glad to have me."

“The apartment is small for the two of us," said John.

"John, when I come back, I would like to ask Clara to marry me. I listed you and Clara as my next of kin and as my beneficiaries on my military paperwork. I want your blessing if it is all right to ask her."

A tear formed in John's eye, and he hugged his friend without saying a word.

"I guess that's a yes," said Charlie.

* * *

That evening Major Jamison dined with Maude at a corner table where they talked long after coffee and dessert. Maude empathized with Edward when he admitted that he had lost his stomach for corporal punishment. In two days, he planned to turn over command and the Fort to Major Randall. Preparations were underway for the trip to Fort Adams in North Dakota before the weather changed.

The next night, Major Jamison met with business leaders from Redwood over the anger the townspeople felt about the closing of Fort Smith.

The main question remained on everyone's mind: Who will help in time of need for protection? The decisions fell to the mayor and the good citizens of Redwood.

The sheriff, mayor, and Major Jamison talked long into the night discussing the necessary transitional requirements.

Back in the kitchen, Isabel and Clara fought back the tears as Maude explained that John had received twenty lashes, and Charlie was taking good care of him. He should be able to be upright in a couple of days. Also, the sentence included John's continued confinement to the barracks until the soldiers left for Fort Adams.

By the end of the month, John would be a free man. Isabel sat on her bed, looking out at the stars that night. She thought, "A few more weeks and we could be together.

Will he want to marry me? Should I say yes? Would I have to give up my job at the hotel to become a married woman? Where would we live? I like having my own money and my private room and my own money to buy what I want."

In her heart, she knew she loved John. She could not stand being apart. Isabel sat up late that night, writing to John. Writing came naturally to her; the more she practiced.

Isabel was developing a way to stay connected to John by writing to him. As a young woman, Isabel wanted him to know how she felt without being too presumptuous.

On Sunday morning, Isabel went to church with Clara for support. Clara prayed for John, and Isabel spent the church services trying to follow the sermon and listening to the hymns everyone seemed to know.

After church, Clara took Isabel's letter and packed some food to take to John. Since Clara was a relative, Major Randall granted her permission to visit John on Sunday afternoon.

Isabel finished cleaning the kitchen and felt restless. She walked across the back yard and alley. She had not seen Sarah for more than a few minutes since the fire, and she needed to talk to another woman. Besides, she wanted to learn how to sew, and Sarah had promised to teach her.

"Sarah?" Isabel called from the doorway to their house.

"Isabel, come in," offered Sarah. She held Samuel in one arm and pulled out a chair at the kitchen table for her friend to sit down.

"Clara went to see John and Charlie this afternoon. I decided to come over and visit with you," said Isabel.

"We just got back from church. Every Sunday, we travel over to the First Church and stay for the noon gathering," explained Sarah.

"I went to church with Clara this morning," explained Isabel.

"Things have been busy with laundry, sewing and taking care of this active one," said Sarah as she smiled and tickled Samuel who laughed back at his mama.

"Oh, he is growing. Look at that adorable smile," exclaimed Isabel.

"He is a charmer," said Sarah.

"Sarah, did you have some time this afternoon to teach me a little about sewing? If I figure it out, I might be able to help you out since you did so much for me for the harvest celebration with my hair and everything," said Isabel.

"Why, I would love to!" exclaimed Sarah.

"It wouldn't be too much bother?" asked Isabel.

"Not at all. Follow me, and we will get all set up to sew and gossip," said Sarah as she walked into the next adjoining room. She handed Samuel over to Isabel and laid a blanket on the floor. Then, she slipped into her bedroom and brought out some sewing supplies along with a couple of projects.

Sarah reached for Samuel and laid him on the floor with a couple of soft animals made from old stockings. Immediately, he picked one up and chewed on it contently. Sarah sorted out her sewing supplies and found a basic nightgown to hem. She started Isabel on a running stitch. Sarah gathered a dress into her arms and sat down in a rocker with Samuel at her feet.

Isabel sat on the sofa and mimicked the stitches with precision. In no time at all, Isabel caught on to the method and worked on the hem.

For the next two hours, the girls caught up on the news around town, the hotel and the Fort. They were able to piece together much information for each other, and the time flew by as Isabel finished the hem, and Sarah completed taking in the dress seams.

Samuel fell asleep, and Sarah covered him up with a blanket without disturbing his slumber.

"I need to get back to the kitchen for the evening meal. Thank you so much, Sarah. I enjoyed this afternoon," said Isabel.

"Any time, girl. You can help me with stitching anytime. Here take these with you. I finished these two dresses and undergarments that Maude gave you. This afternoon was delightful. Tell Clara, hello for me," said Sarah.

Isabel carried the garments in her arms back to the hotel and ran to see Clara.

"How is he? Did you give him my letter? What is the matter, Clara? Is it John?" asked Isabel in confusion.

"It's Charlie. He is leaving. He has to go with the supply wagons to Fort Adams. He leaves Friday," said Clara with tears on the edge of her voice.

"Oh Clara," said Isabel, and she wrapped her arms around the woman's shoulders.

"John is fine; Charlie has done a good job takin' care of him," said Clara.

"Did you give him my letter?" asked Isabel.

"Yes, and he wrote you one back." Clara pulled a folded piece of paper from her pocket and gave it to Isabel.

Her first letter ever in her lifetime sat in her hand. It felt magical. She opened it, hoping she would be able to read it. The handwriting was bold yet showed signs of education.

"Dear Isabel, your letters have been the best medicine I have received. Your words of encouragement boosted my spirits when I have needed them the most. Thank you for taking the time to write. I miss seeing you every day. I want to talk about our future together — You and Me. Your words have given me hope that you still want a future with me. Forever yours, John."

Isabel was able to read every word but "encouragement." Clara smiled tenderly as she quickly looked over the letter.

"Ah, he is a good boy," said Clara as she stood to tie on her apron. It was the signal to get back to work in the kitchen.

Isabel counted the days until John would be free. She reread the letter several times before going to bed. It felt like one of her most prized possessions.

On Monday, she went to the bank to deposit her wages. She took such pride in seeing her bank account grow. Afterward, she bought light blue stationary along with a quill pen and a bottle of black ink.

She needed to write another letter to John. She spent the rest of the afternoon in her bedroom writing the letter and practicing her lessons for Mrs. Beaumont's on Thursday.

On Tuesday, she did some extra laundry, ironed her clothes and tidied up her room with clean sheets and all of her clothes hung in the closet. Isabel did everything possible to make the time go by faster. Friday was coming, and she was impatient.

By Wednesday, Major Jamison said goodbye to the staff, and Maude accompanied him to the train station. The Fort would be packed and ready to leave by Friday.

Charlie packed to leave the Fort, and the army scheduled to release John on Friday morning after roll call.

Clara felt such a mixed bag of emotions. She planned her menu around all of John's favorite dishes for the evening with fried chicken, mashed potatoes, squash, biscuits, and chocolate cake. Clara also worked on food for Charlie's trip. She was hoping to see him on Thursday before he left the next morning.

When Thursday morning had arrived, it was overcast and looked like a storm. Isabel was glad that she had washed her hair the night before and braided it wet. This morning, she brushed it out to make it look softer and fuller. She put on her warm woolen stockings and her uniform with a clean white apron and went down to work.

"Clara, I am so excited for John to be released, finally," said Isabel. Then, she realized too late that it also meant Charlie was leaving.

"Ah, I do miss that boy. I cleaned and rearranged the apartment for the two of us. It has been four years since he has lived with me. I got kind of use to living there by myself."

Isabel had not spent any time thinking about how everything was about to change in people's lives. She had not thought about where John would live after the army.

Suddenly, the back door opened, and Thomas ran into the kitchen. "Did you guys hear the news? Thieves broke into Campbell's General Store last night. They took a bunch of supplies along with boots and clothes."

Isabel and Clara exchanged glances that spoke loud and clear on who one of the thieves might be.

Chapter Twenty

Payback

Drunk for three days, Pichon ate beans from a campfire and slept in a makeshift bunk in the barn of Ernie Walker. Ernie was the local moonshiner who had a steady supply of cheap "corn squeezing's." Most of Ernie's cohorts were sodbusters looking to make a fast buck. Overall, none of them worked too hard.

When Pichon first showed up with Ernie's boys, he held up Old Man Walker in the air by his shirt and threatened to pulverize him for making him sick. Ernie admitted to having a bad batch.

Old Man Walker explained what happened when they rushed the process during the harvest celebration. He assured Pichon that he had good stuff coming out, and for three days, they tested it, mostly at night, while they sleep off the hangovers during the day.

After three days, Pichon headed to the river to clean the stench off his clothes. The cold water made him realized that he was wasting time. Pichon needed a horse, new clothes, supplies for the road, and Isabel. He wanted to sell her for money.

First, he planned on stopping by Isaiah Grant's homestead to offer him one last chance to pay up on his debt.

If he had no money, then Pichon was planning to sell her to the whorehouses in St. Paul. He'd break her in while they traveled, and he would be able to get top dollar for this thorn in his side. She ruined his military career, and he needed to get even with the little tramp and her piss-ant boyfriend, Webster.

* * *

Thomas loaded the grocery supplies into the back of the wagon. When Isabel walked into the carriage house carrying her books, Thomas admired how she showed up every Thursday afternoon right on time to leave for their weekly trip to Mrs. Beaumont's house. Thomas looked forward to Thursday. He and Isabel had become closer as they shared these afternoons.

Isabel was like a sister that Thomas had never had, and Thomas reminded Isabel of Ben, her younger brother. When they were both seated on the buckboard, Thomas reached in his vest pocket.

"Here. I found these," said Thomas. "I thought you might want them back."

Then, he handed her two black buttons that belong to her coat she had received from his Aunt Ruth.

"Oh, Thomas," said Isabel with delight yet surprise in her voice. "I haven't been able to make myself go back there to look for them."

"Now, you don't have to look," said Thomas as he pointed to the buttons in her hand.

Isabel clutched the buttons tightly in her hand and held onto her hat as Thomas urged the horses forward.

When they arrived, Ruth met them at the door with two crates for each of them to carry. They contained some old dishes, and she wanted them stored in the shed. Thomas showed Isabel the carriage house, and then he showed her the shop where he was making a trellis archway for his Aunt Ruth's flowers.

"Wait until you see her flowers in the spring and summer. The whole backyard is full," Thomas said with pride. "Don't say anything about the trellis. It's a surprise. The old one was damaged in a windstorm earlier this summer."

After settling the horses and the wagon into the carriage house, Thomas and Isabel carried groceries to the house. Ruth anxiously waited for them.

"Hurry inside, you two. It is cold out there," Ruth said with delight. She loved having these two come to visit her every week. "Put those groceries in the kitchen."

"Wow, look at that apple pie," exclaimed Thomas.

"Now, that is for later. First, Isabel and I will work on her lessons, and then Thomas, I want you to come back into the house at four o'clock. I made new curtains for one of the upstairs bedrooms, and I need you to help me hang them up," instructed Ruth.

"Aw come on. Do I have to wait until then to eat pie?" complained Thomas.

"Oh, all right. I happen to have some apple bars with frosting here. Would those do?" asked Ruth.

Thomas grabbed her and gave her a big kiss on the cheek. "You betcha. These will do just fine," said Thomas.

After grabbing about four bars in a cloth, Thomas headed back to the shop to work on his project.

When Thomas left, Ruth and Isabel sat down to the dining room table and caught up on the news.

"I wrote a couple of letters to John this past week," said Isabel proudly.

"Oh Isabel, I am so happy for you. See, you can use your writing skills," said Ruth.

"And he wrote me back. I was able to read almost all of it. Clara helped me with a couple of words," admitted Isabel.

"Well, maybe we should look at some reading skills today," said Ruth.

She rose from her chair and walked to the bookshelf. In less than two minutes, she located "Little Women" by Louis May Alcott. "Let's start reading this today and see how you like the story."

For the next hour, Isabel and Ruth read aloud to one another. Ruth helped her to sound out the words, phonetically. Isabel caught on quickly and understood the story of Jo March and her sisters.

"Would you like to take the book, "Little Women" home and continue to read on your own," asked Ruth.

"Could I?" asked Isabel.

"Absolutely. That is what reading is all about. Reading a story about people living different lives in different parts of the world is exciting. If you come across some words, you don't understand, write them down for next week," said Ruth.

Isabel picked up the book, moved her hands over the binding, and then held it to her chest with a gesture of affection for the object.

"Thank you. You are too generous. Thank you," said Isabel.

After an hour of reading, Ruth switched to math and questioned Isabel on how much she understood about numbers.

Isabel explained how her mother would play games with her and Ben down by the river. They would gather stones and make piles of ten stones in each.

Their mother taught them how to count to ten and then count the piles of ten. Sometimes, they would stack the stones or lay them in circles of nine with one in the middle. Isabel remembered the game so clearly.

Ruth began to show her on paper what the numbers looked like and how to add the numbers together.

"This looks like my bank book. Every week the bank teller writes in the numbers and adds them up," said Isabel making a connection.

"That's right," said Ruth.

"I'll bring it next time to show you," said Isabel, proud to be able to share one of her most prized possessions with Ruth.

Thomas walked in a few minutes later as the women were gathering up their papers and books. Isabel laid her reading book along with her primer and writing papers next to the door on the bench, so she wouldn't forget to take them with her.

Walking over to her nephew, Ruth asked, "Are you ready to hang some curtains?"

"Any time you are. The sooner we hang curtains, the sooner we eat pie," said Thomas, smiling at his Aunt.

The three of them headed upstairs to one of her spare bedrooms. Ruth had removed the powder blue sheer curtains and had sewn some pink floral curtains to replace them. Ruth didn't trust herself on a stool, hanging them.

"Isabel, fold those old blue curtains into a box and take them out to the wagon. Ask Maude if she wants them for one of her hotel rooms. If she doesn't, tell her to donate them to the church," instructed Ruth.

Then, Isabel and Thomas proceeded to hang up the large rods over the two windows in the bedroom. The pink floral lightened up the room make it more inviting.

Isabel also thought the sheer blue curtains were beautiful. Maybe, Isabel could talk Maude into hanging them in her room. Isabel felt giddy about the idea of having new curtains. She carefully folded them up and placed them into the crate. Isabel carried it downstairs.

When she looked out the window, it was gently starting to snow. She put on her coat to run this crate out to the wagon.

A beam of happiness radiated from Isabel as she looked towards town. As she glanced at the sunset, she breathed in a deep aroma of the early evening air. She looked up to the sky and thanked her stars for the friendship of Mrs. Beaumont.

Isabel sent an extra prayer for the incredible support she had received from the people of Redwood. At this time tomorrow night, John would be a free man, and she would be with him discussing plans for their future.

She no more than sat the crate down on the ground to open the carriage door when the overwhelming smell of horse manure stripped away the clean taste of the evening air. She fought against the gag tied across her face.

Throwing an old horse blanket over her head, Pichon picked up Isabel and threw her in the back of the wagon like a sack of feed. The final landing on the wooden wagon bed knocked Isabel unconscious.

Unaware of how long she had been in the wagon, Isabel felt jolted back to reality. She was in the back of a wagon gagged and bound with an old wool blanket thrown over her. Stuffed in her mouth was a dirty handkerchief.

She felt suffocated by the smell of horse sweat mixed with the scent of corn liquor. The stench was unbearable as the sour odors permeated through her nostrils.

Isabel felt urine run down her legs as it soaked her dress and her blanket. Mile after mile melted together as she jostled around in the wagon bed. The bumps in the road jolted her to the realization that Pichon had kidnapped her.

She panicked when the wagon stopped for a few moments, but they didn't check on her. Soon, the buckboard was moving again. She contemplated screaming but realized Pichon would halt the wagon and even touch her or hit her to make her silent. The thought of him touching her revolted her; she remained silent, unable to swallow.

* * *

Many minutes passed as the sun went down. Ruth and Thomas came down the stairs and called for Isabel. Ruth walked to the kitchen to cut up slices of pie, and Thomas volunteered to check on Isabel.

Thomas walked out to the carriage house and opened the doors to harness the horses to head back to the hotel. When he opened the doors, the carriage house was empty, the wagon along with the horses.

"What the hell," said Thomas, swearing like a grown man.

He looked around into the fist of Henry Walker. Thomas went down on the first punch, and Alvin added a few kicks to the stomach and kidneys as Thomas curled into a ball. Henry pulled him up by the shirt and hit again, knocking him out cold. The two boys threw him on Alvin's horse. They arranged a blanket over him and took off into the dark.

They rode double leading Alvin's horse over to their lookout spot down the way from the schoolyard. They lifted Thomas off the horse and carried him to the river. They threw him in the ice-cold water face down, hoping he would drown. Then, Henry and Alvin rode off to meet Pichon.

Ruth carried everything into the dining room. She had brewed tea and set the apple pie at each place setting along with forks and napkins. She set out a glass of milk for Thomas and teacups for her and Isabel. It felt quiet in the house. Isabel's books were lying on the bench.

She walked to the back-porch area and opened the door. Ruth tried staring out into the blackness of the night. Snow fell straight down, showing signs of accumulation on her steps. She called for Thomas and Isabel into the night with no answer.

For the first time in a long time of living alone, Ruth became frightened. She was terrified that something had happened to them. She had to get to the hotel and tell Maude.

With sheer determination, Ruth Beaumont bundled up for the elements with a fur hood, gloves, and a woolen scarf tucked into her winter coat. It was starting to snow harder as she walked out the back door. Being 60 years young, she trudged down the lonesome streets, passed dimly lit houses, that cold and dark evening.

Settlers and their wives crowded the hotel dining room. Ruth glanced around the room for Maude and then headed straight down the hallway for the kitchen. She pushed the door open and stood, ready to collapse.

Maude was helping in the kitchen to prepare serving plates. When the kitchen door opened, she looked up in surprise. "Ruth, what in the world are you doing here? What happened?" asked Maude.

The sap seemed to have run out of Ruth the minute she accomplished her goal of reaching the hotel. Ruth slumped into her arms.

"Are they here?" asked Ruth.

"No, we thought they were at your place," said Clara.

"They didn't come in to say good-bye, and they carried boxes out to the wagon, Oh, they were coming back to eat some pie. They didn't come back, and their wagon is gone along with the horses," stammered Ruth.

"How long ago?" asked Maude.

"Maybe an hour by now. Isabel left her books, and Thomas left food behind. She didn't take her scarf. She must have thrown on her coat to carry the crate out to the wagon."

Then, Ruth dropped her head and sobbed as if she had lost her children. The safety of Maude's arms reassured Ruth that she would get help to find Isabel and Thomas. Maude took Ruth up to a room and insisted she stay at the hotel that night.

Ruth gave in without an argument. Maude gathered up a nightgown and some extra toiletries for her room to make her comfortable and then went down to the kitchen to make up some soup and tea to bring up to her.

On the staircase, Maude allowed herself a moment of weakness. She trembled at the thought of something happening to her only son. Maude sent a prayer to heaven and asked for protection for Thomas and Isabel and strength to refrain from killing the person who harms her son.

* * *

Thomas laid crumpled in ice-cold water with snow falling at a steady rate. His head throbbed as he crawled up the bank of the river. Wet, muddy, and pissed described Thomas's mood. Once again, Henry Walker had out bested him in a fight. This rivalry was becoming more dangerous knowing they had left him in the river to die.

His clothes were soaked and stiff as he tried to run toward the carriage house of the hotel. He had to get to Joshua. The carriage house was dark, so he crossed the alley to Joshua and Sarah's house.

"Sarah, tell Joshua to meet me over at the carriage house," said Thomas.

"Thomas, are you all right? You are soaking wet," exclaimed Sarah.

"Don't tell Ma. I got some clothes in the carriage house. Sarah, tell Joshua to hurry."

Thomas crossed over to the carriage house with his teeth chattering. He needed to get out these wet clothes. Thomas started in the bunkhouse by rustling through a trunk with some old clothes. He also started packing.

He needed to convince his Ma to let him go after Isabel. This opportunity was his chance to go out on the trail while it was fresh. He needed to prove he was old enough. After all, he was sixteen, almost seventeen.

First, he needed to convince Joshua. He grabbed his wet clothes and threw them in a pile. He dressed in an old pair of jeans, two shirts, heavy socks. His boots were wet.

He rummaged around for an old pair of cowboy boots. Thomas grabbed his leather gloves and picked out an old jacket.

"Where do you think you're going," asked Joshua standing in the doorway.

"I'm going after Isabel, and you can't stop me," said Thomas defiantly.

"Whoa. What? You're not going anywhere until you tell me what is going on," said Joshua.

"Isabel and I took the wagon with supplies to Aunt Ruth's this afternoon. Aunt Ruth and I were hanging some curtains up, and Isabel took a box of curtains out to the wagon to bring back to Ma. When Isabel didn't come back, I went out to check on her."

"The wagon, the horses, and Isabel were gone. Then, Henry Walker and his brother Alvin jumped me. I figured Pichon grabbed Isabel and threw her in the wagon, and Henry and Alvin waited around to beat me up. I woke up in the river down past the schoolyard with a bump on my head," said Thomas

"Nice guys," said Joshua, shaking his head. "So, you think now that they beat you up, you can take them on single-handedly."

"No, but I have to go after them. I owe it to Isabel. It makes me sick to think she is with them with Pichon," pleaded Thomas.

"Well, you need a plan before you go off, half-cocked," said Joshua. "Let's talk to Dauber. See what he says or wait until morning, and I'll ride out with you after I get John from the fort."

"No. I am following tonight. There is fresh snow, and I can follow the wagon trail. In the morning, you can pick up John at the fort and talk to the sheriff. Then, I'll leave a good trail that you guys can follow. I promise I wouldn't do anything stupid. I will stay far enough back to keep an eye on them until you guys catch up to me," explained Thomas.

"You scare me, boy," said Joshua.

"How's that?" asked Thomas.

"You are starting to make sense," said Joshua as he tousled his hair.

"But now, you have to convince your Ma. That's whole other obstacle."

Thomas grabbed his pack and walked out into the stables. He looked around for his saddle and then turned to Joshua.

"Those sons of bitches stole my horse."

* * *

Charlie had returned to the hotel that evening after talking to Sheriff Dauber about Isabel. Dauber had sent his deputies yesterday tracking the thieves that broke into Campbell's store. Charlie also explained that John has until tomorrow morning, and then he will be discharged.

Both Dauber and Charlie agreed that Joshua needed to the one to tell John. Dauber assured Charlie that he would deputize the men and pay wages along with reward money to bring back Isabel.

Clara had packed Charlie food for several days and had it all wrapped neatly for traveling. Clara and Charlie were sharing a late evening meal at the hotel. Clara felt twisted up inside with emotions, and Charlie listened and assured her everything would be all right.

Inside, he felt sick knowing he would not be here to help look for the kids. Charlie felt torn, leaving when the people he loved needed him.

Before he got ready to leave, he slid a piece of paper over to her that included his address to Fort Adams. Clara smiled and held his hand. She promised to write.

Charlie assured her that he would be home safe after the first of the year. He told her he would have a surprise for her. She looked at him suspiciously, and he just patted her hand. Then, Charlie finished his coffee, kissed Clara goodnight.

Clara went upstairs to check on Ruth and to find out more details of what happened. When Clara arrived at Ruth's bedroom, Maude went downstairs to see if Joshua had any news.

She walked into the kitchen. There was her sixteen-year-old son dressed in old clothes making sandwiches. The unfamiliar determined look on his face warned Maude that this was important.

"Ma, before you say no, I'm going after Isabel," said Thomas with conviction.

"I was going to ask if you needed any help," said Maude as calmly as she could muster. Maude's heart was aching with the realization that her son was growing up before her eyes.

His face looked newly bruised, and his smile was gone. Thomas turned and hugged his Ma and held her tight.

"Ma, it's my fault that Isabel was attacked that night when she walked back from Aunt Ruth's alone. I was supposed to pick her up, and I let the time slip by."

"Thomas, don't blame yourself," said Maude.

"I do blame myself. Don't you see? I owe it to Isabel to go after her. It makes me sick to think of Pichon with her. It's kind of like she is my sister," confessed Thomas.

"Oh Thomas, you have the kind heart of your father," Maude said as she embraced her growing son.

Joshua came through the back-kitchen door and saw Maude helping Thomas pack some food.

"Evening Mrs. Renshaw," said Joshua politely. "Could you spare me for a couple of days while we go after our property?"

"Evening, Joshua. What do you mean?" asked Maude.

"Well, ma'am. These men stole our wagon and three horses, and I would like to see these horse thieves brought to justice."

“I plan on picking up John in the morning and meeting with the sheriff. Then, we will follow Thomas's trail," explained Joshua.

She felt the color drain from her face at the thought of Thomas trailing these thieves, alone.

"Oh, how could she let him go?" she thought. She took a deep breath.

"Sounds like a good plan, Joshua," said Maude, complimenting Joshua.

"Ma'am' it was Thomas's plan," confessed Joshua.

Maude turned to look at the young man standing before her dressed to hit the trail.

She breathed deeply in admiration for the solid head on his shoulders.

"Promise me; you will be safe. Wait for John and Joshua. Let them take the lead in capturing these men," said Maude.

"I will, Ma," replied Thomas as he hugged her tight.

Thomas grabbed his food sack and an old black Stetson off the hat rack. He stepped out into the night. When he reached the carriage house, Joshua had already saddled an older mare. He secured an extra rope, a bedroll and his knapsack of clothes onto the horse.

As Thomas took off toward Aunt Ruth's to pick up the wagon trail. He secretly smiled at Joshua's realization that Thomas was going no matter what anyone said.

He had never loved his mother more than he did that night. Thomas knew that was a tough decision she had to make, to let him go. He wanted to prove to them all he could handle this trip.

Snow continued to fall as he turned into Aunt Ruth's yard and walked into the shop. Fishing around for matches, he found a lantern and lit up the area. Thomas opened up a trunk that belonged to his Uncle and pulled out an old floor-length duster. Then, down on his knees, he unwrapped the cloth that held a six-shooter.

The young man stood up and pulled out the holster and buckled it on. Then, he slid the pistol into the holster. Thomas filled the belt with ammunition.

For the final touch, he found a hunting knife and attached the sheath to his belt. Throwing on the duster over the holster on one side and knife on the other gave him newfound confidence.

He grabbed a canteen from the wall. Thomas stepped out in the snow to fill his container out of the water pump next to the shed. Then, he checked the shed for any other supplies. He turned down the lantern and stuffed the matches into his inside shirt pocket.

Opening the door, he lowered his hat with determination. Thomas mounted his horse and rode off into the darkness to find the trail and Isabel.

Chapter Twenty-One

Surviving on the Trail

Decked out in a new coat, hat, jeans, shirt, and boots, Ivan Pichon drove the hotel's wagon along with their horses. The new Stetson kept the snow off his face, which was now sporting a short grisly beard.

The travelers reached the hidden still by nine o'clock according to Pichon's new pocket watch. The moonshine still was located and hour and half northwest of Redwood.

He and the boys had stored all of their supplies, courtesy of Campbell's General Store, under an old tarp in the makeshift lean-to shed on the property. Isabel was still unconscious when they loaded the wagon with the supplies, including cases of moonshine to sell along the way. The two boys tied a tarp over the wagonload.

As the snow continued to fall, Henry made a fire in the old potbelly stove warming up the inside of the shed. All three settled in for some shuteye, leaving Isabel in the wagon. About seven o'clock in the morning, the snow slowed down, and they started the eight-hour trip on the trail to Calabash.

Pichon drove the wagon through the snow. Henry sat tall on Thomas's horse, and Alvin rode his horse. They tied Henry's horse behind the buckboard. Throughout the day, they stopped periodically to relieve themselves, grab some jerky to chew and refill their canteens. It was slow moving as they broke trail. They avoided the way station on the main road for fear of being spotted.

By two o'clock, the eclectic group stopped three hours outside of Calabash to make camp the second night. Before it got dark, Alvin took off into the woods looking for fresh meat for their supper. Henry headed down to the river to catch some fish before the stream froze over for the night.

Pichon had pulled the wagon off the road and hid the horses behind some bushes in a thicket. Gathering sticks and small branches, Pichon started a fire for coffee. Then, he had an idea; Pichon had a woman who could cook for him. Besides, he thought he better check on Isabel to make sure she was still alive.

Isabel had been in the wagon for almost twenty-four hours. She felt bruised and dehydrated. Disheveled and stiff from lying in one position for so long, her head pounded, and she felt nauseous from the manure smell of the blanket over her head.

Suddenly, Pichon pulled off the burlap bag and threw the blanket to the side, and the light blinded her eyes. Yanking her out of the wagon, he pulled her to her feet. He pulled the gag from her mouth and untied her hands.

"See that river. Clean yourself up. You smell," said the unshaven ex-officer with the big belly. "Then, you're going to cook for us, and don't try anything funny."

With stiff joints, she stumbled down across the rough ground and collapsing on the ground near the shoreline. She slipped her coat, boots, and stockings off and picked up her skirt as she waded into the cold water of the stream.

Isabel was thankful to be out of the wagon. Her swollen lips drank in the icy cold water.

She looked around and saw Henry down river fishing. She turned and walked upstream away from his lecherous eyes. Isabel wanted to wash in private, but she did not dare risk it. Her trust did not extend to any of them.

After drinking more water and splashing water on her face one more time, she reluctantly climbed out of the stream, dried her feet with her skirts, and put her stockings and boots back on her feet.

Walking into camp, she set to the task at hand of cooking for four.

It felt good to stretch and walk around the campsite. She made another trip to the stream to fetch water for supper. Pichon watched her like a hawk as sipped on his coffee.

* * *

Thomas rode the older mare through the night as the snow continually fell, coming straight down. He had picked up the trail of the wagon. Within the first mile outside of town, Thomas followed them to the still. Then, Thomas jumped down and tied his horse; he walked about five hundred yards up to the makeshift, lean-to shed. He waited for them to leave.

He was thankful for the old duster and the big Stetson; it kept the snow and cold away from his body, but his feet were cold. The old leather boots were wet from the snowfall, and his feet felt numb. Thomas knew he needed to make camp with a fire to dry his shoes.

Thomas did not trust this group. He knew they would travel at night to make time, so he stayed on the watch, sleeping off and on again throughout the night. About seven o'clock in the morning, the wagon took off, and Thomas followed.

As daylight approached, he took a different route and trailed them through the woods that ran parallel with the road. He tore off a piece of an old handkerchief and tied it to the bushes where he left the road and trail into the woods.

Working through deer paths, he was able to keep the wagon in view. The riders made camp early in the afternoon, and he saw Alvin head to the woods with his gun. Thomas spurred his mare up to the tree line on the ridge and rode hard across an open field to the next set of trees.

He rode farther up ahead, hoping to find a lookout spot. Then, he would be able to see their campfire and even find a place to make one of his own. Thomas searched for an outcropping or thicket to make a small fire. He checked for wind direction and found a spot.

Then, Thomas started a small fire. He walked his horse down to a spring and filled his canteen. The water was like ice, but it tasted good. He drank more water, refilled his container, and went back to tend the fire.

After tying his horse off to let her graze, Thomas set out his bedroll and propped up his boots to dry. He felt Pichon was not going anywhere for a few hours.

He looked around the small campsite proud of himself. Thomas felt confident in his skills, and he liked having a purpose in tracking. Finally, he allowed himself to catch some shuteye.

* * *

Early Friday morning, Charlie showed up at the doorstep of Clara's apartment and stepped into the front room carrying a green satchel.

"What in the world is this?" said Clara.

"This satchel, my dear, is all the possessions I own in the world, except for my horse, saddle, and gear. I was hoping you could keep it for me until I get back. The fort is going to be empty, and I don't want looters going through my belongings."

"Yeah, sure, you betcha; yah, I'll watch over them," said Clara, impressed with his thorough preparations.

"Are you going to watch the parade? The fort is going through town this morning on its way out. We have to head north and then west to Fort Adams. We will be flying the colors of the regiment along with the flag, and then supply wagons and the troops. Should be a good show," said Charlie.

"I will be watching," said Clara. "What about John?"

"Joshua will be there to tell John," explained Charlie.

Then, in the early morning light, the conversation halted, and they both knew this was the final goodbye.

Without saying a word, Charlie and Clara fell into each other's arms to hug goodbye. Charlie pulled back, reached his hands to her face, and kissed her long and hard.

"Charlie Anderson, you make me feel like a school-girl," exclaimed Clara.

"Well, with that blush on your cheeks, you look like one," said Charlie, teasingly.

Clara laughed and said, "Oh, be off with yah before you're late."

"Bye darling, see yah after the first of the year," said Charlie.

With that note, he climbed down the long staircase and walked toward his horse. He looked up to see Clara standing on the platform.

As he rode back to the fort, Charlie vowed there would be no more steps for her.

He was going to build her the prettiest, ranch-style house, one story with a beautiful big kitchen, just like those he always read about in those dime-novel Westerns. She deserved the best, and he was going to see that she got everything and then some. Now, he had to figure out a way to convince her to marry an old bachelor.

John awoke early to bathe and shave. He dressed in his best uniform and combed his hair back. He had packed everything that belonged to him into an army satchel.

Discharged soldiers were not allowed to leave with their horse. It was Army property. Leaving Chester behind was making him sick. He groomed him last night and said his goodbyes. He knew Charlie would take good care of him.

The thought of Chester shot or killed by Indians was sickening feeling. He hated to see horses left for dead on the prairie, ravaged by carrion birds and wild animals. He brushed the images from his mind.

Charlie rode into the livery and pulled his saddle off his horse. Reality had set into Charlie. He was not very talkative; he had too much on his mind. Charlie told John he had taken his stuff to Clara for safekeeping, and then he headed out to check on the horses.

John's back was healing, but the large wounds were tender. His skin felt tight, and it itched as the scars healed. He did not sleep well last night. John sat up most of the night with a gut full of emotions.

Leaving Chester, saying goodbye to Charlie, leaving the army and deciding where he would start his business weighed heavy on his mind. The only bright spot of the whole night was the times he thought of Isabel. The chance to see her made everything worthwhile. He could not wait to pick her up in his arms and spin her around to hear her giggle. Then, he was going to kiss her, and he did not care who saw them. He was in love.

In just a couple of hours, they would be together planning their future together as husband and wife. He outlined different scenarios on how he wanted to ask her to marry him, but John was afraid when he saw her, he would blurt out the words, "Will you marry me?"

He envisioned the scene. John knew she would be there this morning outside the gate to meet him. Charlie told him that Joshua was coming to the fort to take him home. He would be waiting right after reveille, inspection and the ceremonial lowering of the flag. Then, the polite handshakes, and he would walk out of the fort a free man.

Before he left the livery, he topped off his uniform look with his thin-billed cap and gathered his satchel. He went one last time to the corral to say goodbye to Chester. He walked back into the livery and then said goodbye to Charlie.

"Promise me, you will take good care of Chester?" asked John.

"I will, considering that I am going to travel on him to Fort Adams," said Charlie.

"Oh, I am relieved to hear that. You two always did get along. What about your horse?"

"I hitched her to one of the supply wagons," explained Charlie.

"Now, don't go getting shot full of arrows or buckshot. You don't have to worry about being scalped. There ain't enough hair up there worth scalping," said John laughing.

Charlie started defending himself. "Don't get too big for your britches there, young man. You still owe me for saving your hide."

"I know. I'm going miss yah, you, old buzzard," said John grabbing Charlie in a bear hug.

"I'm coming back," said Charlie shoving him back.

"You better. I hate to see you break my aunt's heart," said John as he smiled.

Joshua was there, waiting when John walked through the gates of the fort, carrying his army sack and his saddle. John smiled from ear to ear at seeing Joshua, and yet, he felt a little let down at not seeing Isabel with him.

He shook his hand. "Thanks for coming to get me. Where's Isabel?" asked John.

Joshua's face was not smiling. He was bracing for the explosion. "She's gone."

"What do you mean she's gone? Where is she?" said John, with his anger crawling up back.

"She's gone. We think Pichon kidnapped her," explained Joshua quietly.

"What?" This news was almost more than John could comprehend. He felt his legs buckle, and he felt weak, nauseous, and pissed all at the same time.

"That rotten son of a bitch. I'm going to kill him. I'm going to beat the shit out of him, and then I am going to kill him," shouted John as he paced back and forth.

"No, you're not," said Joshua calmly.

"Yes, I am."

John tried to jump up on the wagon, with the intent to drive off. Joshua grabbed his arm and pulled him to the ground.

Then, his steel arms held him down. Joshua threw a knee on him and said, "Now, listen to me before you go off, half-cocked."

"Get off of me." John threw Joshua off balance and scrambled to his feet. Joshua sprung up like a cat and grabbed hold of his shirt, throwing him up against the wagon.

"Now, listen to me. That is why everyone wanted me to come to get you this morning because I am the only one big enough to handle your temper," said Joshua gritting his teeth.

"Everyone? Wait, how long has she been missing?" asked John, feeling his temper boiling.

"Since last night," explained Joshua.

"Damn it, Joshua. Why didn't you come and get me?" said John exasperated.

"Thomas took out last night after their trail. They stole his horse and the wagon along with two other horses from the hotel. We think they also stole supplies from Campbell's store," explained Joshua.

"Geez! Thomas? Well, what are we standing around for?" asked John as he climbed up on the buckboard.

Joshua climbed up next to him. "Charlie wants us to see the sheriff. Then, we are to come back to the hotel before leaving. Clara wants to see you. Nobody wants to see you locked up for killing Pichon."

"Let's bring back that kidnapping horse thief and let the law hang him," explained Joshua.

John was shaking; he was pissed. "Shit, since when have you been able to take me?"

"Just now and I was going easy on you," said Joshua as he took up the reins, and they made the two-mile long trip into town to see the sheriff.

Sheriff Dauber looked up from his desk when John and Joshua strode into his office.

Joshua stepped forward and said, "Sir, Mrs. Renshaw wanted you to know that we are leaving for a few days."

We are going after some horse thieves. They stole three horses and a wagon from the hotel."

"And they kidnapped my girl, Isabel Grant who works at the hotel," said John.

"The little blonde that is a waitress there?" asked the sheriff.

John shook his head.

"Charlie stopped last night and told me about Isabel. I already have two men out looking for the thieves that broke into Campbell's store," said Dauber.

"Pichon kidnapped her, and I bet he is with the men that broke into the store," said John.

"How do you know it's the same fellows?" asked Sheriff Dauber.

Joshua looked at John and then answered, "Sir, they beat up Thomas Renshaw last night and left him for dead down in the river."

With that news, John moved over to the window, sick to his stomach, thinking of Thomas and remembering what he looked like the last time he received a pounding.

"I am sorry, sheriff. I was discharged from the fort this morning, and I had not heard that bit of news," said John. "We want to bring them back and have the law hang their kidnapping, thieving asses."

Sheriff Dauber's eyebrows rose up at the direct comment. "Well, don't you suppose the law should go after them?"

John marched back to his desk and said, "Deputize me, and I'll bring them back. Because right now, I want to kill them with my bare hands, and maybe that badge will remind me to bring them back to hang."

Sheriff Dauber opened up his drawer and tossed a tin badge on the table, and then, he grabbed his keys and opened the cage. He handed John a rifle and pistol with a hostler. "Bring them in. I will wire information to the surrounding area."

After they left the Sheriff's office, John and Joshua went to the carriage house and packed for the trip. Clara had clothes laid out for John for the journey and packed food for traveling. Clara brought out more supplies from the pantry, and she hugged and cried the whole time.

"First, I had to say goodbye to Charlie, and my Isabel is gone. There is no Thomas around the hotel, and now you have to leave me. Promise me. You will come back safe and sound. Please," said Clara, with her eyes red with tears.

"Clara, I will. I will be back, and I will bring Isabel and Thomas back with me. I promise," reassured John.

Maude came out to the carriage house, gave Joshua money for expenses, and told him to get what they needed.

"Thank you, ma'am. We'll bring Thomas and Isabel back safe. Watch over Sarah and Samuel while I'm gone."

"I will," said Maude, with tears in her eyes.

"Ma'am, if you need anything, ask Pete or Gus to come help with the horse or carriages," explained Joshua.

Sarah came across the yard carrying Samuel along with a wool scarf for him. Joshua kissed his wife and son and promised them he would be back in a few days.

The men took off on saddled horses tied down each with a bedroll, rifle, canteen, and saddlebags. John and Joshua rode out to Mrs. Beaumont's house to pick up the trail. In the distance, they could see the colors leading the troops to Fort Adams. The fort caravan was heading north, and they headed west following the wagon trail leading out of town.

John and Joshua pushed hard throughout the first day, trying to make up for the lost time. They followed the tracks up to the still. They dismounted and crept up to the makeshift lean-to. There were tracks, but no sign of life.

They followed the wagon tracks until almost darkness overtook them. Then, they set up camp next to the river along a tree line grove. John started a fire to boil water for coffee. Joshua grabbed the canteen to get water from the river.

John had a good fire burning when Joshua returned with the water along with a flat stone for the coffee pot. In the firelight, Joshua noticed dried blood on John's shirt.

"Give me your shirt. We don't need the smell of dried blood, inviting any visitors tonight," said Joshua.

John removed his shirt and revealed the bloodstained bandages.

"My wife is so smart; she packed some salve and extra bandages for you," said Joshua as he continued to dig in his saddlebags.

Joshua set to a routine of cleaning and tending to the open wounds on his friend's back. He used a clean handkerchief to clean the dried blood from his back. Then, Joshua put salve on the lash marks to soften the skin. He wrapped the clean bandages and secured them tightly. He helped John put on a clean shirt.

After Joshua got John propped up on his bedroll, he tossed him a pint of brandy.

"It's from Maude," said Joshua.

"What a woman," said John poured some brandy into his coffee cup.

Joshua gathered up John's shirt and the used bandages. He went down to the river and tried to rinse the blood out the clothing. He knew animals could pick up the scent and follow them. They would have to take turns standing guard tonight.

John stayed up most of the night, tending the fire while Joshua slept. By sunrise, they broke camp, packed up the horse, and prepared for a long day in the saddle.

An hour into their ride, they found a strip of handkerchief tied to a bush. Joshua smiled at how well Thomas had done so far, leaving them a trail.

They headed into the tree line and followed a deer path through the trees, which gave a good view of the road.

John rode up to the top of the ridge to get a good look, and then they rode down out of the tree line looking for the wagon tracks. They found the campsite that Pichon had used. There were several sets of footprints. After resting and watering the horse in the river, they continued following the wagon tracks.

The buckboard had pulled off the road to make camp, and the wagon left a clear trail leading back to the route to Calabash. John and Joshua knew they were closing in, and they needed to cover ground.

* * *

By the second night of camping, Pichon started drinking. He was becoming careless, and he allowed Isabel to remain untied, as long as she cooked for them. Alvin brought in some rabbits and two pheasants. He cleaned them and handed the meat over to Isabel.

She fried the meat and then used the drippings. Isabel stirred in some flour, and in no time, there was gravy. She kept the meat warm in the gravy mixture. Then, Isabel mixed some biscuits with flour, water, and salt, and fried the bread dough in grease. As soon as the biscuits turned a golden brown, she spooned the gravy mixture over them and served Alvin first, which pissed Henry off to no end.

He didn't like Alvin getting all of Isabel's attention. She served up Pichon last throwing in a pinch of dirt into his meal.

Finally, she served up herself and sat by the fire to eat what she could. After supper, Isabel gathered up the dishes to head to the river to rinse the plates.

"Where the hell are you going?" yelled Pichon.

"To do the dishes unless you would like to?" asked Isabel.

"Take Alvin with yah," ordered Pichon.

"No, I'll go help her," offered Henry.

Henry escorted Isabel to the river, sat, and watched her clean up the plates.

"Remember meeting me that day at the harvest celebration. You sat with me under a tree that afternoon, but shoot, you only had eyes for that big sergeant. I saw you with him later that night. You even allowed him to kiss you on the dance floor. You're a hussy, letting a man kiss you like that," said Henry.

Isabel's eyes grew wide at his accusations and insinuations. She remembered that afternoon when Henry had spoken to her and how mad John was. She also remembered the kiss and the magic of the dance floor.

She continued to wash dishes and did not rise to his bait to argue with him.

Henry persisted, "How come you are spending more time with Alvin than with me? You seemed to be showing him more attention."

Finally, Isabel spoke calmly, "Alvin brought meat for supper, and he brought me some water to clean the meat. He has just been helpful."

"Well, tomorrow night, I'm going to catch us a bunch of fish, and I'll clean them for you, okay? said Henry, trying to win her favor.

"That would be nice," said Isabel, almost finished with the dishes.

"You sure are pretty," said Henry, smiling at her.

"Thank you, Henry. Would you help me carry these plates back?"

That night around the fire, Pichon and Henry drank from the supply. Alvin was working on a snare for a rabbit. Isabel finally felt bold enough to ask Pichon about his plans for her.

"Are you taking me back to my pa?" asked Isabel.

"Of course, I am. I want the money your pa owes me."

"What if he doesn't have any money?" asked Isabel.

"Then, I plan on taking you to St. Paul and selling you to the whorehouse. I ought to get a pretty penny for a virgin like you. That is if you still ARE one by the time we arrive in St. Paul," said Pichon, feeling like a rutting hog, the more he drank.

Pichon decided he wanted to get her liquored up tonight and fool around with her. He stood up and grabbed Isabel, pulling her to her feet. He grabbed the jug and poured liquor down her throat. Isabel thrust her tongue against the opening of the jar, causing it to spill. Some of the vile tasting liquor ran down her throat. She gagged and choked on the alcohol and then coughed and spat, trying to vomit.

Tears ran down her face, and Pichon said, "Damn it to hell, I hate it when a woman cry."

He plopped down disgusted and left Isabel lying on the ground crying.

"Wait a minute," said Henry. "You said that if her old man couldn't pay, that I could buy her for my wife."

Both offers made Isabel's skin crawl. Her throat burned, and her stomach felt nauseous.

"She is mine, and I'm getting the money for her. Besides, you ain't got any money," said Pichon laughing at Henry.

"I can sell my pa's whiskey if you don't drink it all up, you, lousy souse," said Henry.

"Watch, who you're calling names, boy," said Pichon, standing up to Henry who was now on his feet.

"I am not for sale," screamed Isabel. "You cannot just buy and sell a person. That is not right."

"Listen here, you little bitch." Pichon walked over to her, grabbed her arm, and came close to her face. "I call the shots here, and I need money. I gave you a sack of coins once, and you spent it on fripperies.

"I did not. I put it in the bank," said Isabel defensively.

"Don't you beat all? Why didn't you give me my money when I asked for it?"

"Because you told me I could keep it. You are the one who rejected me, remember. All you have done is make my life miserable. You have interrupted every chance at happiness. You found a way to ruin my life. You are a pig, and I am so glad that I didn't have to marry you," screamed Isabel, and then she spat in his face.

Before she knew it, Pichon backhanded her in the mouth and sent her sprawling to the ground. Alvin stood up in anger, and Henry was shocked at how quickly Pichon had hit her.

Isabel started crying. She could taste blood in her mouth. She stood up, ran over to the wagon, and cried. The three bachelors stood there, stupefied on what to do next.

Pichon grabbed the bottle and cussed a blue streak on how stupid women are.

Alvin was shaking with anger and knew he had carried that feeling with him since the start of the trip. This guy was bad news, and he did not like traveling with this piece of shit.

Henry didn't know what to think because he felt caught in the middle. He grabbed his bottle of whiskey and walked off towards the river.

Isabel crawled into the wagon bed and covered up with the horse blanket, praying he would get so drunk and pass out and not think of touching her.

She cried herself to sleep, thinking that she will never see John, Thomas, or any of her friends ever again.

Thomas sat in the dark and listened to the entire fight. He had all he could do to refrain from shooting Pichon. Thomas had promised his ma and Joshua that he would wait for backup, but the guys had not caught up to him yet.

Thomas devised a plan that night as he sat in the woods and waited for them to get drunk and pass out. He rested next to a tree and slept off and on for a few hours.

By the middle of the night, the camp was quiet. Slowly, he crept down to the horses. Thomas wanted his horse.

He left the two for the wagon, but he quietly untied his horse along with Henry and Alvin's.

Thomas walked the horses back to his campsite and staked them out. Then, he went back with branches and erased the snow to hide their hoof prints.

From listening to Pichon, Thomas knew the next town was Calabash. He took off in the middle of the night, rode his horse, and trailed the others along behind him. It was sunrise when he arrived at Calabash, and he headed for the livery. He took Henry and Alvin's horses to the livery and explained that his friends wanted them stabled here until they arrived.

He assured the liveryman that his friends would pay for their keep. If not, the owner could always keep the horses in exchange for payment. It was early in the morning, and the old horse wrangler from the livery agreed.

Thomas rode out on his horse and trailing his mare packed with supplies. Thomas found a spot to watch for Pichon, wishing he could be there in the morning when they discovered the horses gone. He liked being out on the trail.

That morning, Isabel woke up to hollering and recognized Henry's voice.

"The horses are gone?"

"All of them?" asked Alvin.

"No, they left the horses for the wagon, but Renshaw's horse, my horse and Alvin's are missing. They took our horses," screamed Henry.

Isabel secretly smiled and thought, “maybe now, you know what it feels like when other people take your belongings”.

Then, she realized; they were here. Her heart skipped several beats at the thought of rescue.

She felt a surge of courage slide up her back. Isabel wanted a life with John, and she was going to fight for it. She loved him, and Pichon was not going to stop her from achieving this new life.

Last night, she went to sleep, knowing that she was destined to spend the rest of her life with either Henry Walker or sold to a whorehouse in St. Paul. It felt hopeless, and she thought that she would never see her friends again, let alone become the wife of John Webster.

This morning she woke up to the elation at the chance of rescue. She chastised herself for ever doubting that John would come after her. She should have never questioned him. He loved her, and she loved him.

She heard everyone picking up camp, and she scooted out of the wagon. Alvin was loading the bed of the buckboard. Isabel told Alvin she needed to relieve herself. She and he both blushed as she quickly went down by the river.

When Isabel came back, Pichon grabbed her hands and began to tie them up tight. He shoved the gag back in her mouth and tied on another handkerchief.

"So, you think your boyfriend is going to save you. Don't be too sure," snarled Pichon. Then, he shoved Isabel into the wagon, covered her with a blanket, and tied down the tarp over the supplies. Isabel had overheard their plans to travel to Calabash to sell whiskey and camp outside of town that night.

Henry sat next to Pichon in the wagon, and Alvin rode in the back with Isabel. There was no conversation amongst the travelers. Pichon was in a foul mood this morning between being hungover and duped during the night. The taste of humiliation hung in his mouth.

They drove toward Calabash. Pichon figured about two hours by wagon, and they would be in town. He planned on setting up a campsite outside of town away from suspicion, and then, he would go in late in the afternoon to sell some moonshine.

While he drove, he tried to decide whether he would take Henry with or not. Since Webster was following him, it was hard telling who would be with him. Pichon needed to devise a plan to take Isabel and use the horses from the wagon.

He would have to steal a couple of saddles since the sons of bitches took those last night. On horseback, he and Isabel could cover a lot more ground. The wagon was slowing them down.

They camped on the northeast side of the town in a grove of trees. Alvin went into the woods to use his new snare, and Pichon and Henry set up camp. Isabel remained tied in the wagon. Alvin had pulled the blanket off her and helped her sit up when they were removing supplies.

Landmarks looked familiar. Isabel had ridden to Calabash only a few times with her dad and Ben for supplies. As she watched from a distance, she was surprised to see the new construction in the town.

Settlers had built several new, two-story houses behind the business on Main Street. One of the houses even had a white picket fence around the back yard.

Suddenly, she saw them. She saw John and Joshua riding on the road into Calabash. Her heart was beating out of her chest.

She looked around and realized Henry and Pichon were busy with the horses and camp to notice their arrival. Now, she had to figure out how to get free, to escape and get to John. There had to be a way.

Chapter Twenty-Two

Crossing Paths

For several hours, Thomas watched for Pichon and the boys to roll into Calabash. Finally, he saw the wagon move past the outskirts of Calabash and pull back, way into the tree line on the northeast side of town. Soon as they found a spot, Pichon made camp. Thomas spotted Isabel's white hair as she was sitting up in the back of the wagon. It was a relief to know she was safe for now.

As Alvin headed into the woods to set his snares, Thomas rode, with the mare trailing behind, in the opposite direction of Alvin. With the horses, he chose a secure spot to make camp. Thomas needed some sleep, and he knew Pichon would not be moving until dark.

Pichon threw down his bedroll next to an old maple tree and settled in for some sleep. Henry followed suit. A few minutes later, Alvin was back.

Walking over to the wagon, he covered Isabel with the blanket, and then he re-tied down the tarp. He also took an extra precaution and tied her feet together this time using a piece of rope he had found. Moments later, the camp was asleep except for Isabel. She felt so trapped under the heavy blanket to the point of suffocation.

Isabel had seen John and Joshua. John had traveled and tracked down Pichon. Her nightmare would soon be over, and she planned to return to Redwood, to her new hometown. Isabel missed her friends, the customers at the hotel, and her room.

The more she thought, the more she realized it meant nothing without John. In her eyes, John looked so handsome riding that horse.

Until now, Isabel had only seen him in his uniform. Today, he wore jeans and a long duster with a dark brown cowboy hat. The thought of him warmed her inside, and she felt mad with desire. She needed to get free and find him.

Maybe by dark, when she went to the river, she knew that it was only a day's journey to her childhood home. Mentally, she worked through the plan, trying to remember all of the landmarks to the cave and the homestead. Isabel had only been away three months, and yet it seemed a year since she was with her family. Oh, how she missed Ben.

While she thought and schemed, she continued to work against her knots, but it seemed to make them tighter. If she could escape tonight, when Pichon and Henry went into town to sell the moonshine, she could be home by morning to see Ben.

What about her Pa? Her feelings of joy stopped in her throat at the thought of the last time she saw her Pa at the train station. He had sold her to Pichon, a man he knew, and yet he sold her for a few stinking dollars and for what? Whiskey? Sure, as hell wasn't food or supplies.

Would she be glad to see him? Could she forgive him? She laid in the wagon bed as these thoughts circled her mind until finally, she dozed off dreaming of John's arms wrapped around her, protecting her from harm. The afternoon sun had warmed up the horse blanket creating a cocoon of warmth as she slept.

* * *

After the trail left the ridge with several hoof prints, John and Joshua followed the trail to the main road into Calabash. In the back of their mind, they hoped Thomas had not met up with trouble. The men rode into town to the livery to rest the horses and get something to eat. As they were paying the liveryman for the day, John asked the old cowboy some questions.

"By chance, have you seen a wagon with an older man and two young men on horseback and possibly a young girl come into town today?" asked John.

The old cowboy named Rusty looked at the two travelers, "Who wants to know?"

"I do," said John, as he showed him his badge.

"Nope, can't say I have seen that combination today. I did have a young feller wearing an old black Stetson, and he was trailing three horses. He stopped by early this morning," said Rusty.

It was Joshua's turn to question the old man, "What kind of horse was he riding?"

"Oh, a nice black quarter horse with a star on his forehead. He left two horses here at the livery. Said his friends would be in to pay for them later. Told me that if his friends didn't pay, I could keep the horses in return for payment," answered Rusty.

Joshua and John smiled and shook their heads in disbelief. They knew it had to be Thomas. He had somehow gotten his horse back and possibly stolen the other horses. It reminded them both not to underestimate Thomas. They could not be prouder of him than at that moment. They just beamed at his ingenuity.

"Don't suppose you're the two friends wanting these here horses?" asked Rusty.

Joshua walked over to the corral to see if he recognized any of the horses belonging to the hotel., but he didn't see any of their horses. Joshua shook his head at John.

"No, they aren't ours, but we might know who brought the horses in here. Which way did he head out of town?" asked John.

"Well, he left riding the black horse, and he was trailing a mare, tied down with supplies. He rode north out of town," explained Rusty.

"We're going over to the saloon to ask around, and then get something to eat before riding on. We'll be back," said John.

Joshua fished a couple of coins out of his pocket to cover the care for the horses. The old liveryman led their horses inside to a stall to give them some oats and rub them down.

The two men walked over to the town's only saloon. It was afternoon, and a few older gentlemen were playing cards in the corner. They walked up to the bar and ordered a couple of beers. The beer was cold and wet, and it slid down effortlessly.

"Say, barkeep," said John. "Captain Pichon? Does he ever travel through here?"

"Captain Pichon?" questioned the barkeep as he searched his memory. Polishing a glass gave him time to size up these two big men standing before him. He decided that he would want these two on his side if a fight ever broke wide open.

"You know him?" asked John. Joshua kept his eyes on the card game as well as the front door.

"Yeah, he's been in here before," said the bartender, remembering this past August when he roughed up Isaiah Grant. "Usually, he tries to sell some rot-gut moonshine or watered-down whiskey to me. He likes to gamble. Mostly, Pichon gets in a fight over cards after he has been drinking too much."

"You have seen him around here lately?" asked John. He finished his beer as he waited for the barkeep to answer.

"Nah. Been about three months, since I have seen him."

“He had a fight with a local over some money he owed Pichon, but I haven't seen him since."

"Thanks. Know where we can get a good meal around here?" asked John.

"I can make you some steak and eggs if that'll be all right," said the bartender.

"Sounds good," said Joshua.

"Can I get you a couple more beers while you wait?" asked the bartender.

"Sure, couple more but bring coffee with the meal," said John.

After the bartender left, the men found a place to sit down with a view of the street. They took off their dusters and tipped back their hats.

"Damn it to hell," said John to Joshua. "That had to have been Thomas. If he don't beat all."

"I can't wait to hear him tell the story," said Joshua with pride.

"I think after this we should get directions to Grant's homestead and ride out this afternoon. Pichon might be on edge after an incident with the horses. He knows we are on his trail, and we are closing in," said John.

"I think that's a good idea. We can cover some ground before nightfall. Hopefully, we meet up with Thomas soon," said Joshua, who had been worrying about Thomas for days.

The bartender brought out two platters with sizzling steaks and several eggs. Then, he came back with steaming hot cups of coffee. The men ate with their eyes shut most of the time as the meat melted in their mouths.

Joshua threw down some money on the bar, and both men complimented the barkeep on the wonderful meal. After leaving the saloon, they headed back to the livery to get their horses.

"Say there, cowboy. Can you give us directions to a homestead owned by a fellow named Grant?" asked John.

"Isaiah Grant?" asked Rusty.

"Yeah, you know him?" inquired John

"Yeah, he lives about a day's ride away from here. Follow the river north and east until you see a big outcropping of limestone. Turn north and follow it around until you see a pretty, little valley, and his cabin is back in there," explained Rusty.

"Thanks," John said as he led his horse into the open area to check his cinch and straps.

The old cowboy followed John out past the big double doors of the livery. "Isaiah, in some trouble?" asked Rusty.

"No, his daughter's been kidnapped. There are three of them, and they stole some horses, a wagon, and possibly some supplies."

"We believe these men are heading this way," explained John.

"Isabel?" asked Rusty as he turned pale.

"You know her?" asked John.

"When they were little, she and her brother Ben used to hang out here until all hours while their Pa drank up their money. She was a cute little thing. Felt so bad for those kids.,"

Rusty got pensive as he thought about the Grant family. He took a couple of deep breaths before he continued.

"Their ma's crazy. She sometimes lives up north away with some old Sioux Indians. Don't see much of Isaiah any more. I don't think he is doing very well.

Ben comes to town about once a week to sell eggs and cream. He usually picks up whatever scrap lumber he can find. I hire him to muck out the stalls and pay him with feed for his animals. He's a good kid," said Rusty, looking out over the edge of town.

"Well, I plan to marry that cute little thing, and I'm going to arrest that kidnapping, horse-thieving' son of a bitch. Then, I am going to haul his ass back and see the ex-Captain Pichon hung," said John.

"Yes, sir, I do believe you will. I'll keep my eyes open for them. If I see Isabel, I tell her you are looking for her," said Rusty, extending his hand.

"Webster, John Webster," said John, shaking his hand. "Thanks, cowboy. By the way, have you got a sheriff here in town?"

With that question, the cowboy spits on the ground. "I wouldn't trust him as far as I could throw him. Don't waste your time. He's a piece of shit."

Joshua finally spoke, "Please to meet you, sir. We're both liverymen by trade, and that opinion is gold in my book."

The old cowboy smiled up at Joshua and shook his hand. Then, John and Joshua mounted their horses and headed north out of town.

* * *

With the campsite secured back in a thicket of bushes and trees, the wagon and horses were undetectable from the road, yet he could look through the branches to see if anyone was traveling. Unfortunately, it was almost dark when Pichon and the boys woke up at their campsite.

Pichon needed to head into town to sell some moonshine. He gathered up a clean shirt and walked to the river to wash up and change.

Henry and Alvin felt groggy after sleeping for so long. Alvin headed to the woods to see if he had caught anything in his snare.

Henry stirred the fire and gathered some small kindling to reignite the campfire. There was some coffee left in the pot that needed reheating.

When Pichon came back to camp, he had on a clean shirt. He draped his other shirt over some bushes to dry. Alvin came back with two rabbits. He sat next to the fire skinning and cleaning off the meat for supper.

"Where do you think you're going?" asked Henry.

"I'm going into town to sell moonshine and make some money. Might even play some cards," answered Pichon in a positive mood.

"That ain't your moonshine to sell. That belongs to us, me and Alvin," said Henry, who was tired of reminding Pichon and tired of being broke.

"You're a kid; nobody's going buy from you," said Pichon as he raked his hands back through his hair.

"What? You're going to take the wagon and the moonshine and leave the rest of us here with nothing?" said Henry, getting more pissed as he spoke.

"Yeah. Alvin's working on some meat for supper, and then, you got Isabel all to yourself. Should I leave you a bottle?" asked Pichon as he sweetened the pot.

"Alvin can watch her. I'm going to town with you, and if you sell any moonshine, it is my money, mine and Alvin's. Got that," said Henry to Pichon's face.

"Fine," said Pichon, thinking that he needed to get rid of the boys. They were slowing him down. In the end, Isabel was his to sell along with the money from the moonshine.

Henry went off to the river to clean up, with his temper brewed almost to a boil. Alvin was tired of Pichon calling all the shots and being ordered around like a servant. He was the only one who ever supplied any food for the group. Alvin never felt like he got enough to eat.

Pichon walked over to the wagon and unloaded the supplies. He undid the tarp, grabbed the blanket off Isabel, and pulled her out of the back-end of the buckboard. He saw her feet bound with rope; he picked her up, carried her over next to the fire, and sat her down.

Isabel sucked in her breath as Pichon carried her. She cringed since she was so close to him but tried not to let it show on her face. Isabel did not need to make him mad.

Sitting next to the small fire, Isabel tried to piece together what was going on around the campsite. The sun was setting, and the evening was approaching. She noticed Pichon had on a clean shirt.

Moments later, Henry appeared with wet hair all slicked back. Pichon continued to empty the wagon, and he threw the old horse blanket at her. Alvin kept quiet as he worked with the rabbits.

Isabel realized they were leaving; they were going to town to sell the moonshine. Her heart raced; this was her chance to escape.

She needed to talk Alvin into untying her so that she could go into the bushes, and then she would follow the river. In the distance, she could see a huge orange moon rising. She sent a prayer upward in her own words thanking the Lord for a full moon to light her way.

Pichon and Henry got in the wagon and yelled at Alvin "Stand guard over Isabel and don't let anything happen to her. We'll be back later tonight." With that, they took off out of the thicket and headed southwest toward the road to Calabash.

As soon as they were out of sight, Isabel tried talking through her gag to Alvin. He looked at her skeptically. Then, finally, he pulled down the handkerchief, and she spat the gag out of her mouth.

"Thank you. Can I have a drink of water?" Isabel asked politely.

Alvin looked around for the canteen and walked over to her.

With her hands tied, she tried to hold it up to her lips. He helped guide it to her mouth. Some ran down her front as he poured too fast. Isabel choked and coughed.

Finally, Alvin spoke, " If I untie you, will you make me some biscuits and gravy using that rabbit meat?"

"Of course, I will Alvin," said Isabel.

"And you promise me you won't try anything funny," said Alvin accusatory.

"Of course not," said Isabel as innocently a possible. "Let's get started. I'm starving."

Alvin untied her feet and hands. Then, he walked back to the river to get fresh water to clean the meat.

Isabel smiled as her plan fell into place. She gathered up the supplies and started making biscuits. She stoked the fire, gathered more wood, and Alvin finished cleaning the meat.

She roasted the rabbit meat and then used the grease to make gravy. She cooked another piece of meat in the second pan using the fat to fry the bread dough. She made Alvin plate after plate of biscuits and gravy until finally, he said he had had enough to eat.

He relaxed with a smile on his face and said, "Miss Isabel, you sure is a good cook."

"Thank you, Alvin," said Isabel as she moved quickly around, gathering up dishes and secretly placed the extra biscuits in her pockets.

"I'm going to go down to the river and to do these dishes. Ah, Alvin, I need some privacy to clean myself up. Okay?" asked Isabel.

Alvin blushed at the thought of womanly needs, and he mumbled okay as he unbuttoned his pants and leaned back with his head against a tree, filled to the brim. She handed him a cup of coffee and then took the pot with her to wash.

Looking around to adjust her eyes to the darkness, Isabel carried the dishes down to the river. She set the plates down and scanned the area. Quietly, Isabel stepped into the water and walked upstream to the embankment.

Crossing into the brush line up into the wooded area, she scurried around the bend. Isabel ran across the open field up into the shadows into the next tree line. She ran for all she was worth not stopping to look back.

It felt invigorating to be free, and her destination was the cave. If she could make it there, she could rest and maybe even make a fire. Would her Ma be there, or would she be at the cabin with Ben and her Pa?

By morning, she would go to the homestead and find Ben to warn him that Pichon was coming to collect his debt from Pa. The urgency of her task pushed her forward. She continued to run like a child through the woods, making good time.

Alvin rested near the campfire until the embers died down. He felt a chill in the air, and he stood up to gather firewood to throw on the fire. He got a good blaze going and looked around in the dark. She was not back yet.

"That bitch," said Alvin in disgust at his naïve knowledge of women.

Grabbing his rifle, Alvin took off toward the river. When he got down to the shoreline, he walked along the water's edge. Finally, he found the dishes, and they were still dirty. He realized that she had run off in the dark. He looked around along the shoreline to see if he could find any tracks. nothing. She had vanished.

Alvin sure as hell did not want to go chasing after her in the dark, and he did not want to face Pichon. Pichon was going to kill him.

The fear crawled up his back; Alvin knew he was a dead man for sure. He remembered how quickly the ex-captain had hit a woman for talking back. Yep, Pichon was going to kill him. Alvin stumbled back to the campsite and tried to think about what he should do first.

Everybody always ordered him around all of his life; he never had the chance to think for himself. He was tired of being everybody's gopher. He was old enough to make his own decisions.

He thought if he had a horse, he'd gather up the supplies and take off on his own. The more he paced, the more he realized that he wanted to shrug off the whole business of kidnapping, head out west on his own to trap and hunt. This kidnapping was not going to end well. Alvin realized that he was either going to be shot by Pichon or hung by the law, and he didn't like his odds.

Alvin gathered up the supplies, stacked them up behind a couple of bushes and doused the fire. Then, he took off on foot with his rifle toward Calabash to steal a horse.

Chapter Twenty-Three

Landmarks

Carrying his rifle, Alvin walked to Calabash to find a horse. The last thing he wanted was for Pichon or Henry to see him. The big livery barn was on the edge of the town with several horse corrals. He crouched low in the darkness along one of the corral fences. As he approached the back of the barn, he spotted his horse. It was in the corral closest to the livery door.

Crawling through the rail fence, he inched along the wall of the barn closer to the door. Listening for voices, he waited in the dark. Slowly, he approached his horse and reassured him that they were leaving.

"Who's out there?" said Rusty.

Alvin froze and then moved around to the other side of his horse. He climbed through the split rail fence and drew his rifle as he approached the old cowboy. Alvin outweighed the old wrangler by fifty pounds, and this was his first job by himself.

"This horse belongs to me, and I'm taking it. My brother, Henry or Pichon can pay the bill," said Alvin with quivers in his voice.

The cowboy knew that fear and inexperience was a deadly combination. This kid was nervous with the gun in his hand and did not look that bright.

"Sure. You go ahead and take your horse," said Rusty.

The old cowboy did not want a fight. He walked over to the gate latch and swung it open, allowing Alvin to leave with his horse.

When Alvin was checking the straps and the cinch, Rusty asked, "Where you headed?"

Henry's response would have been "None of your business," but Alvin was thinking for himself. He mounted his horse and said, "West, where a man can be by himself and not get in any trouble."

Alvin rode out of town and headed back to the campsite to gather up supplies into the saddlebags. He planned to use the moonlight to ride out away from Calabash and head west putting as many miles as possible between himself and Pichon.

* * *

When Thomas woke up, it was dark. He realized that he had slept too long. The moon was high in the sky, and he was starving.

"Shit. Shit. Damn it." Thomas started cussing like a soldier.

His weakness for sleep pissed him off to the moon. A cold campfire, no warm food, and no trail left him beyond angry.

What if Pichon had already driven by and he missed them? Walking to the edge of the campsite, Thomas checked on the horses and looked around in the distance. He could see the glowing yellow lights of Calabash

Thomas broke camp and packed everything on to his mare, Ada. He mounted his quarter horse Roy and rode the tree line towards the last spot Pichon had set up camp. He was hoping to find the wagon tracks. As he rode, Thomas cursed himself out for being so careless to lose their trail. Now, he was worried about Isabel.

Thomas felt the effects of the past three days. Irritability, hunger, aches, and exhaustion from lack of sleep took a toll on Thomas's sunny outlook on life. He realized the cold weather was helping him to stay clear and focused as he rode.

Finally, he reached the shadows of the pine trees on the ridge, tied the horses loosely and approached by foot. There was no campfire light, but he could smell smoke through the trees.

It was eerily silent, and every time he moved, Thomas made more unnecessary noise. He erred on the side of caution and took his time as he crept closer to the campsite. What? No one was at the campsite. There was no wagon, no horses, and no Isabel. Now, he was worried.

In the moonlight, Thomas saw wagon tracks in a field of brome headed south toward the road to Calabash. Suddenly, he heard a rider approaching. Thomas scrambled up the ridge to secure a lookout spot.

It was Alvin, and he was riding his horse. Thomas watched as Alvin searched in the bushes. Discovering his stash, Alvin packed all of the supplies into his saddlebags.

Thomas's mind tried to process the questions flying through his brain. What happened? Where was Isabel? Why does Alvin have all the supplies?

Thomas sat quietly, not moving a muscle as he watched Alvin pack his horse. Then, Alvin grabbed his canteen and headed to the river. Thomas finally let out the breath that he had been holding.

Alvin came back from the river carrying the coffee pot, a couple of pans, plates and coffee cups. He stuffed them into the saddlebags.

He searched around the campfire, found some loose rope, and tied the coffee pot to his saddle. Finally, Alvin grabbed a couple of rabbit skins next to a tree and rolled them up into his bedroll. He made one final check of the stripped-down campsite. All that remained were two satchels and two bedrolls leaning against the tree. He threw the old horse blanket over his shoulders and mounted his horse.

Then, Thomas watched in amazement as Alvin pointed his horse west and rode out of camp. He rode in the shadows of the tree line.

Thomas watched until he was out of sight. The satchels and bedrolls had to belong to Pichon and Henry, but why the split?

With a glint in his eye, Thomas had an idea. He was sure there was room on the mare for two more satchels and two more bedrolls.

The young tracker slid down the ridge and grabbed their packs. He climbed back up to where he had tied the horses. Thomas knew it served them right to spend a night on the cold ground.

* * *

Isabel kept running through the night. Stopping at times to rest, she drank some water and ate a cold biscuit. Her feet were wet. The temperature continued to drop throughout the night as the moon rose higher in the sky. She needed to keep her feet moving; her skirt was stiff as she walked through the trees. She was so thankful for the black wool coat; she used a dark handkerchief to hide her hair.

As she climbed higher on the back ridge of the outcroppings, Isabel move cross-country knowing the wagons and horses would have to travel around on the road.
She stopped for a moment to look at the beautifully bare trees and the tall black evergreens lining the ridge.

In the moonlight, she saw the limestone outcroppings, and she knew she was getting closer to the valley where Isaiah and Ellie Grant had their homestead. A pang of homesickness knotted in her stomach; she was afraid of what she was going to find tomorrow.

Would Ma be there? Will Ben be all right? Will Pa be around? What would I do if everyone was gone? She knew John had to be somewhere in the area.

Isabel's feet continued to move forward, pushing her muscles in her legs to carry her. Finally, she reached some rocks and knew she needed to rest. The moon was dropping from the apex of the sky when Isabel found a grassy knoll.

She allowed herself to sleep until sunrise before she pushed forward. As she closed her eyes, she pictured the night of the dance in John's arms. She remembered looking into his beautiful green eyes and admiring his sun-bleached hair combed gently to the side. She felt the sensation of his arms around her as his strength pulled her in for their first intense kiss of passion.

Suddenly, Isabel's eyes sprang open, and she realized she had fallen asleep. She felt cold, and her feet were numb. Her eyes saw the moon moving to the west.

The dawn was only a couple hours away. She needed to keep moving, to fight through the cold, and to push on towards her home. She ran through several fields of grass until she came to the tributary of water. Isabel had to cross the stream to the embankment to continue.

This time she took off her boots and stockings. Then, holding her skirts up high and carrying her shoes, Isabel waded across the icy cold water. After climbing up the embankment, she sat on a flat rock and dried her feet.

Dawn was approaching, and familiar landmarks became more vivid as Isabel looked around at the landscape. Once she finished tying her boots, she felt ready to continue. Something caught her eye.

Looking down, she saw something familiar — a small rock formation of piled rocks, piles of ten. Upon closer inspection, she found the circle of stones, a circle of nine with one in the middle. Isabel knew where she was.

She picked up her skirts and ran across the wide-open expanse of wild grass to the next tree line. There next to the tree line was a rock wall with intricately carved steps leading to the cave. It was her mother's cave.

The cave was where her mother used to hide all the time. Ellie brought the children up there for days on end. She kept supplies there, so she and the children lived in the darkness of the cave for days. Her mother told them they were hiding from bears, soldier, Indians, or whatever else she conjured in her delirium.

Isabel climbed the rock steps and stopped at the entrance to smell for anything unusual. The cave smelled like home, full of an assortment of herbs.

She listened for animal sounds. Nothing. She inched back farther into the cavern feeling along the wall for anything familiar.

Bumping something near the ground, Isabel reached down and felt the wool of a blanket. She lowered to her knees and found a mat. Then, her hands felt around, and Isabel found a basket.

Carrying the basket, she moved back to the opening to investigate. Inside the basket was a leather pouch with matches and dried moss for starting a fire. She set the woven basket down and set to the next task. Isabel climbed down the steps to gather firewood and kindling.

After three trips, Isabel proceeded through the familiar routine of starting a fire. Using a stick, she orientated herself to the layout of the cave and found the ring of rocks. The growing daylight helped to shine through several cracks in the ceiling. Before long, the fire was blazing inside the cave.

To Isabel's amazement, her mother filled the cave with dried plants. The herbs were strung along on a homemade rack. There were woven baskets filled with leaves and dried beans. Her mother had been working and possibly living in the cave. Built up off the floor, Ellie's bed contained a beautifully woven Indian blanket with bright red and yellow stripes and goose-down pillow.

Isabel walked down the back corridor and looked into the back corner of the next room. Rocks were stacked up representing the graves of her younger brothers. Tears flowed down her face at the sadness of their early deaths. She moved back to the fire, sat down on the mat and hugged the old wool blanket close to her chest as she said a prayer for each of her brothers, hoping they were safe and happy in heaven.

* * *

Through the night, Thomas positioned himself above the campsite waiting for the wagon to return. Thomas wanted to see the fireworks when Pichon discovered Alvin and Isabel gone.

The moon was high in the sky when Thomas heard it approaching. Finally, the wagon arrived at the campground. Henry drove the buckboard up to the site and jumped down.

"What the hell? The fire is out. Alvin? Alvin, where are you?" yelled Henry.

Pichon laid in the back of the wagon, passed out drunk. He drunk his fill at the saloon and lost his money in a card game. Then, he got into a fistfight, which was followed by getting thrown out of the bar. Henry helped Pichon to the wagon and threw him in the wagon bed before leaving to go back to the campsite.

Henry walked around in the moonlight and realized their supplies were gone. Isabel and Alvin were gone. The bedrolls, their satchels, and food supplies were gone.

Luckily, they had taken their rifles with them when they went to town. The extra ammunition was in their satchels. Henry had sold some moonshine while Pichon was in the saloon, so Henry had some money, but he was not going to let Pichon know.

Henry walked back to the wagon and yelled at Pichon, "Get up. All of our stuff is missing. Alvin and Isabel are gone."

Pichon sat up in a drunken stupor and slid out of the wagon bed. He rubbed his face and then tried to focus on Henry's words. "What are you caterwauling about?"

"Alvin and Isabel are gone, and our supplies are missing. Gone. Everything is gone," screamed Henry. He paced around in disbelief that Alvin would leave him and take everything.

"What the hell are you talking about?" said Pichon.

"Look around," said Henry. "They're gone."

Pichon stumbled forward to realize what Henry was saying. His mind was unable to understand what had happened. He lashed out with his hand and slapped Henry, "This is all your fault, you, stupid kid."

Henry fell to the ground. "Leave me alone, you, son of a bitch," said Henry. He grabbed the blanket covering the moonshine and went over to start a fire.

Pichon climbed back into the wagon bed and passed out within moments.

Henry tended the fire with a dark look in his eyes. Henry was pissed. His anger brewed as he tried to process the turn of events. Finally, Henry settled in on the ground near the fire.

Thomas stayed up the rest of the night watching and waiting for them to leave. The sun rose, and Pichon was broke. He had no money; no supplies, just moonshine left. He and Henry were down to the wagon and horses. Henry found some dirty dishes down by the river but no coffee pot and no food supplies.

Anger and hostility boiled over Pichon in the morning. He swore on a death warrant on Alvin, that if he ever finds out, Alvin let her go. He vowed to kill him.

Pichon stumbled toward the river as Henry avoided him. Harnessing up the horses to the wagon, Henry cussed out Alvin for leaving him. He was even more pissed knowing Alvin had left him with Pichon.

Pichon walked to the side of the wagon and inventoried the pittance of supplies. Shaking his head in utter disgust, he grabbed a bottle of moonshine and climbed into the wagon seat. Henry jumped up into the driver's seat, and the wagon pulled out of the campsite. They took the long way around to avoid Calabash and then, they headed north to the valley of Isiah Grant's homestead.

Thomas stayed to the ridgeline keeping the wagon in view. It felt good to be back riding Roy. By trailing the mare, packed full of supplies, it made him look like a mountain man, a trapper.

He liked this lifestyle except for the lack of food. He reached into his pocket and pulled out a sliver of the remaining jerky out of his pocket.

* * *

Isabel sat by the fire for a long time before standing up to meet the day. She dried her stockings and boots by the warmth of the fire.The sunrise showed through the valley, and the morning dew twinkled in the sunlight.

Isabel realized how close she was to seeing her brother, Ben. She decided to leave a message that she was here. She knew that Ben and her mother would recognize the sign.

She gathered pebbles and small rocks. In the doorway of the cave, she stacked three piles of ten and then a circle of nine with one in the middle. Isabel checked the fire and spread the coals out. Then, with one last look, she climbed down the stairs and headed toward the homestead. Her feet felt lighter than air as she ran towards her home. She glided past trees and knew which path to take next.

Julie Granger

The intricate path was well worn. When she reached the final tree line, the house and barn came into sight. Isabel gasped and stopped to soak in the view. Someone repaired the house and the barn; they looked sturdier than Isabel remembered.

Cautiously, she approached the house and moved around the corner. Her heart slid to safety with no sign of any horses or a wagon. Secretly, she hoped John had found the place. Isabel moved closer to the door.

She opened it up and called, "Ben? Pa? Ma? Is anybody home?"

"Isabel? Is that you?"

Chapter Twenty-Four

The Homestead

Isaiah Grant never recovered from selling his only daughter to Captain Pichon to pay off his gambling debt. It was the final straw. He worked, hustled, and schemed to provide for his family, but hard living caught up to his body and his mind.

He knew he could not work as he used to on the lumber line. Isaiah had become involved with Pichon, who was only interested in making easy money, and easy money had a price.

He also blamed himself for his wife's mental condition. Isaiah wore the guilt of not being at home when soldiers attack his wife. After the rape and the difficult delivery of a baby, Ellie was never right in the head after that.

Ellie was so frightened of people that she would run off to a cave. She would scamper across the open meadow across the river as if the demons themselves chased her. The wide-eyed look of fear became etched on her face. After many days in the cave, she came back very sullen and reserved as if she felt bad for her behavior.

Sadness had descended on Isaiah like a heavy blanket of guilt when he returned home. He lost interest and never left the place. The bottom had dropped out of his world.

At age fifteen, almost sixteen, Ben picked up the pieces. He no longer had Isabel to rely on for help with the chores. Ben took care of his Ma and Pa. He needed to provide for what remained of his family.

Weekly, he would ride to town looking for odd jobs for money or supplies. He mucked out the livery for grain for the animals and swept out the bar for money and a meal. He traded eggs, milk, and cream for groceries like flour, salt, and coffee. Back home, he picked apples and berries, went hunting and fishing every day. He dried meat and made jerky for the winter.

Ellie stopped by for a couple of days at a time to check on Isaiah and bring him herbal medicines. When she brought the Indian blankets, Ben knew she had been spending time at the old Indian encampment with Grandma Red Bear.

Ellie never spoke much but set into working to help the boys. She baked bread and washed clothes, and then, Ellie disappeared again for three or four days.

During the weekly trips to town, Ben gathered scrap lumber from the new construction in Calabash. He had one mule and a wagon that hauled back the load. He worked to fix up the barn, and the house, to make it sturdier for the upcoming winter. Chopping wood was an everyday chore, and every night, Ben fell into his new bed in the barn exhausted.

Ben woke up early that morning. Today, he had planned to go deer hunting, hoping to bring back venison. He finished chores and then went to the house to make his Pa some breakfast. Ben opened the door to the dark cabin. Isaiah was sleeping. Ben walked into the kitchen, started some coffee, and sliced some bread. The bread was getting low, and he had not seen his ma for several days.

If he had good luck hunting this morning, then he could check the cave to be sure she was all right. While Ben waited for the coffee to boil, he woke up his pa.

"Pa? It would help if you got up, Pa," said Ben.

"What for?" answered Isaiah.

"I'm going deer hunting today. I made some coffee, and there is some bread on the table," explained Ben.

"I'm not hungry," said Isaiah as he turned over to go back to sleep.

"No. Not today," said Ben. "It is a beautiful morning, and I need you to help me today."

“Can you sharpen these knives? We'll need to butcher out the deer and try to smoke the meat."

With that note, Ben helped his dad get out of bed, and he sat him up at the table. He poured two cups of coffee and set the bread on the table along with a crock of butter. Ben set out the knives and a whetstone on the table.

"I should be back by dark. There is some stew from last night if you want," said Ben. He finished his cup of coffee and grabbed the heel of the bread. Then, on impulse, he leaned down and hugged his pa.

"Thanks for helping me today. I'll be back." Ben put on his hat and his dad's coat to head into the woods.

"Check the north ridge down by the river for deer. I always had good luck there," said Isaiah.

Ben smiled and went to the barn to grab his gun. He packed burlap bags for the meat and checked for his hunting knife. Then, he threw in ropes to secure the deer. Ben slung over his head his satchel, his ammo pouch, a canteen, and his gun. He led his horse out of the backside of the barn, trailing his mule, Sadie. Then, Ben headed north on the trail along the tree line.

* * *

Isabel was so afraid of what she might find at the homestead. She never realized that there would be improvements. It made her admire Ben all that much more. As she approached the house, she knew the final step was to open the door and face her family.

"Isabel? Is that you?" called out Isaiah.

Isabel stepped through the doorway of her childhood home onto the dirt floor. It took a few seconds for her eyes to adjust to the darkness of the cabin. Then, all of her anger dissipated when she saw him in at the table looking frail.

"Pa, I'm home," said Isabel. She ran forward to the table and threw her arms around his neck. "I missed you and Ben and Ma. How are you?"

"Better now," said Isaiah with a smile.

"Where's Ben? Is he out in the barn?" asked Isabel.

Isabel sat down at the table and stared at the knives lined up in a row with the whetstone and a rag next to her father's arm. The windows had new wood around them, bracing them up. The window in the back allowed light through the house. The house was neat and tidy, and she smelled the remnants of a stew.

"He went hunting early this morning. Your ma hasn't been here for a few days," said Isaiah sadly. Then, he looked at Isabel's appearance. "Girl, are you all right? What happened to you?"

Isabel explained to her father that she escaped from Pichon and followed the river back to the homestead.

"Isabel, I'm so sorry for what I did to you. Can you ever forgive me?" said Isaiah with pleading eyes full of tears.

"Yes, Pa. I forgive you, and I want to thank you," said Isabel, surprising herself yet realizing it was true.

She had met John, learned how to read and write, made new friends, earned her own money, and gained her independence.

"What? You're thanking me?" said Isaiah in disbelief.

"Yes, I would have never met John nor learn how to read and write. I have a bank account, and I earn my own money working in the dining room at the Redwood Hotel.

"What are you doing here? Where is Pichon?" said Isaiah with fear in his voice.

Isabel told her Pa the whole story. She told him about his rejection, his court-martial, his kidnapping, and now Pichon had no money.

"He was coming here to collect his debt, or he planned to sell me to the whorehouses in St. Paul. That is why I escaped from Alvin and came here. John and Joshua are in the area, and I am not going with Pichon ever again. I am going to marry John Webster if he ever asks me," said Isabel with determination.

"What am I going to do, Isabel? I don't have any money. Your brother has been supporting us. Your ma stops by every few days to check on me," explains Isaiah.

"Everything is going to work out. You'll see. John will be here soon, and he wouldn't let anything happen to us," said Isabel, feeling a rush of warmth just thinking about John.

"I sure hope you're right about that young man of yours," said Isaiah.

"Are you hungry? I learned how to make the best biscuits in Redwood from Clara, John's aunt. She is the lady that I work with at the hotel," said Isabel with pride.

"That would be great. I need to finish sharpening these knives for Ben. Sure, hope he gets a deer," said Isaiah as they fell into the routine of everyday conversation.

She stoked the fire in the kitchen with kindling and then went to the woodpile to carry in an armload of wood. Isabel reheated the coffee and found the leftover stew to warm up on the stove.

She started in on some biscuits with flour, water, and lard. The biscuits turned out as light as a feather, and the creamy butter melted on them. It felt good to be sharing a meal of stew and biscuits along with some coffee.

Isabel recognized that her father looked tired and encouraged him to lie down while she cleaned up the kitchen. Isaiah felt sleepy after the big meal. He walked into his bedroom to lie down, but he could not sleep. Pichon was coming for him.

Opening a drawer, he found his pistol. Isaiah checked it for ammunition and loaded it. He placed the gun under a pillow. Isiah laid down to rest his body, but his mind became more active as he thought about the pending situation.

Isabel went out to get water and heated it on the stove to do dishes. She cleaned with a passion knowing she was helping Ben. After she finished the dishes and knowing her father was resting, she wandered out to the barn.

To her surprise, Ben repaired the barn with used lumber that looked new, and the inside was neat and orderly. Ben had created a bunk bed for sleeping with Indian blankets on both beds. He framed the windows and repaired the stalls.

The haymow had a full floor with no holes to fall through when playing up there. There were oats in the bunk for the mule and corn for the cow. The chickens had a new scratch pen and laying boxes for eggs.

She was impressed with Ben's carpentry skills. She was so proud of him and could not wait to see him. Isabel remembered the location of some apple trees. She decided she was going to treat her father and Ben to some pie along with a nice supper. She took off in a run toward the makeshift orchard.

Isabel gathered as many apples as her apron skirt could hold. She walked back to the house, excited to bake.

The rest of the afternoon Isabel made apple pies, apple turnovers and apple butter along with applesauce. She realized they lacked cinnamon, but the cooked apples made the cabin smell like home.

Isabel found some potatoes in the root cellar and a roast in the smokehouse. She gathered more wood and more water to clean up her mess. It felt so wonderful to be at home.

Her hard work paid off when her father walked into the kitchen and said, "Boy, something smells wonderful around here."

"I did some baking today. I have supper started, but I need some milk. Ben is not back, so I'll take care of chores," said Isabel.

"It is so nice to have you back Isabel," said Isaiah feeling better than he had for a long time.

"You just sit there and enjoy a slice of pie and some coffee, and I will be right back."

Julie Granger

Isabel grabbed a pail and walked to the barn. It was late in the afternoon, and she looked out across the fields to see if she spotted any riders coming up the road. John should have been here by now. Ben was gone, and the night was approaching.

Isabel fell into the routine of doing chores. The sunlight through the windows provided plenty of light. It felt good to be in the warm barn.

She milked the cow and gathered eggs. She walked back to the house carrying two pails, one with milk and one with eggs. She walked through the door and heard.

"Hello, Isabel. Come in and close the door.

Chapter Twenty-Five

Showdown

It was Pichon with his pistol drawn sitting next to her father who was sitting at the table. Isabel stepped through the door and left it open. He was eating her pie right out of the tin.

"Come in, Isabel," said Pichon. "I was just explaining to your pa how you ran off and worried us," said Pichon. Then, he wiped his mouth on his sleeve and crumbs of pie crust clung to his week-old beard.

"By the way, what'd you do with Alvin?" asked Pichon.

"Nothing," said Isabel glaring daggers at this pathetic excuse of a man. "Why? Where is he?"

"We don't know. You were the last one to see him," said Pichon.

"I don't know what happened to Alvin. After I took off running, I didn't look back. I never saw him the rest of the night. I figured he was with you and Henry," explained Isabel.

She looked over at Henry leaning in the corner by the door. He looked sullen and pissed at the world. Pichon saw her holding two pails, so he decided to give her an order to show who was the boss around her.

"Now, you go in that kitchen and make us something to eat, and then, we will talk terms on this debt your father owes me," said Pichon, waving his pistol at Isaiah.

She could tell that he had been drinking. Isabel went into the kitchen, eyeing the open back door. The family hardly ever used that door.

She bustled around the kitchen, and her mind whirled with activity. "Where was John? Where was Ben? Would Joshua be with him?"

"I need some water for coffee," said Isabel, ready to go outside with the pail.

"You stay here. Henry, fetch her some water," said Pichon.

Henry bristled at the fact that Pichon was bossing him around, how he hated him. He wanted to be in charge. Henry walked out of the house, carrying a pail for water.

He thought to himself, "Serve him right if I would git in that wagon and drive out of here and leave Pichon to fend for himself. Maybe that's what Alvin had done. When I find Alvin, I'm going to beat the tar out of him for leaving me."

* * *

John and Joshua had followed Pichon and Henry as they traveled to the homestead. John worried with no sign of Isabel and wondered where she could be. They had stayed well north of the road on the top of the ridge. They stayed far enough back as not to arouse suspicion. From a distance, they saw the homestead, and they spotted Henry getting water.

They continued the trek on foot, moving ever closer to the place. They spotted the barn; trailing their horses behind them, they found a spot amongst some bushes to tie them. Suddenly, John and Joshua heard a rider approaching, and they stayed low amongst the shadows of the forests.

The rider was a tall young man on a brown mare. He was trailing an old mule with a deer strapped across the back, and he rode to the barn.

Ben tied the horse and mule next to the water trough in the makeshift corral. He started the process of working with the deer carcass to remove the hide when he heard a noise. He grabbed his gun and crept up to the barn.

Looking out the window towards the house, Thomas crouched in the barn with his rifle drawn. Thomas had followed Pichon and Henry to this homestead. He kept his horse up on the west ridge, and he walked down behind the barn.

Thomas came through the barn and set up a lookout to the house. He saw Henry getting water. Thomas sat there patiently with his stomach growling. He reached in his pocket and found a small bit of jerky. Then, he felt a jab into his back

"What are doing in my barn?" asked the voice holding the rifle.

Thomas wanted to turnaround, but he knew enough to turn slowly.

"Put down the weapon and turn around real slow," said Ben.

"I can explain," said Thomas laying his rifle down on a mound of hay.

He looked into Ben Grant's face. Thomas's face lit up with a big grin.

"What's so funny?"

"You. You look just like Isabel, your sister, only you're a boy," said Thomas.

Ben Grant was taller than Thomas with sun-bleached blonde hair. His eyes were dark brown, and his skin was tan from the sun. His well-built frame showed muscles in his face and neck.

"Isabel. You know Isabel. Where is she?" asked Ben.

"She is in the house. I'm Thomas," said Thomas as he offered to shake hands.

"Isabel works for my ma at the Redwood Hotel in the dining room."

Ben lowered his rifle and then shook hands with Thomas.

"What is Isabel doing here? I thought she left to marry some officer. She left without telling me anything," said Ben with a twinge of hurt in his voice.

"Your papa sold Isabel as a mail-order bride, and Pichon rejected her. Then, he got court-martialed out of the army. This past week, Captain Pichon and the Walker brothers kidnapped Isabel, and I have been following them for three days," explained Thomas

He moved to the window to watch for any movement.

"Henry and Pichon are in the house with Isabel. Is there anybody else in the house?" asked Thomas.

"My papa," said Ben.

"Pichon is returning her, and he wants the money your pa owes him," said Thomas with brutal honesty.

"We don't have any money. Is Isabel okay? Is she in any danger?" asked Ben with concern.

"She might be, but I've got a plan," said Thomas with a smile on his face.

Thomas talked rapid-fire, filling in details. He told him about Henry and Alvin Walker, and how they stole his horse, beat him up, and left him for dead in the river.

"We need to lure Henry out here to the barn and then jump him and tie him up. That would leave Pichon by his lonesome," said Thomas.

"I like the way you think, Thomas," said Ben.

Ben started looking around for a place to jump Henry, and then he spied a pile of old burlap feed sacks. They both gathered up some rope, and Thomas asked for a couple of handkerchiefs for a gag.

John and Joshua grabbed their rifles and checked their guns for ammunition. They moved forward towards the back of the barn. Joshua peaked in a window and could see Thomas talking a mile a minute with his hands flying to the tall blonde that rode in on the mare. Joshua worked his way over to John, who was also looking into a window.

"These boys are up to something. Let's make ourselves known. I don't trust Pichon, and it could turn ugly in a hurry," said John.

"Good idea," said Joshua as he followed John's lead into the barn. John and Joshua walked in through the back door of the barn.

"All right, what are you boys up to?" asked John with a gruff voice.

Ben turned around and watched these two huge men walk into his barn. Thomas ran over to both men and slapped them on the back.

"Where have you two been?"

"Man, you look like crap," said John. He noticed the dark circles under his eyes.

"You're looking pretty ugly yourself with that scraggly beard," said Thomas.

"Hey, Little Man, it's good to see you. You did all right following them," said Joshua ruffling the scruff of his neck.

"So, what's going on? Where's Isabel? Fill us in on what you two are planning," said John, and then he looked over at Ben.

John stopped talking and realized he was looking at Ben, Isabel's brother. John walked over and extended his hand. "Hi, I'm John Webster, and this is my friend, Joshua."

Joshua tipped his hat, and Ben nodded back.

"You must be Ben. I've heard so much about you from Isabel," said John.

"Oh yeah, this guy is in love with your sister, and he is going to marry her if he ever gets up enough nerve to ask her," said Thomas blurting to the world.

John cuffed the hat right off his head, and Thomas ducked out of his way, smiling. To Thomas, it felt good knowing these guys were here to help. He had missed them.

"So, let's hear this plan," said Joshua.

Thomas explained the details. John and Joshua smiled at the ingenuity of the ruse. Then, Thomas got serious. "But remember all of you, this is my fight."

"We'll be here to back you up, but you need to realize that if Pichon comes out, we're taking over. I don't trust that son of a bitch," said John, reminding Thomas how fast this could turn serious.

Set in their place, the boys started making noise to scare the chickens. Ben stood by the house and barked like a dog.

Inside the house, Henry and Pichon were eating the roast, potatoes, and biscuits Isabel had made for her family. There was silence at the table. Isabel stayed busy at the cupboard working with food. She had lost her appetite and had no desire to sit with Pichon.

"What's all that noise out there?" asked Pichon.

"Sounds like a dog," said Henry.

"Well, I'm eating. You go out and see what it is?" ordered Pichon, pouring himself more coffee.

"Why do I have to?"

"Because I said so, now get," yelled Pichon.

"I'm sick of you ordering me around," yelled Henry.

Isabel and her father exchanged glances, and Isabel's heart was a flutter. Either Ben was back, or it was John. She could not explain the dog sounds. Isabel stayed busy by the cupboard, putting away food.

Henry got up disgusted. He grabbed his hat and his rifle and went out to investigate the noise.

Ben saw him coming and motioned to Thomas who got into place.

Henry looked around the house and saw nothing. Then, he heard the dog barking in the barn. Henry walked through the door and looked around the barn.

The barn door closed, and Ben stepped forward. "Put down the rifle," said Ben with his gun pointed at Henry's back.

As soon as Henry laid down his rifle, Thomas jumped Henry from behind, throwing a burlap sack over his head. The two boys took him down, sat on him, and pulled his arms behind his back.

Henry put up a good fight, and it was all the two of them could do to hang on to their prisoner. Finally, they got his hands tied and then his feet. They set him up, but not before Thomas gave him a severe kick in the stomach.

"That's for stealing my horse, you rotten piece of shit."

Henry was leaning against a post when they pulled the bag off his head, and Henry's jaw dropped with shock at Thomas.

"You thought I was dead, didn't you? You piece of crap. You left me to die." Thomas kicked him again and followed with a blow to the face.

John held back Joshua's arm and then said quietly, "Let him get it out of his system."

Finally, after a couple more blows and kicks, John and Joshua stepped forward. Joshua put a hand on Thomas' shoulder, and John picked up Henry's rifle. Ben stepped over to the window, kept a lookout for Pichon. Thomas shrugged off Joshua's hand and walked away.

Thomas had one more part of his plan to implement. He took one of Ben's handkerchiefs and rubbed it in some horse manure. He walked over to Henry, stuffed it in his mouth, and tied the other bandana around his mouth to keep it in.

"There, you piece of shit, chew on that for a while," said Thomas.

John, Joshua, and Ben all turned around, afraid to even smile at Thomas's antics. Henry laid in the hay groaning and cussing at Thomas. Thomas walked over to John and said, "Okay, what's next?"

Inside the cabin, Pichon paced the small cabin room, waiting for Henry to return. He knew something was not right. Webster was here; Pichon just knew it. He thought, Webster, that son of a bitch, stole their horses and their supplies. Hell, Alvin could be sitting in jail somewhere, and now they have Henry.

He didn't like his odds.

John realized that just as Henry was Thomas's fight; Pichon was his fight. He wanted Isabel safe and in his arms. John wanted Pichon out of their lives.

"I'm going to call him out," announced John to the other three.

"What?" asked Thomas.

"Joshua, back me up. I'm going out there, and I am going to talk to him, challenge him or whatever else I got to do to draw him out," said John.

"There's a back door by the kitchen, but we never use it. I could try to get into the house from behind," said Ben.

"Don't trust him, son. No telling what he could do," said John, looking into the eyes so similar to Isabel.

Joshua and Thomas both selected spots for back up, and each one checked their ammunition. John walked out of the barn to the middle of the yard.

"Pichon . . . Pichon. Get out here. I want to talk to you."

Nothing. John waited and called again. "Pichon, you piece of shit. I am here to arrest you on charges of kidnapping and thievery."

No sound came from the cabin.

"Pichon, I am coming in," said John with his rifle drawn.

Pichon stepped out of the cabin with a butcher knife held to Isabel's throat. John just about fainted at sight.

His eyes saw the fear in Isabel's face, and his green eyes zeroed in on Pichon as anger gurgled in his throat.

"Let her go, Pichon," said John stepping closer with his rifle drawn.

"No. Get on your horse and ride out of here. I'm staying right here with Isabel," said Pichon.

"Shoot him, John," pleaded Isabel.

Pichon covered her mouth with his hand and pulled her head back farther, exposing her throat.

"Give me the knife," said John as he inched closer. "Put the knife down, and nobody has to get hurt."

Then from next of the house, Joshua shows himself with his rifle pointed at Pichon.

"Grant owes me money," said Pichon.

"How much? I'll pay the debt," said John bargaining with him. "Joshua's got the money, and you can have it and ride out of here. Just let Isabel go."

"What do you think I'm stupid? You'll hunt me down," snarled Pichon, looking around at Joshua.

Joshua took out the money pouch and held it up to him. Then, he threw it in front of him and returned his hand to his rifle.

"Drop the knife; let her go. You can have the money. I won't follow you," negotiated John.

"Let her go, Pichon," said Isaiah Grant as he leaned up against the open doorway of the cabin with his pistol in his hand.

Pichon glanced over his shoulder and saw that Isaiah had a pistol drawn on him.

"Give me the knife, and no one gets hurt," said John walking closer to Pichon. He was within steps of being able to grab Isabel from Pichon's grasp.

Isabel held her breath, and she felt the cold blade leave her neck. Pichon disingenuously looked as if he was handing the knife to John. Instead, Pichon turned and side-armed the butcher knife right at Isaiah as he fired his pistol.

Isaiah fell, clutching his stomach.

"Nooooo," screamed Isabel.

Then, everyone heard the blast of gunfire, and Isabel felt the warm splatter of blood on her face as she fell.

Chapter Twenty-Six

Her Family

Isabel opened her eyes. Pichon was lying on the ground dead, and she looked at her pa who was still alive but bleeding. Ben was kneeling next to him. Isabel looked around, unable to catch her breath, and then she saw John.

Isabel scrambled and pulled herself away from the dead limbs of Pichon. She scurried over to John and embraced him with tears running down her face.

Isabel kissed him all over his face and cried. "Are you all right?" said Isabel.

"Don't mind me. Are you okay?" said John, searching Isabel's face, seeing the bruise on her cheek.

Then, Isabel followed John's eyes as he saw her mom looking disheveled, holding a buffalo gun aimed at Pichon.

"That son of a bitch raped me," said Ellie Grant.

No one said a word. Ellie leaned the buffalo gun against the cabin and moved over to Isaiah.

During the face-off, Thomas held his spot on the edge of the house and had a good aim on Pichon when he felt the tap on his shoulder.

He turned to look into the face of an older woman dressed in several layers of clothes with long white braids.

"This shot is mine," said Ellie Grant with her eyes blazing. She stepped into view with a buffalo gun, and when Pichon opened his arm to throw, Ellie let him have it.

Thomas saw the blood splatter. The explosion of blood and skin tissue was more than his empty stomach could handle. He dry-heaved along the side of the house. Using the back of his sleeve, he wiped the taste of bile from his lips.

When Ellie realized Pichon was dead and Isabel was alive, she moved over to Isaiah.

The knife punctured his side just under his lung. Isaiah was losing blood, and Ellie needed to get it under control. Ben and Ellie helped Isaiah into the bedroom.

"Isabel, I'm fine. Go check on your pa," said John.

Isabel looked into his eyes, and John reassured her with a big smile, and then she ran into the cabin. Her mother was boiling water and gathering rags. Isabel cleared the table.

"Does Pa need stitches?" asked Isabel

"Yes, too many to count. Stoke the stove and keep the water boiling," ordered Ellie.

Ellie sorted through her sewing kit, looking for a needle and thread. She went back into the bedroom with clean rags to pack the wound. Within moments, Ben carried out a pan with the blood-soaked clothes to wash.

Ben and Isabel stopped their chores and looked at each other. Time stood still as they realized that this was the first, they had seen each other in over three months. Isabel rushed toward Ben and hugged him, realizing he had grown to be taller than she is.

"I missed you," said Ben.

"I've missed you, too. You've grown. You're taller than I am," said Isabel.

Isabel poured cold water over the rags in the pan. and then she asked Ben for more water.

"I also need more wood for the stove. Are you hungry?" asked Isabel.

Ben smiled at her, and she realized what a silly question to ask him. She set to the task, knowing that her mother needed to care for her Pa.

Isabel stoked the stove and set a kettle on top. She started chopping the leftover potatoes into the pot, cover them with a little water, and added the venison roast beef that Ben had brought in to the cabin. Isabel chopped wild onions and added salt to the stew. She looked around in the root cellar for carrots or extra potatoes to add. She mixed some biscuits and started more coffee.

When the water was boiling, she carried the kettle into the bedroom. Her pa looked so gray in color and so fragile lying in bed.

Ellie had an oilcloth under him. She continued to stitch his side; Isabel carefully wiping the excess blood as she went. Her mother packed the wound with bandages and tied the wound with a strip of bedding. Isaiah laid bandaged in the bed, leaving him looking old and vulnerable.

Ben made several trips for Isabel carrying water and wood into the cabin. Then, he told Isabel he would be outside taking care of venison.

Seeing death up close and personal was overwhelming to Thomas. At sixteen, he had no experience with death face to face. Pichon, the man he had followed for three days, was alive one moment; then, one powerful shot blew his chest apart, and he was dead.

In his embarrassment of vomiting, Thomas left the scene to retrieve the horses and the wagon Pichon had stashed in the woods.

Thomas brought their horses and buckboard into the yard for the night. The men wrapped Pichon's body in a tarp and placed it in the wagon. Joshua and John agreed to sleep outdoors to protect the body from wild animals.

Thomas and Ben took the horses to the barn for feed and a rubdown. Thomas checked on Henry to be sure the ropes were holding. Brushing down the horses was always calming to Thomas when he was upset, and he needed time to think.

Joshua needed to retrieve their horses for the night. John watched Joshua as he walked towards the barn. It was getting dark as John turned and walked into the small, dark cabin.

Isabel had everything under control in the kitchen when John entered through the doorway. She smiled and rushed over to him.

"Here sit down," said Isabel, fussing over him. "Do you want any coffee?"

"Sounds good," said John.

Finally, Ellie walked to the kitchen. Isabel grabbed the wash pan from her mother. She gave her a fresh container of hot water. Ellie washed herself up and then dished up a bowl of broth and took it into Isaiah.

John's eyes stayed focused on Isabel as she prepared a meal for everyone. He drank in her beauty as he longed to touch her soft skin. He admired her long porcelain white hair that she pulled back into a loose braid. John almost chuckled when he realized it was a hell of a way to meet your future in-laws for the first time.

Isabel smiled at the scene of John in her home at her family's kitchen table She was proud of her Ma. It made Isabel feel small and childlike in her presence yet grateful. She was so thankful for her Ma, Pa, and Ben; they were family, her family.

Isabel coaxed everyone, including her Ma to come to the table to eat something. The smell of homemade biscuits and stew was hard to turn down after days of traveling. Six of them sat around the table and filled each other in on their role in the ordeal.

Ellie sat and listened with delight. She knew John loved Isabel by the way he looked at her daughter. Finally, Ellie said, "Isabel, I found your pile of stones at the entrance of the cave."

“I remembered when we used to make piles of rocks when you kids were younger. How did you think to leave those piles?"

"When I ran away from Alvin, I hiked across the ridge and followed the river into the valley. I found some of the piles of rocks where we used to play."

"From there you found the cave. You remembered?" asked Ellie.

"I found it this morning. It smelled wonderful with all the drying herbs in there," said Isabel.

"When I saw the pile, I knew you must be here," said Ellie. "I'm glad I decided to come back to the cabin. I'm glad that I did what I did."

No one said anything, but in the back of each of their minds, the questions of justice tumbled around. How will they explain the death of Pichon? Will Ellie be charged with murder? Will a judge believe she was trying to save her daughter's life? Who will take care of Isaiah?

Silence became extended until Thomas spoke, "Do you suppose I should bring Henry something to eat?" said Thomas.

"Henry? Oh my gosh, I forgot about him. What happened to him?" asked Isabel.

Then, the boys told Isabel and Ellie how they captured him in the barn and tied him up tight.

"I used one of Ben's handkerchief and put horse manure on it. Then, I stuffed it in Henry's mouth and tied it around his mouth," admitted Thomas.

Everyone at the table laughed at Thomas's description of the incident. Isabel stood up and made a plate of food. "Thomas Renshaw, you take this out there to Henry. Ben go with him and keep an eye on him," ordered Isabel, feeling like a big sister to two younger brothers.

When Ellie finished her supper, she went back into the bedroom. Isaiah Grant rested comfortably with Ellie set to watch over him for the night.

The stitching had taken a while with Isaiah. Ellie worried about infection setting in and whether a fever would take over during the night. She planned to stay right by his side.

The boys retired to the barn, and John and Joshua made up a fire in the yard. They laid down their bedrolls and propped up against their saddles.

Isabel finished cleaning the kitchen and brought her mother a fresh cup of coffee. Then, Isabel walked out of the cabin carrying an extra blanket. She sat down next to John. Isabel curled into his chest and laid her head on his shoulder. She was not leaving no matter how much he protested. John never protested. It felt right to have Isabel in his arms.

Morning came, and the group gathered outside of the house. Ellie spoke first, saying, "I want to take Isaiah with me to the old Indian camp to winter over with them. Grandma Red Bear can help me nurse him back to health."

John answered, "Ma'am, I think that is a fine idea, but first, you need to go to Calabash and give your statement to the sheriff concerning the death of Pichon."

Ellie looked up at John and everyone waited as Ellie weighed the odds.

"We will all go with you and give our statements as well. We need to turn the body over to the undertaker," continued John.

Ellie looked straight at him, "I don't like townsfolk, and I don't like soldiers."

"Please, Ma. Have the doctor look at Pa and give the sheriff your statement. Then, you and Pa can travel to the encampment to stay with Grandma Red Bear for the winter," said Isabel, trying to bargain with her mother.

"Ellie, she's right," said Isaiah from the doorway of the cabin.

Everyone was so surprised to see Isaiah up and dressed. Ellie and Isabel fussed over him.

"I'm sore, but I ain't dead," said Isaiah, sitting on the outside bench next to the cabin.

"So, help me, Isaiah Grant, if you tear out those stitches," scolded Ellie.

"Then, you'll go, Ma?" asked Isabel.

Ellie looked at Isabel and John and then at Ben. "Ben, you need to go back with Isabel. I'll watch over the animals through the winter."

Everyone agreed and set to task packing supplies. Ben hitched their mule to the wagon, and Ellie made a comfortable bed for Isaiah in the back. Ben planned to drive their buckboard to Calabash with Ellie seated up front. He would trail his horse behind the wagon.

John stepped forward to the wagon bed where Isaiah laid. He took his hand and shook it. "Sir, we have not formally met, but I am in love with your daughter. I want to ask your permission to marry her if she will have me," said John.

Tears ran down Isabel's face as she listened to John talking to her father. Isaiah smiled and squeezed John's hand. "If Isabel loves you, that is all the reason I need. Have you asked her yet?"

"No, sir, not yet," confessed John.

"Well, you have my permission, young man," offered Isaiah.

John turned and looked into those soft brown eyes clouded with tears. He walked over and took her hand. Then, in front of everyone, he knelt on one knee and said. "Isabel Grant, will you marry me?"

"Yes, John Webster, I will," said Isabel as she smiled. Tears of joy ran down her face.

Cheers went up from the party as Isabel's folks smiled. John stood up and hugged Isabel.

"I love you," whispered John in Isabel's ear.

"I love you, too," said Isabel softly.

Hugs, kisses, smiles, tears, and slaps on the back entwined the close-knit family and friends as everyone offered congratulations.

It was time to leave the homestead. Thomas drove the hotel wagon with Pichon's body and Henry sitting next to him, trailing his horse behind the buckboard. John and Joshua rode their horses, and Isabel rode the other mare of Thomas's. Ben drove the buckboard with his parents sitting next to him. He had tied his horse to the wagon.

Their nightmare was over, and the sun shined down on the happy couple.

It was late afternoon by the time the travelers rode into the livery in Calabash. Isabel insisted that Isaiah visit the doctor's office first. John and Joshua helped Isaiah to the doctor's office. Isabel and Ben held on to their mother as she hid under her shawl. Thomas took the wagons and the horses to the livery for the night.

The doctor welcomed the travelers into his examination room in his house. Eulah May, his housekeeper, set to boiling water and making coffee for the late-night guests.

After his examination of Isaiah, Doctor Palmer looked over his glasses and said, "Who did the stitching?"

"I did," said Ellie Grant.

"Mighty fine work, ma'am," said the doctor. "You ever need a job you just let me know."

Then, he smiled and winked at her. Ellie blushed at the compliment. They agreed it would be best for Isaiah to remain with the doctor overnight. He gave him some pain medication to help him sleep.

Then, Joshua and John asked Doctor Palmer if they could speak to him privately.

"Of course, let step back here in the kitchen," said Doctor Palmer.

Ellie, Isabel, and Ben remained with Isaiah.

Joshua insisted that John have his bandages changed and checked for infection. John reluctantly agreed, knowing the devastating effect infections can cause.

Doctor Palmer and Eulah sent to work changing his bandages and cleaning his wounds. Doctor Palmer insisted on stitching up two of the lash wounds that had split open and were still oozing.

When they finished, John thanked him and paid the doctor's bill, and then they all went down to the sheriff's office.

When they arrived at the door, John turned to Ellie and Isabel and said, "Let me do the talking." He opened the door, and the ladies walked through into the small office of the sheriff of Calabash, followed by Joshua and Ben.

"Hello there. What can I do for you?" said the sheriff of Calabash. He was a tall, oily-looking cowboy. He had been drinking in his dirty, cluttered office.

"I am John Webster, and this is my fiancé Isabel Grant and her mother, Ellie Grant."

"Are you Isaiah Grant's family?" asked the sheriff.

"Yes, they are. We just came from the doc's office, and Isaiah is resting comfortably there. Sheriff, I was deputized by Sheriff Dauber in Redwood to go after Ivan Pichon."

John showed him his badge, which surprised Isabel. "Pichon kidnapped my fiancé and stole horses, a wagon and supplies from the Redwood Hotel and Campbell's General Store."

"I know. I got a telegram from the sheriff a couple of days ago to be on the lookout," said the sheriff as he sorted through papers on his desk.

"Well, Pichon is dead and in the back of our wagon down at the livery. We need to take his body to the undertaker," explained John.

"What happened?" asked the sheriff.

John went on to explain the events that lead to Pichon's death.

The sheriff listened and stroked his face as he tried to piece together the facts.

"Let's go see the body," said the sheriff.

They walked back to the livery where Thomas was waiting along with Rusty. The sheriff walked over to the wagon and saw Henry tied up, and then he lifted the tarp to reassure himself the man was dead.

"Ma'am, if I may ask, what type of gun did you use?"

"It was a buffalo gun that I found. I kept it stashed by the woodpile to shoot at bears," explained Ellie.

"Yes, ma'am. I don't believe that gun was meant for close range," explained the sheriff. "You folks staying in town tonight?"

"We planned to get something to eat first and then camp outside of town."

"Well, I'll take the horse thief off your hands and throw his ass in jail," said the sheriff.

Thomas and Ben pulled Henry down out of the wagon.

"Man, you smell, son," said the Sheriff.

Everyone started laughing as Henry was led away by the Sheriff of Calabash. Rusty gave them directions to the undertaker.

They decided to meet at the café at the end of Main Street after the men took the body to the undertaker's house. After supper, Ellie insisted on staying with Isaiah at the doctor's house. The rest walk back to the livery and set up camp.

Isabel slept once again in the crook of John's arm. She laid her head on his shoulder and rested peacefully. For the second night in a row, John slept through the night holding Isabel in his arm, and it was the most restful sleep he could ever remember.

In the morning, the sheriff met with the Grants and John to discuss the ramifications of Pichon's death. His ruling on the report stated:

"The deceased had prior offenses, which led to a court-martial by the United States Army and along with several charges of robbery. Ellie Grant defended her family from the man who kidnapped her daughter. There will be no charges brought against Ellie Grant."

He handed a copy of the report to John to give to Sheriff Dauber. Then, both men shook hands. He escorted the ladies out of the office. In front of the doctor's home, they loaded Isaiah into the wagon bed. Isabel and Ben reassured their pa that they would send money to the Calabash bank on his behalf for food and supplies.

"I will not hear of it. I will earn my way. Ben, you have cared for me long enough. Your ma is going to get me healthy this winter, and we are coming back in the spring to work our homestead. You kids save your money," said Isaiah.

"Pa, the money will be there if you need it," said Isabel. "Please, let us do this for you. Promise me; you will spend the winter taking care of yourself."

"Now that I know you are both safe and in good hands, I feel so much better. I am sorry, Isabel for all the trouble I caused you," said Isaiah, lying in the bed of the wagon.

"I love you, Pa," said Isabel, with tears running down her cheeks.

"I love you too, Isabel," said Isaiah, squeezing her hand.

The small Grant family hugged one last time. Then, Ellie took the reins of the mule and led them out to the road towards the trail that led to the Indian encampment. The rest of the travelers started down the main road as they began the six-hour journey back to Redwood.

It was dark when the dusty, tired and cold travelers rode into Redwood. Joshua and the boys took the horses to the livery for oats, rubdowns, and warm shelter. The travelers stumbled into the dining room of the hotel, looking for warmth, coffee, and Clara's cooking.

Hugs and tears of joy surrounded Isabel and John from Clara and Maude. When the boys walked into the dining room, Maude clung on to Thomas and swore he had grown two inches overnight. Thomas looked older and tired from the trip.

Ben hung back as he witnessed the love and affection of Isabel's friends. Joshua joined the party with his young son in his arms and his wife by his side.

Loneliness laid like lead in Ben's stomach. Isabel and John were glowing with happiness as they told their friends the news of their engagement.

Clara hauled out food and desserts along with coffee for the weary travelers. Ben and Thomas sat down and commenced to eat everything in sight. Clara soon made Ben feel right at home as she fussed over him.

The party finally broke up as everyone said goodnight. John and Isabel stood in the back hallway by the kitchen and back stairway.

John slowly reached with both hands to hold Isabel's face, and he leaned in to kiss her mouth as gently as he could. The passion of this kiss took on a life of its own as the warmth of sparks ignited. Isabel wrapped her arms around his waist and pulled him even closer to her body.

Isabel's mind was spinning, and her legs felt weak as she searched and explored his mouth with her lips. She felt overwhelming love for this man, and she never wanted this moment to end.

John felt such raw emotion as he kissed Isabel. His tongue searched her soft mouth, and he nibbled on her lips, still wanting more. Feeling her body pressed against his brought out more desire. He knew he needed to refrain. Finally, they pulled apart and captured their breath as they continued to hold one another close.

"Tomorrow, we will make plans after breakfast, and we will have the rest of our lives to be together," said John.

"I don't want to be separated from you again. I love you with all my heart," said Isabel.

"I love you too more than you know. I loved you from the first moments I saw you," confessed John.

"I knew from the first time I saw you in the train depot that you were the soldier I was supposed to marry," said Isabel remembering that first day in the depot lobby.

They kissed again until finally, they said their goodnights to each other with the promise of meeting tomorrow at breakfast.

When Isabel returned to her room that night, she carried warm water with her. When she undressed, she realized she would have to boil her clothes to get them clean again. She washed until the warm turned cold, and she put on a clean nightgown and slid into clean sheets.

She laid in bed and took inventory of all of her loved ones. Her ma and pa were together and safe for the winter. For the night, Ben bunked in with Thomas. Thomas set up a cot in his room. Tomorrow, they would help Ben get settled into the carriage house.

Maude had said goodnight to everyone, and Joshua, carrying their son, walked arm and arm with Sarah back to their home.

John went back with Clara for the night to the apartment they shared when he was a young boy. Tomorrow, John and Isabel would begin searching for their first home together as well as making wedding plans.

All was right with the world.

Chapter Twenty-Seven

Wedding Plans

John wanted to wait until Charlie returned to get married. Waiting gave John and Isabel two months for their engagement. This time allowed them to plan for their wedding in January and look for a place to live. Also, they were able to celebrate the holidays together as a newly engaged couple.

When John returned from Calabash, he turned in his badge to the Sheriff and turned down his offer to be a deputy. He told him that he was engaged and ready to start his life with his fiancé. Sheriff Dauber felt a twinge of jealousy knowing the life of a sheriff is not for a married man.

John wanted a building for a store for his leather goods and outfitting supplies. He looked for a storefront with a possible apartment upstairs. He found two different storefronts that were available, but the bank had rented upstairs apartments for the winter. For now, John worked with his tools out of the back of the livery with Pete and Gus.

When people heard John was back in town and working at the livery, the work orders filed into his workbench. He had harnesses to repair along with boots and shoes. He had orders for new leather gloves for Christmas along with leather belts.

The first weekend back, John took Ben with to set traps. The next morning, they went back to check their traps and successfully caught some minks. He worked on a beautiful pair of warm black leather gloves with mink cuffs for Isabel for Christmas.

He made Ben a leather-tooled belt for the new pants Isabel had bought for him. John loved every minute of the day; there were not enough hours in the day to get everything done. Every order he finished meant more money in his pocket.

John waited for his pension from the U.S. government. Fortunately, he had plenty saved in the bank. Isabel was perfectly willing to live in an apartment as long as they were together, but John wanted a house to call his own.

He secretly hated apartment living. At 6"3", the rooms felt too confining. He wanted space to call his own. In the spring, he wanted to start building his own house with the help of his friends.

Isabel and Thomas helped Ben set up the bunk room. The three of them cleaned and rearranged the furniture. Joshua cleaned up a small stove for heat. The boys helped him set it up to work. Isabel brought out clean bedding and blankets from the hotel; Thomas found some winter clothes for Ben.

With pride, Isabel showed Ben her bankbook and explained the lessons she had received from Mrs. Beaumont. Isabel insisted on going to the bank and using some of her money to buy Ben a new pair of boots, long underwear and a new hat. She loved being able to introduce him to friends in town.

Isabel had made a new home for herself in Redwood. Ben saw that she overflowed with happiness. On Thursday, Isabel and Thomas insisted that Ben come with them to Mrs. Beaumont's for the afternoon.

Ruth was overwhelmed with joy to see the youngsters. She hugged and smooched on all of them until she cried. She held them so tight in her arms and sang her praises to the Lord for their safe return.

That afternoon, Isabel and Thomas told Ruth of their adventure over apple pie. Ben enjoyed hearing Thomas tell stories of the three days he tracked Pichon and the Walker brothers.

Isabel, Thomas, and Ruth felt relieved to finally piece together the knowledge and timelines of what had happened. Ben enjoyed the pie while the three of them caught up on the last time they had seen each other.

* . * . *

Isabel loved working at the hotel through the holidays. Maude decorated the lobby and dining room in such a festive manner. It made the hotel, even more, inviting for the customers. At night, candlelight warmed the dining room as customers gathered for their evening meals.

John continued to stay with Clara in her apartment. She had heard from Charlie once in two months. He ended the letter telling her he would be home after the first of the year. She missed him and prayed every night for his safe return. She baked up a storm at the hotel to keep herself busy.

Late at night, when she could not sleep, she would work on her new dress for Christmas. The material was worsted linen in a deep burgundy red color. She dreaded going through another holiday alone, yet she was happy for John and Isabel. It became a vicious circle of missing Charlie and feeling sorry for herself.

During the afternoons, Isabel worked on her wedding gown with Sarah. The material was a beautiful ice blue satin with a fitted bodice.

The gown had long fitted sleeves, and a full skirt. The wedding reception was to be held at the hotel complete with the holiday trimmings and candlelight. Her brother, Ben, would be ushering her down the aisle of the church, and Sarah was to be her matron of honor. Joshua was the best man.

Church members gave her a beautiful bridal shower complete with gifts for a new household. John and Isabel also received gifts during the holidays from friends and loved ones.

Isabel's room was becoming crowded with generosity. She was counting down the days until she would become Mrs. John Webster.

* * *

Late one evening on January 3, 1877, the hotel was quiet. A few remaining customers sipped on their coffee after finishing their evening meal. Charlie stumbled into the dining room at the hotel with Pete and Gus behind him.

"Clara? Clara?" bellowed Charlie Anderson, who had recently retired from the Army. He jumped up on to the table, yelling for Clara. "Where is that beautiful woman?"

"What in the world is going on out here?" says Clara, drying her hands on a dishtowel.

"Clara, darling, will you marry me?" says Charlie from the top of the table.

"What in the world? Are you drunk?" said Clara, tilting her head in disbelief.

"Yep, drunk with love," responded Charlie.

"Get down off of that table before you fall," said Clara like an old mother hen.

"You come up here and kiss me, and tell me, yes, you will marry me," said Charlie, teasingly.

"Oh, Good Lord." Clara laughed with embarrassment.

"Pete and Gus held out a chair for Clara. Holding their hands, she carefully climbed up on the chair onto the dining room table.

Charlie took her hand in his and said, "Will you marry me?"

"Yes, you, old sweetheart."

He kissed her hand and said, "Thank you, darling."

Cheers went up from the dinner crowd. Maude walked down the stairs to see Charlie and Clara standing on the table in the center of the dining room.

"Now, let's get down before we fall," said Clara.

"Not until you kiss me." Charlie took Clara into his arms and kissed her long and hard on the lips, and she whispered. "Welcome home."

Pete and Gus helped Clara down from the table, and Charlie followed as others applauded and smiled. Charlie swatted her behind and said, "Now, rustle me up some grub there, woman."

"Oh, you shyster." She smiled from ear to ear, and everyone laughed. Drinks began to flow, and pats on the back and handshakes came from everywhere as Charlie gave everyone in town something to talk about in the morning. Charlie Anderson was glad to be home in Redwood and marrying the girl of his dreams.

Chapter Twenty-Eight

Wedding Preparations

A few days after the New Year celebration to ring in 1877, Thomas and Ben were sitting in the bunkhouse room in the carriage house. They devised a plan to build a bunk bed similar to the one Ben had made in his barn on the homestead. They had talked through all of the arrangements and ideas for storage for both of them.

Thomas wanted to convince his Ma to let him move out of the hotel and into the carriage house with Ben. Thomas would be seventeen at the end of January, and he was hoping his Ma would let him make a move.

"Did you hear that noise?" asked Thomas.

"Yeah, sounds like a party at the hotel," commented Ben.

"This time of night? Something's going on. C'mon let's see what it is," said Thomas, jumping off the bunk.

Thomas and Ben trotted across the open lot from the carriage house to the back door of the hotel by the kitchen. They walked down the dark corridor to the lit dining room.

When the boys turned the corner, they saw Charlie and Clara standing on the dining room table kissing each other. Thomas started smiling and then told Ben.

"Charlie just got back from setting up an Indian outpost in the Dakotas."

"Is he Clara' boyfriend?" asked Ben quietly.

"Yep," said Thomas proudly. He looked for his Ma in the crowd, and he walked up behind her. "Ma, what's going on?"

"Charlie just proposed to Clara, and she said yes." Then, Maude grabbed a bottle of blackberry brandy and started pouring glasses for a toast. The celebration had begun.

John and Isabel had been out walking that evening after her evening shift. John wanted to show Isabel a storefront that was available with an apartment in the back.

"What do you think?" asked John as he pointed out a corner storefront. "We could live in the apartment until spring when we start building our new house. Together, we could convert it over to a shop for leather goods to sell," explained John.

Isabel peeked through the windows, and the store looked large and spacious.

"Will it be hard to heat such a large space in the winter?" asked Isabel.

"We will build our bedroom and kitchen in the back for privacy. I'll make it cozy and warm; it will be our first home together," said John, hoping Isabel would agree to the arrangement.

"I think it is perfect. It will give us space for our things and time to plan our new home," said Isabel.

Under the crisp winter sky, John took Isabel into his arms and kissed her with gratitude. "Thank you for being so open for an adventure. I promise you I will work so hard," whispered John softly into her ear.

"You mean we will work hard together," said Isabel feeling the strong arms of John around her.

"I love you so much the soon-to-be Mrs. Webster," said John.

"I love you, too, Mr. Webster," said Isabel.

She pulled his face closer to kiss his lips. She felt a rush of strong desire overtake her body. A rush of heat pulsed through her as she devoured his lips.

John's head spun with desire. Isabel's innocent passion made him almost forget his manners as a gentleman. He wanted her in every way humanly possible, and he wanted her now.

His lips nibbled on her lower lip as they slowly pulled apart gasping for air.

"I don't know if I can wait much longer for Charlie to get back," whispered John as he held her lithe body next to his.

She felt his desire against her leg, and her mind swirled with the unknown, yet it felt so right to be in his arms. She knew she would never tire of kissing him.

As they walked back, they stopped by the livery. The lights were dark, and Pete and Gus were gone. They hurried back to the hotel, hoping nothing was wrong. John and Isabel walked into the hotel as friends and family gave the first round of toasts to Charlie and Clara.

Isabel rushed to hug Clara. She was especially glad to see her smiling and crying. Isabel knew how worried she had been about Charlie and how much she had missed him.

John could tell Charlie and Gus had been drinking. Pete even looked a little rosy in the cheeks as he smiled. John's heart swelled with love for these men. He bear-hugged all three of these old guys. When he got to Charlie, he swung him around and let out a holler to the rooftops with excitement.

"I am so happy to see you back in one piece, you, old buzzard," shouted John.

Next, John hugged his Aunt Clara until she cried tears of joy. Clara locked arms with John and pulled him into the kitchen.

"Are you okay that we are getting married?" asked Clara as she looked into her nephew's eyes.

"I am so happy for you, Clara," said John, as he hugged and lifted her off the ground.

"Yeah, I am happy," she said, catching her breath. "Where will you live after you get married? You and Isabel can stay with me, and Charlie and I can wait to get married."

"Now, don't you be worrying about me. I may have found a storefront for us to live in and fix up for ourselves.

In the spring, I am going to build my own house. We can live in the back apartment for now. I will keep working out of the livery until then," explained John.

"Oh, I am so happy for you two. I knew it would work out okay," said Clara with relief in her voice.

Clara and John carried more glasses out to the dining room, and people made more toasts to the happy couple into the wee hours of the morning.

The next morning Redwood was abuzz with the news of Charlie and Clara's engagement. Clara looked radiant that morning as she greeted everyone.

For breakfast, the dining room filled with well-wishers, and congratulations came from friends in the community.

That morning, Thomas and Ben drove over to Mrs. Beaumont's house to bring her back to the hotel to join in the festivities. Ruth hugged her friend and cried gentle tears when she saw how happy Clara was.

"Please Ruth, will you stand next to me as a witness when I get married?"

"Yes, I will," said Ruth, with tears in her eyes.

The hotel door opened with John and Charlie walking in from the cold. They doffed their winter coats, hats, and gloves.

"Just the beautiful bride we were looking for," bellowed Charlie. "Good morning, darlin'."

"Good morning, dear. Sleep well?" asked Clara as she patted his hand on her shoulder.

"Sleep like a man in love with a smile on my face," said Charlie, who made everyone laugh.

"Where is my beautiful bride?" John called out.

Isabel came walking out of the kitchen and into John's arms.

"Good morning, beautiful," said John as he hugged her.

"Say, girls, we have an idea," said Charlie.

"I know every girl dreams of their wedding day. Isabel, what would you say to the idea of Clara and I sharing the same wedding anniversary as you and John?"

John smiled at Isabel, "What do you think? Would it be okay with you if they got married along with us next Saturday? It would be a double wedding ceremony with a reception here at the hotel to follow."

Isabel looked at John, Charlie, and finally, at Clara. The boys' faces were glowing. Clara looked back at Isabel and shrugged her shoulders yet showed panic at how much there would be to do.

Isabel said, looking at Clara. "I think it would be fine if Clara doesn't mind sharing the day."

Clara stood up, walked over to Isabel, hugged her, and whispered, "I loved to share an anniversary with you both. Thank you, Isabel."

"Then, it is settled. We are getting married next Saturday afternoon. C'mon John, we got a lot to do," said Charlie.

The girls started laughing and rolling their eyes. "They think they got a lot to do. C'mon Isabel, get some paper, and let's start planning," said Clara.

* * *

The next week was fraught with details. John closed the deal on renting the storefront from the bank. Charlie helped John clean the storefront, and every afternoon, Thomas and Ben hauled items and boxes over to their new place. Isabel had gifts from the bridal shower, and Mrs. Beaumont donated some old furniture along with other household goods.

Pete and Gus ready the carriages for the wedding with newly grease axels and conditioned leather seats and toppers. Gus groomed the horses, and Pete added shine to the hardware.

Charlie bought himself a brand-new suit with a white shirt and tie. He even picked out a new pair of black boots. Charlie picked out the wedding rings. He chose two full gold bands. Clara agreed to go to Campbell's General Store for a fitting, but Mr. Campbell told her to wait until their wedding day to see the actual ring.

John and Isabel chose silver wedding bands, and they had them inscribed with the word "Forever."

Every night, they sat in the storefront and admired how much they accomplished each day. The walls to the bedroom were in place, and the kitchen had a stove and a table with two chairs.

During the days, John and Charlie worked on building a bed frame and headboard along with shelves for the kitchen.

Isabel, Sarah, and Samuel sat in Sarah's kitchen, working on the silk flower bouquets. Sarah had brought out her bag of miscellaneous fabric. Sarah showed Isabel how to gather the material and form a flower.

Clara also wanted a simple hair ornament with silk flowers to match her dress. Clara had decided to wear her dark burgundy red Christmas dress. She added a detachable ivory lace collar along with lace wristlets. She told the girls she wanted her bouquet to be shades of pink silk and ivory with ribbons to match.

Isabel loved the idea of creating silk flowers and accessories. Sarah thought she was talented with the craft of making and arranging the flowers.

"When I was little, I would gather wildflowers and make bouquets to carry around with me. I would stick them in old jars and bottles to brighten up the house or the cave. I forgot how much I enjoyed working with flowers," said Isabel softly.

Deep inside, Isabel was thinking about her parents and how she wished they could be here for her wedding. Winter travel in Minnesota was not feasible. Knowing they were safe with Grandma Red Bear for the winter was reassuring.

Ben was giving Isabel away, and he was nervous. The idea of walking down the aisle with everyone staring at you was the last thing he wanted to do.

"Everyone is going to be looking at your sister. You're too ugly to look at for very long," laughed Thomas.

Ben caught him off guard with an Indian wrestling move that John had taught him. Thomas realized Ben was starting to improve on some of his hand-to-hand fighting skills. Ben was taller than Thomas and had longer arms.

"Who's ugly now, dirt face?" answered Ben. Their nightly workout of sparring had begun.

Ever since the Walker brothers had first blackened Thomas's eye, Thomas had insisted that Joshua teach him how to fight. Joshua was a big strapping black man with arms of steel.

Joshua humored Thomas until Thomas thought he was winning and bam! Joshua reminded him how much he still had to learn.

John also took both boys under his wing and taught both of them some fighting skills that he had learned in the army. Ben was a natural with knife fighting and a quick learner with wrestling moves.

Maude stood in the doorway of the carriage house watching Thomas and Ben wrestling in the dirt.

"Thomas Renshaw, do you think Louisa has all the time in the world to wash your clothes. She has enough to do with the hotel laundry without you creating more."

"Ah Ma," said Thomas, flashing that big grin at his mother. "We were just practicing."

"Well, I need to talk to you about Saturday. Ben, if you will excuse us, I need to talk to my son for a few minutes. C'mon, let's go back to the hotel," said Maude.

"I am not trying on any more clothes," said Thomas.

"Okay," relented Maude. "Besides, I already have your clothes picked out for Saturday." She and Thomas walked back to the hotel arm in arm.

Ben dusted off his pants and his shirt. He headed back into his room and lit the lantern. Then, Ben grabbed the books and paper Mrs. Beaumont gave him.

He felt foolish, making circles, swirls, and copying letters, but the arithmetic book fascinated him. Ben worked on the numbers and the simple problems.

He hoped she had another arithmetic book for him. Ben wanted to finish this one before Thursday.

He needed to ask Thomas whether it was essential to learn how to read. He was sure Thomas would be straight with him. It was late when Ben finally turned down his lantern.

* * *

On Friday night, all of the male members of the wedding party including Thomas and Ben gathered at the livery to toast and celebrate the final day of bachelorhood for Charlie and John. The younger boys felt proud to be included in on the festivities. Hard apple cider and whiskey jugs made the rounds. A warm, soft fire glowed from the forge.

"Here's to John and Charlie. Long may your love last," said Pete.

"Thank you, Pete," said John. Charlie asked Pete to stand up for him since John was escorting Clara down the aisle.

"Here's mud in your eye. You both have my deepest sympathy," said Gus.

John took hold of Gus around the head, "You are the most disagreeable cuss. Always the proverbial bachelor." Everyone laughed, watching the two of them.

Gus and Thomas were the ushers for both ceremonies. Ben was escorting Isabel down the aisle, and Joshua was standing up for John.

"Speaking as a happily married man and soon to be a father again, I want to wish you both happiness. You both deserve it," said Joshua.

Joshua received slaps on the back and handshakes all around. John filled the glasses again as the men continued to make more toasts. Thomas and Ben decided that this was the best part of a wedding.

Down at the hotel, Maude had invited the women into the dining room that night to present Isabel and Clara with a gift. Ruth poured red wine, and Maude served everyone at the table.

Samuel played contently in the corner with blocks. Sarah sat next to him.

The women were congratulating Sarah on the impending birth of a new baby in the spring. Isabel was so happy for her friend as they sat next to each other at the table.

"To Clara and Isabel, we all want to wish you all the happiness in the world. Cheers!" said Maude. "We would like to present these gifts to each of you," said Maude, proudly.

Maude wrapped the packages with such beautiful ribbons that Isabel hated to open the gift. She and Clara carefully opened the large boxes. Inside each box was a beautiful nightgown set. Each had white lace necklines on the gown with a matching robe.

Isabel blushed as Clara laughed right out loud, "Oh good heavens, Maude. You are going to give the man a heart attack with all this lace," said Clara.

"I was hoping by you wearing this it would make Charlie's heart race; I wasn't aiming at a heart attack," said Maude. All the girls giggled as Ruth poured more wine for everyone.

Isabel blushed as she fingered the lace. She loved John with all her heart, but this nightgown brought the wedding night to the forefront of her worries. She had meant to talk to Clara or Sarah, but time had gotten away from her. Here it was – the wedding night was tomorrow night.

Maude noticed how quiet Isabel had become looking at the nightgown and robe. Then, Maude realized she does not know what to expect. Maude walked over to Isabel and whispered, "We'll talk later."

Isabel smiled at her with relief. The girls were talking and laughing as Clara told stories. Isabel tried to relax, but in the back of her mind, she had many questions.

By ten o'clock, all of the women decided they had had enough wine, and tomorrow was a big day. They were surprised the men did not come into the hotel yet.

Clara headed back to her apartment, carrying the beautiful package. Ruth stayed that evening in the hotel, and Sarah went back to her home to put Samuel to bed.

Isabel went up to her room. She moved most of her personal belongings to the storefront this week. The room felt empty. It would be the last night sleeping in her hotel room. She loved her little room; it had always been her refuge.

Maude knocked at Isabel's door, and Isabel opened it. The beautiful nightgown laid open in the package on her dressing chair.

"Do you like the gown?" asked Maude.

"Oh, yes. I have never seen anything this lovely. Thank you," said Isabel.

"Listen, Isabel," said Maude as she took her hand "You don't have anything to worry about with John. You love him, and he loves you."

"I know he does, but Maude, I don't know what is supposed to happen on the wedding night. It is like everyone else knows, but I don't," said Isabel.

"You just let nature take its course and follow your heart. I am sure John will be gentle. Take your time and enjoy the lovemaking that happens between a man and a woman. I remember when I first married Thomas's father. I was scared, and he was patient," said Maude.

"How did you know what to do?" asked Isabel.

"You need to trust your instincts and surrender yourself to your husband. Trust in your love and John. You will be just fine," said Maude.

"Thank you, Maude . . . for everything," said Isabel. As Maude was opening the door, Isabel blurted a question that had been nagging her some time.

"Maude, can I work at the hotel after I'm married?" asked Isabel.

"Why, of course. I would love to have you continue to work. Let's see how it goes this spring."

"If you decide to cut back your hours with the new house and the new store, remember, I will always welcome your help," said Maude with tears in her eyes as she said goodnight and scurried down the hallway to her room.

Isabel undressed, put on her old cotton nightgown, and crawled into her bed of clean sheets for the last evening of looking up at the stars shining over the town of Redwood. She smiled to herself. "Tomorrow, I become Mrs. John Webster."

Suddenly, there was a noise on the staircase. Isabel threw her uniform dress over her nightgown and stepped out into the hallway.

It was John and Joshua carrying Thomas upstairs to his bed.

"What in the world?" said Maude.

"Now Maude. He is fine. He has just had too much apple cider," said John in a rough whisper.

"Apple cider, my foot. He smells like a whiskey barrel," said Maude.

John and Joshua laid Thomas down on his bed, and then they started laughing. Maude grabbed a pillow and shooed them both out of his bedroom.

"Go' on now both of you," said Maude trying to be stern at two men who don't usually drink.

"Where is Ben? Is he all right?" asked Isabel.

"Yes, Miss Isabel. We already put him to bed in the bunkhouse," said Joshua.

Isabel didn't wait for them; she went down the stairs and out the back door across the yard to the carriage house.

"Ben, are you all right?" said Isabel.

Isabel walked into Ben's room, and he was lying on his bed with no covers. Isabel grabbed a quilt and covered him up on that cold January evening. She added some wood to the stove and then she checked on Ben, again.

"Ben, are you okay? Talk to me," asked Isabel.

"Hi, Isabel! This was the best night. You know what? I'm never getting married. I am going to be like Gus and Pete," said Ben. "Besides, I don't even know any girls my age.

Isabel shook her head. It is the first time she has ever seen her brother drunk. Ben laid back down and went fast asleep. She thought, "Why do men do such stupid things like this?"

John appeared in the doorway, "Is he okay?"

"He is fine. I hope you guys will be all right tomorrow," said Isabel eyeing her fiancé.

"I'm sorry, Isabel," said John. "We did have fun tonight."

"Yeah, a little too much fun, I see," said Isabel trying to scold her husband on his last night of bachelorhood.

"I am sorry. Don't be mad. Just kiss me and let me know you are not mad, and I'll go home to sleep by myself for one more night," said John in one, long sentence.

Isabel smiled and walked into his arms. He smelled like whiskey and staggered when he walked.

"Just one and off you go," said Isabel. She kissed him on the lips and took off walking towards the hotel. He grabbed her hand and pulled her back into his arms.

John bent down and gave her a deep, meaningful kiss full of desire. He wrapped his arms around her narrow waist and pulled her in tight.

"Goodnight soon-to-be Mrs. Webster," said John with a grand dip backward. Isabel squealed and was set upright on her feet. John bowed and turned to walk back to the apartment he shared with his Aunt Clara.

Julie Granger

When Isabel opened the door to her room, she leaned against the closed door. She stood in the dark and smiled.

"Tomorrow is my wedding day."

Chapter Twenty-Nine

Truly Blessed

Thomas woke up with a hangover that would kill a small horse. All he wanted to do was sleep the day away and block the bright sun from shining in his room. The white winter sun reflected off the four-inch snow cover.

It was a gorgeous winter day for a wedding. Maude stood in her hotel room looking out at the beautiful Minnesota landscape. She smiled to herself; she was going to run those two young men ragged today.

Maude knocked on Thomas' door early Saturday morning. "Thomas, get up and get dressed. We have so many things to do this morning, and I am going to need your help," said Maude.

All she heard was a groan as she opened the door. Thomas had placed the pillow over his head to block out the light and noise. Maude sat on the bed and laughed at her son's misery.

"Why?" said Thomas, peaking at his Ma. "Why do men drink? Why? If they feel this miserable in the morning, why do they do it?"

"Good question, young man," said Maude. "But if you act like a man, you are going to get up and work like one today."

"Now, get dressed and go down to the kitchen and drink some coffee. How about some greasy, runny eggs?" said Maude laughing out loud as she went down the back staircase.

Isabel woke with the sun. She rolled over, pulled up the warm covers to her chin, and smiled. "Today is my wedding day! I am going to be Mrs. John Webster. Isabel Webster. I am so glad Ben is here with me for today. Ben."

Isabel suddenly remembered Ben and last night. She threw on her woolen dress, slipped on her boots, and grabbed a shawl before dashing down the back staircase. Isabel ran across the backlot to the carriage house to check on Ben.

Just as Isabel suspected, Ben felt awful and thought he was going to die.

"You aren't going to die. You are going to walk me down the aisle. Now, get up and get dressed. Then, go over and have your breakfast. C'mon, Ben, it's my wedding day," said Isabel.

"All right, I'm getting up but only for you," said Ben as he realized how happy and excited his sister looked.

Thomas and Ben drug their old carcasses into Clara's kitchen for breakfast.

"Well, look who tried to keep up with the men last night," said Clara. "You two look terrible."

"Well, if it makes you feel any better, I feel terrible. No eggs this morning, Clara," said Thomas as he plopped down on a stool next to Clara. He laid his head on the cupboard.

She set the coffee in front of both of them. Then, she stirred up an old hangover cure. She took some tomato juice from the pantry and added some horseradish, pickle juice, salt, and pepper.

"Here drink this down," Clara.

"What is it?" asked Ben.

"It is for hangovers," said Clara.

The boys looked at her suspiciously and then drank down the concoction. Then, they managed to drink their first cup of black coffee.

Within moments, they both made a mad dash for the back door and vomited. They threw up their toes for a good three minutes.

Sheepishly, Thomas and Ben came into the kitchen. Clara had warm pancakes waiting for them. "Now, don't you feel better. You boys have a busy day, and we can't have you getting sick on us," said Clara as she swished around the kitchen.

"Did you do that on purpose?" asked Thomas.

"No, why, of course not," smiled Clara. "If I wanted you to throw up, I would have thrown in a raw egg and some vodka."

Both boys groaned in pain at the thought of eggs or vodka. They hated to admit it, but they did feel better after vomiting and then eating a breakfast of pancakes.

Within the hour, the boys had the buckboard harnessed and ready to go to the church. Maude, Ruth, Clara, and Isabel rode in the wagon with Thomas and Ben to the church. The boys carried in boxes of supplies. The room was set up for church.

The first thing was to widen the aisle to accompany two people. Clara set the centerpiece of flowers on the makeshift altar, and streamers adorned the entrance.

In less than an hour, the group transformed the schoolroom into a beautiful site for a double wedding ceremony.

Isabel stared at the beautiful centerpiece of white satin roses. Clara came up and stood next to her. "It is beautiful, Isabel."

"I think so, too," said Isabel.

"C' mon ladies, we have much to do this morning," ordered Maude. Everyone smiled and hand in hand, they left the schoolhouse to head back to the hotel to finish the last-minute details.

At the hotel, final preparations were underway for the reception. Louisa, who works in the laundry with her daughters, were all moved into the kitchen today.

Clara needed help with the preparation of the food for the reception. By eleven o'clock, Maude chased both brides out of the kitchen to get dressed.

Sarah worked with Isabel's hair in Maude's room to heat the irons for her hair. Each curl was pinned with care as soft tendrils curled about her face. Then, Sarah helped her into the light blue satin gown that she and Sarah had carefully designed and sewn these past two months. In her hair, Sarah pinned a garland of tiny white rosebuds, light blue and white ribbons.

"Let me take a look at you, girl. Oh, Isabel. You are beautiful," exclaimed Sarah.

"Do you think John will think so?" asked Isabel.

"If he doesn't like what he sees, then he doesn't deserve such a gem," said Sarah as she picked up her supplies.

"Sarah, I was wondering if I could ask you a question?" asked Isabel.

"Sure. You know you can ask me anything," said Sarah.

Suddenly, there was a long rap at the door. "Isabel, are you ready?"

Isabel's brother, Ben, was waiting outside her door. Sarah gathered up her supplies and hugged Isabel.

"I will see you at the church. Don't worry. I will be right beside you. Everything is going to be fine."

Sarah opened the door and smiled at what she saw. Ben Grant stood straight and tall in a new white dress shirt, black pants, shined black boots, and in his hands, he held a new black hat and an old piece of bundled up leather.

"My, don't we look nice, Mr. Grant," said Sarah smiling at Ben. Ben looked down feeling a blush coming to his cheeks.

"Thank you, ma'am," said Ben softly. After Sarah walked down the hallway, Ben stepped into the doorway and looked at his sister.

She was beautiful. With her hair pinned up on her head, Ben thought it made her look stunning.

"Here, let me straighten your tie," said Isabel, needing an excuse to fuss over her little brother.

"Before we go to the church, there is something I need to give you."

"Ah Ben, you didn't have to get me anything," said Isabel sweetly looking at how neatly he had combed his blonde hair.

"Well, actually, this is from Ma," said Ben.

"What?" Are they here?"

"No, nothing like that. Here. Ma wanted you to have this being the oldest and all. She said to give this to you when the time was right. I guess this time is good as any," said Ben. He held out the bundle of soft leather.

It was the family bible.

"Oh, Ben, how thoughtful. Look. There are names and dates of marriages, deaths, and births. There are our names and your birthdays. Ben, you are going to be sixteen at the end of this month," said Isabel.

"I know. Two days after Thomas turns seventeen. My birthday is January 28, and his birthday is the 26th. Look at this Isabel."

"Your birthday is in February on the fourth. You will be eighteen years old," said Ben.

Impressed with Ben's reading ability, Isabel smiled at him. "This was very nice that you gave this to me on my wedding day. It means a lot to me, especially since Ma and Pa can't be here. Promise me. We will take a trip this spring to see them."

"Promise," said Ben. "Now, we better get going. Everyone is downstairs waiting,"

Isabel had everything packed, and she looked around the room one last time.

"Ah, Isabel. . . you look beautiful."

"Thanks, Ben. You don't look bad yourself."

"I am nervous. I hope I don't mess things up for you," said Ben.

"Stop worrying. You will do just fine," said Isabel dabbing on some perfume from her purse.

She and Ben picked up the last of her personal belongings and placed them in her satchel. Carrying the bag, Ben walked in front of her and helped her down the stairs.

When Isabel emerged from the hallway into the lobby, all conversation stopped as they turned to look at Isabel. She was breathtaking.

Ben realized he had nothing to worry about anymore. Thomas was right. Everyone would be looking at Isabel.

Clara and Maude were the first to break the ice and rush forward to embrace Isabel.

"Oh, my goodness. You look beautiful. The color is exquisite on you. Turn around and let's get the full effect of the design," asked Maude.

Isabel gave a little twirl of delight in the open area and then stopped to look at Clara.

"Clara, if you aren't the blushing bride. I love your hair. Did Sarah do this?" asked Isabel.

"No, Ruth helped me this morning. Do you like it?"

"We added a vinegar rinse to make it shine," whispered Clara, revealing one of her beauty secrets.

Clara looked stunning in her burgundy dress. She added lace to the collar and sleeves. She wore pearl drop earrings, and Ruth arranged her hair in a pompadour style up-do, which highlighted her dark brown hair.

Gus came through the lobby doors all cleaned up and looking miserable. "Let's go, gals. Otherwise, you all are going to be late for your wedding."

The warm January afternoon provided a beautiful ride to the schoolhouse grounds. In the first carriage, Pete drove Ruth, Clara, and Isabel.

Gus followed behind with Ben, Thomas, and Maude. Joshua and Sarah pulled up behind them as they drove down Main Street. The brides waved to bystanders on the street, who called out "Congratulations!"

The brides-to-be waited into the cloakroom of the schoolhouse. Everyone took their seats, as Miss Pederson, the schoolteacher, played the piano. Pete and Ruth strolled down the aisle to the music, and they took their place next to Charlie.

"Are you ready, Aunt Clara? Here's your chance if you have changed your mind," said John teasingly.

"Ready as I ever will be and no, I am not going to change my mind. I love Charlie with all my heart," said Clara with conviction.

"That's good enough for me," said John.

Miss Peterson held the chords on the piano as everyone stood. When the bridal processional began, John walked Clara down the aisle to give her away to his best friend. Charlie could not take his eyes away from Clara.

Charlie thought, "my, but she is a fine figure of a woman. This woman is too good for me. She deserves a better man. Dear Lord, help me to be a good husband."

Charlie and Clara only had eyes for each other and did not remember too much of what the minister said. Pete had to nudge Charlie to break him from his trance enough to say, "I do," which brought giggles from most of the guests.

At the end of the ceremony, Charlie's hearing improved when the minister said, "You may now kiss the bride."

Charlie leaned in to kiss the sweet lips of his bride. Clara giggled, and she blushed before leaning towards Charlie to make it official.

"Ladies and gentlemen, it is my pleasure to introduce Mr. and Mrs. Charlie Anderson," announced the minister.

Cheers and applause went into the air as the newlyweds walked down the aisle. Pete and Ruth followed the new couple to the entrance.

They were the first to congratulate and hug the new couple. The minister walked down the aisle and quietly spoke with both couples explaining that they all needed to sign the marriage license after the next ceremony.

Then, the minister and John took their place in front of the congregation as the piano player continued to play. Ben had sat next to Thomas during the first ceremony, but he knew it was his turn. He stood and walked down the aisle towards the coatroom.

Isabel was the most breathtaking bride of the year. She epitomized the concept of a winter romance. This exquisite porcelain bride wore a gown in light blue satin with silver fur trim. Her V-necked dress had a jacquard stitched bodice with three satin-covered buttons.

Ben held out his arm as he had seen John when he escorted Clara. Ben stood a head taller than Isabel, and their likeness was uncanny. Isabel's smile beamed as she glided down the aisle on Ben's arm. The winter sun shimmered off her satin gown. The soft light caught the strands of porcelain white hair as well as the ribbons cascading from her bouquet of rosebuds.

John gasped when he saw Isabel standing in the back of the room. The light gave her an angelic look that made his knees weak. She was beyond breathtaking, and this angel was about to become his wife.

"Steady, John. Don't you be passing out on me," warned Joshua quietly.

"Who gives this woman to be married to this man?" asked the minister to the congregation.

Ben stepped forward and said, "I do." Then, he placed Isabel's hand into John's outreached palm.

Isabel's heart swelled with pride. She was so thankful to have Ben by her side on her wedding day. It was more than she could have asked for in her dreams.
She turned and smiled at John. Inside, she vowed never to leave this man's side, to always be there for him.

Isabel and John exchanged silver wedding bands and kissed longer than the minister thought was appropriate.

"Humph. Ah, Ladies and gentlemen, it is my pleasures once again to this time introduce Mr. and Mrs. John Webster.

John and Isabel never even made it down the aisle. The entire congregation rose to their feet with applause after the announcement. Kisses and hugs showered the young couple.

The wedding party and guests drove down Main Street. They made a loop through town before pulling up in front of the Redwood Hotel. Both brides were swept up and carried through the lobby doors to begin the reception.

Drinks, toasts, food, and music flowed through the dining room as guests chattered and laughed with one another. Ben discovered another one of Thomas's talents.

Thomas Renshaw was the hit of the party. After eating an extraordinary number of sandwiches and pieces of cake, Thomas danced the night away with every woman at the reception.

Isabel was able to coax Ben on to the floor for a half a dance.

Then, she realized how uncomfortable he felt. She feigned the excuse of being thirsty and gave Ben the reason to leave the dance floor to get something for her to drink.

"Sorry, Isabel. I ain't much of a dancer," said Ben as he apologized to his sister.

"I wasn't much of a dancer either, Ben," confessed Isabel. "Charlie taught me this fall at the harvest celebration." Isabel smiled wistfully remembering the night. It was the first time John had kissed her.

Thinking about the kiss caused a tingling feeling deep in her stomach. She searched the room for John's face.

She spotted him talking to Pete and Ruth in the corner. She smiled invitingly towards him, and he picked up the message loud and clear. He excused himself and walked straight towards Isabel.

"What do you think of slipping out the back? Is it too early to leave?" whispered Isabel to John.

John leaned into her whispers as he wrapped his arm around her tiny waist. "I am ready to go if you are. Let's say our goodbyes, Mrs. Webster."

Isabel walked over to Maude to explain that she and John were leaving.

"Isabel, you still need to throw the bouquet," urged Maude. "Let's gather everyone into the lobby and then, you throw the bouquet from the staircase."

"C' mon everyone. It's time to throw the bouquets," said Maude to the crowd.

Clara went first up the grand wooden staircase behind the front desk. The single girls had gathered in the front with the men watching from the back. Clara smiled and made a big production of preparing to toss it over her shoulder when she quickly turned around and threw it straight to Ruth Beaumont.

Everyone laughed at Clara's antics.

"Looks like your gal just caught the bouquet," remarked Gus to Pete.

"Looks like it. I guess I'd better go and congratulate Ruth. Not every day does one catch the bouquet," said Pete, smiling from ear to ear.

"Humph," grumbled Gus. He walked further back and found a spot next to the door by the lobby.

It was Isabel's turn to throw the bouquet. She promised the onlookers she would throw it over her shoulder. She walked up three steps and turned her back to the crowd.

"Hey, Ben, why don't you go up and catch the bouquet. If you catch it, you are the next one to get married," said Thomas.

He playfully shoving Ben to the front, causing him to bump into some older ladies.

"Knock it off, Thomas. I ain't catching no bouquet. Why don't you?" sassed Ben, and the boys began to scuffle.

Clara saw Thomas and Ben shoving each other and knew Thomas had started it. Isabel launched her bouquet high into the air as Clara scolded the boys. "Thomas Charles Renshaw. You behave."

At that moment, Thomas's biscuit-grabbing reflexes took over at the sound of Clara's voice as he snatched that bouquet right out of mid-air.

Everyone stopped to look at Thomas, who was just as surprised as he was at what he had done. The crowd burst into a roar and applause; the men slapped Thomas on the back congratulating him.

Thomas looked at Ben, who was laughing with Gus. Thomas walked toward Ben, and Ben backed up towards the front lobby door.

The door to the hotel opened, and in walked a vision of loveliness.

Ben saw the most beautiful young woman with jet-black hair done up in ringlet curls. Ben peeked out the side of his eye towards Thomas; he was a goner. Thomas lost all recollections of sound and time as he stared into her deep emerald green eyes.

Arabelle Spencer had seen that look before on men's faces, and she was not interested. Besides, he was simply a young boy holding a bouquet. She turned and smiled at the tall blond who was directly trying not to look at her, which made her inquisitive.

"How do you do?" said Arabelle extending her hand toward Ben.

Gus felt his fright just standing next to Ben.

"How do you do, Ma'am? Name is Gus Anderson. How can I help you?"

"How do you do, Mr. Anderson. My name is Arabelle Spencer, and I need a room for this evening."

Maude also saw the lovesick look on her son's face and rolled her eyes. She stepped forward as more passengers from the stagecoach entered the lobby.

"Good evening, everyone," said Maude. "Let's see if we can't get you all a room."

Passengers from the Overland Stage Coach were windblown and wet. Fallen tree limbs from the last snowstorm blocked the stagecoach road and the railroad tracks. The passengers climbed over the fallen limbs and walked the last mile into town.

When the wedding guests heard their story, the women offered warm coffee and a sympathetic ear. The passengers only had the luggage that they could carry with them. Maude found rooms for everyone, but the stagecoach driver.

"Maude, he can bunk down at the livery since John wouldn't need it tonight," said Gus.

Wedding guests laughed and looked around for John. The young newlyweds were nowhere in sight. Many of the guests smiled wistfully remembering their wedding night and what if felt like to be young and in love.

As the passengers made their way into the lobby, John and Isabel gathered their belongings. Then, they slipped down the hallway toward the back door of the hotel. Squealing with delight, they held hands and ran across the back lot and down the alley toward their first home.

When they arrived at the back door, John opened it with the key from Mr. Wainwright. He swept Isabel into his arms and carried her through the doorway. The building was pitch black. John set Isabel down on the feet, and he fumbled in the darkness for a match. Soon, he was able to light a lantern.

John continued to light the oil lamps until the backroom apartment shown in golden light. Isabel nervously removed her cloak and set down her satchel. John proceeded to make a fire in the kitchen stove.

Isabel smiled at the warm glow of the kitchen. John went out back to fetch a pail of water to set on the stove. Isabel filled the coffee pot and the teakettle with water for the morning.

These minor chores seemed to add to the nervousness they were feeling.

On the table, Maude had set a bottle of blackberry brandy and two small glasses with a card that said: "Enjoy."

"Whoa, let's slow down," said John looking at Isabel in the glow of the lamplight. Then, he spotted the card and read it looking at the table. "Would you like a glass of brandy, Mrs. Webster?"

"Why yes, I would, Mr. Webster," said Isabel, giggling under her breath.

John handed her a glass half full and said, "Cheers to us and our new home."

"Cheers to us and our new life together," said Isabel as the crystal brandy snifters rang in unison.

Isabel sipped the blackberry brandy, and John threw his back in one gulp. John grabbed the bottle and filled his glass again.

"Would you like some more?" said John.

Isabel felt the burn down her throat and then held her glass out for another refill. She felt so nervous that she hoped the brandy would relax her body.

John finished off his second glass and smiled at Isabel. "Are you as nervous as I am?"

"Yes, even more so," said Isabel. "The brandy was a good idea."

Isabel drank her second glass straight down and burped, causing both of them to belly laugh right out loud.

"I am not a very experienced drinker."

"That's okay. I'm not either. Do you want any more?" asked John.

"Maybe one more," Isabel giggled.

After glass three, John stood up to stoke the stove, and then he reached out for Isabel's hand.

Isabel looked into his green eyes and knew inside she trusted him. She loved this man with all of her heart. He led her into the bedroom and pulled her into his arms and kissed her gently.

"I love you, Isabel," said John softly in her ear.

John pulled hairpins from her head, allowing her porcelain white hair to flow down her back. He wrapped his hands into the flowing curls and pulled Isabel closer to his chest. He felt his heart beating uncontrollably. John's lips softly kissed her forehead, her cheeks, her lips, and her neck.

Isabel rotated her neck and closed her eyes, feeling lost in pleasure. Isabel turned her back to John, who awkwardly unbuttoned her wedding gown. With ease, the dress slid off her arms and down over her hips to pool on the floor. Isabel turned to unbutton John's shirt.

Once his shirt fell to the floor, John swooped Isabel into his arms and laid her across the bed. He dropped his trousers and laid down beside her.

"Isabel, I love you. I promise you I will try to be the best husband in the world," said John, with love in his voice.

They began to kiss slowly. Then, passion took over, and the newlyweds knew tonight that they did not have to stop.

Isabel felt an overwhelming desire in the pit of her stomach, and she began to kiss John on his ears and down his neck with her hands, exploring his muscular body. She straddled him and knelt on her knees. Playfully, she continued to kiss him with wild abandonment.

John wanted to go slow, but her innocent desires were more than he could handle. He followed her lead and buried his hands in her long white hair. He kissed her long neck and with his hands, removed the straps of her chemise, exposing her white breasts.

When his mouth encountered her breast, he heard a soft sound escape from her lips. Isabel stopped, stood up, and with the move of an experienced harlot, she removed her chemise and pantaloons to offer herself entirely to her new husband.

John shed his last layer and climbed on top of his wife, promising to be gentle. In a sweeping movement of desire, John entered Isabel. He tried to be patient, but the fit was tight and yet perfect.

He grabbed her around the waist, buried his head into her neck, and shuddered with delight. He kissed Isabel and held her tight as she entwined her legs around his.

Isabel smiled to herself and now knew what everyone else knew. The act itself was intimate yet enjoyable, and she couldn't wait to try it again. Luckily, the new bride did not have to wait too long.

She and John made love the rest of the night holding each other in their arms never wanting to let go.

The morning brought a new routine to Isabel. She felt John's arms around her, and as her eyes open, she silently sent a prayer to the Lord thanking him for her wonderful, kind husband. Isabel counted her blessings and felt grateful for her new friends and family. She closed her eyes and curled deeper into the arms of her husband. She was truly blessed.

The End

About the Author

I thoroughly enjoy living in Iowa with my husband, Les and our dog, Sam. I want to especially thank my family and friends who has supported me every step of the way on this journey. I am blessed and grateful beyond words. God is good.

I hope you enjoyed my first novel in the Redwood Series, *Porcelain White*. *Emerald Green* is the second book in the series. This frontier novel has many of the same characters you have grown to love in *Porcelain White*.

In the second book, jealousy and envy develop as Arabelle Spencer arrives in Redwood to fulfill her mother's legacy of opening a dress shop. Arabelle uncovers evidence of her mother's untimely death. Life becomes more dangerous for the people she has grown to love.

Emerald Green is scheduled for release in 2020. Watch for updates and announcements at my **Website**: juliemgranger.com.

All things are possible with God.

Mark 10:27

Porcelain White

Made in the USA
Middletown, DE
02 November 2019

77859282R00137